T

Lisa St Aubin de Terán was born in London in 1953. At the age of sixteen she left school to marry. She and her exiled Venezuelan husband travelled for two years in Italy before returning to his family home in the Andes. During her seven years in South America she managed her husband's sugar plantation and avocado farm, and based her first novel, *Keepers of the House*, on this experience. She then returned to England with her daughter, and now lives with her family in Umbria in Italy.

Lisa St Aubin de Terán's novels are *Keepers of the House* (1982), which won the Somerset Maugham Award, *The Slow Train to Milan* (1983), which was awarded the John Llewellyn Rhys Memorial Prize, *The Tiger* (1984), *The Bay of Silence* (1986), *Black Idol* (1987), *Joanna* (1990) and *Nocturne* (1992). She has also published a volume of poetry, a collection of short stories, *A Valley in Italy: Confessions of a House Addict* (1994), and, most recently, *The Hacienda: My Venezuelan Years* (1997).

BY THE SAME AUTHOR

Keepers of the House
The Slow Train to Milan
The Tiger
The Bay of Silence
Black Idol
Joanna
Nocturne
A Valley in Italy: Confessions of a House Addict
The Hacienda: My Venezuelan Years

LISA ST AUBIN DE TERÁN

THE PALACE

PAN BOOKS

First published 1997 by Macmillan

This edition published 1998 by Pan Books
an imprint of Macmillan Publishers Ltd
25 Eccleston Place, London SW1W 9NF
and Basingstoke

Associated companies throughout the world

ISBN 0 330 33689 4

Copyright © Lisa St Aubin de Terán 1997

The right of Lisa St Aubin de Terán to be identified as the
author of this work has been asserted by her in accordance
with the Copyright, Designs and Patents Act 1988.

All rights reserved. No part of this publication may be
reproduced, stored in or introduced into a retrieval system, or
transmitted, in any form, or by any means (electronic, mechanical,
photocopying, recording or otherwise) without the prior written
permission of the publisher. Any person who does any unauthorized
act in relation to this publication may be liable to criminal
prosecution and civil claims for damages.

3 5 7 9 8 6 4 2

A CIP catalogue record for this book is available from
the British Library.

Typeset by SetSystems Ltd, Saffron Walden, Essex
Printed by Mackays of Chatham plc, Chatham, Kent

This book is sold subject to the condition that it shall not,
by way of trade or otherwise, be lent, re-sold, hired out,
or otherwise circulated without the publisher's prior consent
in any form of binding or cover other than that in which
it is published and without a similar condition including this
condition being imposed on the subsequent purchaser.

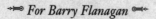
For Barry Flanagan

I

The sun was rising on a May day in 1860, and when it had burnt a complete circle through the pale morning mist, I, Gabriele del Campo, was to be executed by firing squad. The guards often came and took men away before the corn gruel made its early round. Once the slap and clatter reached our cell, everyone was safe for another twenty-four hours. It was mostly their own side that they shot. We, the enemy, were left to rot between the damp stone walls and the gathering pools of slime. There was little talking there. Life was a routine shrouded in suspicious silence. All our heroics seemed to be reduced to mildew and numb despair. We survived in that dank atmosphere like transmuted forms of pond life. At best, when some rapport was made, we lived like toads croaking to each other sporadically across a trench of mud. As the shuffle of the gruel can and its ladlers approached, the deserters in our cell stared down at the slippery floor in dull-eyed fear. They were picked at random on these morning calls. They were not forewarned as I had been the night before.

The first light made its mark on the grey veils outside the small barred window that was our only source of light and air. I had watched what was left of my world parade past there. It was a world of boots and shoes. No one was ever visible above the knee. The men and officers, priests and prisoners were all reduced to pollarded marionettes; headless puppets scuffling, walking, marching, and creeping round a forgotten backwater of the war. My sentence made no sense to me, not that I had tried particularly to fathom any reasons. My winter of captivity, the damp, the cold, the appearance and disappearance of boys from the cell were always less interesting than the sour smell of the tepid slop we ate twice daily. My own left foot was chained nineteen links away from an officer called Vitelli who was unlike any of the other inmates. Had I been less confused, I might have noticed him earlier, but I hadn't. Everything was unreal to me until that day of my proscribed death.

I was immune to thought, and unable to share the fear of the huddled deserters. The first flicker of my plight came not with the footsteps or the turning of the key, but from comparing the pierced fragment of sky to my mother's one grey sheet. I imagined that worn smoky stretch of mended linen being scorched by a rogue spark as it dried by her fire. I felt her dismay at the marring of her most prized possession. Then I felt a foretaste of her grief for me, and with it came a sharp pain in my chest and a reluctance to breathe that rendered me unable to answer my name. It was called again.

This is the chronicle of my rebirth; the vision of my life after death. If you will let me be the custodian of your attention for a while, I will tell you how I entered the world of paradox. I will lead you from the prison where I was free to dream (and dreamt to keep my sanity) to the liberty of obsession. Such terms are other people's words. I will use my own, beginning with what would have been my last night.

I lay on my part of the stone shelf in the darkness unable

to sleep because of the cold cramps in my shins. In my village, the hay for the mules would have long since been gathered, and the barley and corn would both be almost ripe. The first tomatoes would be swelling green on their fragile stalks, drinking in the daily sun. These were the months of drought and heat. Only this holy stone seemed to recognize no seasons. Despite my tiredness, I lay there, holding myself and thinking about a woman. Then I felt a gentle movement; a tide beneath the ice. I knew that Vitelli was awake too. He never pulled on our shared chain when he was awake; only when he slept would he draw me unconsciously towards him as though trying to reduce the gulf that always separated us despite our enforced intimacy. I could sense his eyes blinking, registering the visible and the invisible in an uncanny way that he had. Vitelli would not be thinking about a woman; there was something Jesuitical about him that seemed too austere for that. He was a man of ideas and ideals. I used to think that all we two had in common were our nineteen links of chain and our predicament. We were both prisoners of war, held at the pleasure of the Vatican States. We had fought for Garibaldi and the Red Shirts, me for wages, he for his belief. Now, camp follower and colonel found themselves sharing a bed, married under cover of night, their bodies joined in heavy wedlock.

Donna Donatella, you never would lift your silken skirts for me. No, and you never even lifted your eyes. I am twenty-two now, I was a mere child then, but I have always longed for you. The New Year frosts were no worse than the ache I have felt for you because of my unworthiness. I served my apprenticeship for you. I cut my fingers to the bone learning to carve in stone. I can carve angels' wings with more skill than many an artisan. Is it the remoteness of my memory or my own failure to exist that will not lift your skirt even in my dreams? There is no illicit waft of the orange flower water you sprinkled on your petticoats; one sniff would do. Even the hem of your gown seems weighted with stone.

So I hugged myself and lay as still as a quietened lunatic, waiting for the sun to edge through the barred window and lay its light across my lap like slices of golden polenta so I could breakfast on memories of home. First the scorch mark and then the slivers of light. Instead, while it was still half dark, there was the snapping of bolts being drawn and the rattling of keys. Two black silhouettes entered. They merged together. I heard a voice reverberate around the cell, seeming to come from under my feet and under the stone shelves. It was a disembodied voice that had learnt my name. It said it, chopping up the syllables, cutting the threads that joined me to my life. There was an accusing silence when I should have answered, 'Present.' I felt the tension gather around me. I imagined, but could not see, the deserters anxiously looking away, reprieved for another twenty-four hours. The bald one would be chewing his ragged sleeve to contain his glee. I had seen him do it on so many mornings.

'Hurry up,' the voice insisted.

I felt myself sleepwalking across the cold floor. The chain on my leg tugged but seemed unable to stop me. After only a moment, it let me go. A jab in the side from the guard's rifle butt made me want to cry. My feet moved but not even the chain would come with me. The filtering light I had been waiting for arrived. I fumbled with my boots, bowing my head to disguise the tears I felt gathering.

'Leave the boots, boy,' a guard said, not unkindly. 'Boots are hard to come by.'

He was crouching beside me; close enough for me to feel his cap against my wrist as he unlocked the shackle from my ankles. I placed my boots neatly together under the granite bench with their long laces spilling like entrails from their gaping holes. I wondered who would wear them next, and if, like me, he would waste his life. I tried to distil things from my twenty-two years, but they shrank like handled gossamer in my trembling hands.

My body continued to sit hunched on the edge of stone, but my spirit began to creep around the lightening corners of the cell, searching for traces of the cobweb that had, or might have, been me. The voice was hurrying me, taking me away before I had begun to exist. I felt the presence of Donatella both as a grown woman and as a child. I knew that she could not see me; I did not exist for her any more than I existed for myself. I was invisible, more so than a spider retracking its web. Once, and once only, had she smiled at me, and while the pair of guards jostled me to my feet, I refound that smile from many years ago.

Instead of comfort, though, it caused me a pain so sudden I felt stripped and vulnerable. My eyes stung with remorse and shame. Donna Donatella, if only all eyes could be as blind as yours to my plight, then at least I could crawl out of this place unnoticed, with my fears and yearnings hidden away.

Vitelli, the colonel, would have his mask around him now: that cloak of I don't know what to cover his nakedness. He would know how to walk out of this cell to the firing squad, keeping that smile safe. He would have more than his old mother to miss him. Would mine miss me? They'd shoot more than a body if they shot Vitelli. I realized that he had secrets, hundreds and hundreds of secrets which he would hold to himself and take with him to his grave. If time itself were to freeze, I would go back and speak to him, and listen and try to glean something of the mystery. I put my hands to my face to try to push back my tears. A fist or a rifle butt was prodding me away when I heard his voice, Vitelli's voice, floating around me: 'Come back soon, friend, I'll be waiting for you.'

Strange words to a condemned man; yet I took them gratefully and covered my face with their implications. My feet walked again and my eyes were dry. I even hurried along the low corridor. I was ready to go wherever those guards took me and I would do what had to be done, and then I must get back to Colonel Vitelli. It's a bad thing to keep a friend waiting.

Outside, the sun had already risen. It felt hot, so hot that I wanted to close my eyes but they were fixed open like the propped eyes of a dead child. The firing squad was shuffling restlessly. I heard some of the soldiers murmur as two stepped forward with a length of rope.

I no longer wanted to be ignored, I wanted to be noticed, and I was disappointed when I realized that the murmur was merely one of discontent at having been kept waiting. The rope took my hands away from me and jammed them against splintered wood. The wall behind me was pink and pock-marked like my paternal uncle's chest. At New Year and Easter he would come to our house and scorn our hospitality, surveying our meagre stocks with bleary eyes while drinking our wine and tapping his bubbling, grappa nose. Zio Luciano, the one prosperous member of our family, would sit in our midst, isolated by his success. I was forced to kiss his cheeks, touching his pitted face and smelling his stagnant breath in the hope that he would 'do something for me'. Zio Luciano, lost to all and sundry by his pride, yet never able to break away entirely from the tug of chestnut bread and the smoky squalor of a labourer's kitchen. Condemned, I stood condemned to be pressed against a giant version of his damaged pink flesh, pressed against it for ever with my dry lips welded to his oozing flesh.

A long-beaked priest came hurrying to me, looking as though he had just been turned forcibly out of bed. The last rites dropped from his lips with a mumbled haste that had nothing to do with me. I tried to say some words of prayer to make up for the lack of comfort from his speech, but responses were hollow even inside my head. 'Pray for us sinners now and at the hour of our death.' Where was the 'us'? I was alone, and I'd mumbled the lines so many times, with much of the indifference of the priest, that they held no meaning and no solace now that the hour of my death was come.

I didn't want to die. I didn't want not to have lived. There was lavender vetch growing in the grass in the courtyard. The grass and cobbles were cool under my bare feet. A soldier came with a piece of cloth to tie around my eyes. I rolled my head from side to side and he withdrew. I saw a first flicker of interest there. He must have thought that it was pride or courage that made me reject the blindfold. I couldn't speak, I didn't trust myself to, but I feared the touch of a hand against my face, even the rough hand of a stranger. It would have reminded me of my mother's coarse hands on my skin, touching my brow for fever.

Death was a word with little meaning that morning. It was something that happened to neighbours, to newborn babies and brothers and sisters and soldiers with numbers less fortunate than mine. I had seen dead men laid out with flowers or lying abandoned in ditches. To me, though, it was just a word, a trigger of tinder to spark off my meagre memories. A smile, a touch; they were not enough to soothe the numbness of my brain. The priest had taken flight, glutted on another sinner. My foot had crushed a stalk of vetch, bruising the mauve petals. I felt a sudden tenderness and looked up to try to scan some fellow feeling from the soldiers lined up in front of me. I no longer felt invisible, nor even blind. Something stirred in my blood, awakening my senses to the world.

I saw the two rows of black eyes, the eyes of unknown girls waiting to be asked to dance. The round black expressionless eyes that sometimes stared out of winter faces. I heard frogs croaking in a distant pond. The backs of my hands rubbed on the coarse cloth of my breeches, chafing. I swallowed mildew on my tongue. Somewhere beyond the wall there must be a wealth of broom. The eyes stared hopefully, impatiently.

I remember something pressing on my heart with the weight of a waterfall. There was a riot in my chest which I mistook for death; but the moment passed, and another chest, an officer's, stood close up to mine. There was a choke of cordite. I felt a momentary elation. This is the *coup de grâce*, I thought; this is it. Instead, he lifted my head up by my hair, looked into my face and then released me. No word was spoken. Beyond him, the squad was jabbering like gathered starlings until some new order sent them away.

Such was my rebirth and my first death. Whatever reasons there may have been for that charade of an execution, I do not know. It may have been a mere caprice of the garrison, for it is hard to believe that it took place on Vatican instructions. At that time, I had scarcely heard of His Holiness, the Pope, so how could His Holiness have heard of a captured soldier as insignificant as me?

'Fire.'

Nor can it have served as a tool in my interrogation. For questions had been few. It was clear from the start that I served Giuseppe Garibaldi and fought for the Resurgence: I had my scant uniform to prove it, my streaked scarlet blouse. 'Would anyone have the wealth to ransom me?' When I told them, no, they shook their heads and said more's the pity. The diet had been especially devised for the poor and the disinherited, recipes to jog the memory: might not any cousin, godfather or well-wisher be constrained to take pity on a famished prisoner? It could not have been worth the powder used to extort any secrets from me by means of a mock execution. I was a mere boy and, although an artisan, so clearly of peasant stock that there could have been no booty to be shared between the guards on my account. As to secrets, I had none but my love of Donna Donatella and the names of a few girls who had granted me favours in the woods around Urbino.

So I was reborn by virtue of a meaningless trick. When I was taken back to my cell, I had lost not only my fear but also my indifference, and I determined never to merit such a sense of wasted time again. I would ask Colonel Vitelli to teach me all that he could. I had already learnt how to make music out of blocks of stone, how to shape necks that a hand would involuntarily reach out to stroke, how to make faces that could hold a stare for hours. I knew the anatomy of rocks and little else. Now I'd piece together the bits of Vitelli's teaching like the fragments of a broken statue, until I'd made a new man.

That was the course of my life for the remainder of my time in that Vatican prison. Imolo Vitelli became my friend and mentor. I copied his ways, his wisdom and his fopperies. I learnt to eat with his silver instruments, and to speak another language than my own, trading my Eugubino accent flecked with Urbino for the Tuscan tongue.

My head filled with this new knowledge. I became aware of everything and everyone around me. On the one side, I was shackled to Imolo Vitelli; on the other, to my own sensitivity. The former told me of his ideas and his hopes for a united Italy. He told me of a new Italy built on stones of Independence, Unity and Liberty. He told of the Austrian invaders and the need to oust them. He spoke of Mazzini and Cavour, but mostly of Garibaldi himself, whom he worshipped. Garibaldi, who held Italy first and Italy last.

Vitelli also told me a little about his own family, the Marquises of Borbon and the Counts, who later became

Dukes, of Gravina. They had mostly been loyal to King Charles Albert and supported his clerical leanings, so a rift had grown between them; Vitelli preferred to dwell on Byron and Foscolo, the rise of the Movement, his own views on the past, and his hopes for the future. He told me for what and for whom I had been fighting. I learnt of the tyranny of the Austrians, of the 'Attempt of '48', of the rout and the flight to South America. Vitelli fired me, not with a round of dummy bullets, but with desires and aims. I wanted nothing better than to return to fight with him, persuaded that it was better to die for freedom than to live a slave. But such dreams were tempered by a round of corn slop and cabbage broth, and the small grid that gave access only to a world of boots.

Sometimes, finding myself so full of life and so ensnared, I would be battered by despair. At first I had no weapon with which to combat it. It sat on me as heavy as a slab of granite. I could no more break its surface with my head and fists than I could dent a piece of Carrara marble without my tools. At such times neither Vitelli's advice nor Donatella's memory was enough to keep me from that dry-land drowning.

One by one the deserters were taken from our midst and shot against that wall. There were two men and a boy, anxious for their crops and families. Had I met any one of them in a ditch the year before I might have bayoneted him without so much as a backward look. Locked through a winter and a summer with them, I saw that if there truly was an enemy, they were not it. The men who slunk away from the Pope's forces to tend their crops and feed their families were no enemies of mine, nor the other deserters, those fired by Garibaldi's rhetoric who died for freedom. I saw in each, as he was led away, the suspicion that slavery had not been so bad after all. Faced with the wall, many longed to be living slaves rather than dead idealists. So, those who fought against the Red Shirts, were they really any different from the frightened boys, or from me? There were so many deserters with their hidden sympathies and hidden tricolours. The Pope did not absolve those who were caught red-handed. Confessions were the order of the day, but forgiveness had been temporarily deleted from the Padre Nostrum.

I tried to carve an angel in my mind to block out their padding footsteps and their whimpering and the dull thud of coffin nails banging through makeshift lids. But where once I had been able to carve a calm face in stone, now I could carve only one likeness, and that was so far from the angelic that it filled me with disgust. Each time my mind took up the octagonal handle of an imaginary chisel and began to work, the beak-nosed bird of ill omen, the prison padre, stared out of my block. I thought of him rushing through his so-called prayers with my cell mates who had died, and I shuddered for them. The angel would have been my own prayer, and something to keep me sane. But my head was a desolate place and as barren as the bare hills of Le Marche. Until I began to build in it, only vultures nested there.

The palace started as a single vaulted room and grew in proportion to my despair. It began as an exercise to keep my mind from its melancholy, then it became a dream and a necessity. They say that all the great fortresses are weakened and destroyed in times of war. They say that buildings always suffer for the follies of men. If that is so, then I have broken a natural law: for I built a temple in my head with cut stones and mortar from that prison cell. Its hallways were as lofty as a cathedral, and the arch of each window as supple as a bow. Its corridors were the passages of my own brain.

Whenever I despaired of leaving that damp cell, I reopened the designs (all drawn and measured in my head) from the kitchens to the cupola; and I roamed through the palace of my invention where there was neither tyranny nor ignorance. No one can pass by immune to its beauty. Even Donna Donatella would raise her lovely eyes to admire its façades. I marvelled at my creation.

There was a room for every man who had spoken a kind word to me, from old Nicola who showed me where the best porcini mushrooms were hidden in the woods, to Taddeo, my childhood friend. There was a room for my old master, who taught me to hear and then to draw out the voices in the stone. Born in Gubbio and moved on by the Curia to Urbino, he had been a master craftsman. He had a room as ornate as the tomb he carved for Cardinal Lerici. There was a cabinet for my Zio Luciano, panelled in chestnut, fitted with a thousand cunning drawers, places to hide his coins and his grappa. There were rooms for all my favourite dogs – but no stables: there will be no hoofprints on my floors. There were rooms for my mother to fill with her sick sisters. And rooms for the four girls who granted me their favours and rooms for those whose promises were left unkept. The deserters from the Vatican States all have a resting place. But the best rooms and the most magnificent were the suites reserved for Donna Donatella. The days were long and the nights were longer, but the sum of the details and decoration for my palace were longer still.

II

Darkness is a soft stone staircase. Darkness is an Etruscan tomb with layer after layer of descent down damp tufa blocks. Darkness is being caught on the narrow stairs with a dead candle, feeling the friable tufa grating and crumbling in my hair. It is tunnelling through thousands of years of dead air, groping towards the lowest chamber and the bones. My master sent me into several tombs. He used to prod me with his staff, forcing me into the underworld with a candle end for comfort. When that light failed, as it always did, I had to choose between his wrath and the beating that I knew would follow if I didn't continue going down and down, and my fear of the dark. There were tombs, he said, where suits of golden armour, shields, goblets and jewels had been unearthed. There were tombs, he said, where a boy as small as me could make his way through the disintegrating tufa and discover treasures that would make my master a wealthy man.

But I was afraid of the dark and afraid of the bones. Even when the passageways were not filled with rubble and sand, I was more afraid of that darkness than I was of my master.

The walls were damp in our prison cell and the air was close, and sometimes that darkness was everywhere, inside and out. I swallowed it with the fetid air of the communal pail that slopped and stank. That lack of light crawled into my ears like a trail of slow ants and dulled all sounds to the poised silence of the night.

Then prison was about waiting: not waiting to be free but waiting for the night to end, for the darkness to cease. Time cheats in the night. It defies measurement. On good nights, I could judge the time by the numbness in my feet: the weight of my shackles sent my feet to sleep as regularly as a clock might chime on a bell tower. Hour by hour, the two lifeless lumps who shared my legs with me demanded attention. They woke me to tend them, which I did with the care of an elder brother, lifting now this one and now that, easing the iron anklet to let the blood run more freely.

In our cell there were ailments enough, sores and cuts, coughs and flux. Men lost their hair by the handful and seemed to mourn it almost as much as their lost freedom. Teeth came loose unaided, lying sometimes for days embedded in the slimy patina of the floor. Vitelli suffered intermittently from a severe ague, which sent him muttering in his sleep and wandering in his mind. Of all the inmates, I was the healthiest for I hardly felt a day of fever. While others weakened, I thrived like a land crab growing fat on the spoils of a battle. I flourished in that tomb of living bones. What would my master have said if he could have seen me? After so many aborted descents I was finally lodged in a room of bones.

The others in the cell, for all their suffering, seemed less bothered by their irons than I. The rusty anklets chafed less. Vitelli and I spoke of the grazes and scabs around my ankles. He suggested ways of alleviating both the swelling and the cuts. He was always careful never to jerk our communal chain but, beyond that, his concern about my exiled feet was the beginning of an intimacy that transfused the essence of his being into mine.

When I returned to my cell after my mock execution, Vitelli announced, as a guard locked me into my shackles, 'That walk will have done them good. It's the lack of blood circulation that bothers them most and there's nothing like a walk to set that straight.'

On my return shuffle from the yard to the cell, my body, from the knees up, had felt curiously numb, while my feet had gone as wild as though two sacks of fireworks had been tindered into countless shooting explosions. As a parting shot, the guard threw me my boots. I was bending over them, grappling with the laces prior to reimprisoning my feet, when Vitelli spoke again. Speech was not a currency used in our cell. Words acquired a great significance and even the simplest gathered with a power that I could not define. By firing so many rounds of observation at the neutral third party of my feet, a conversation ensued and each phrase forged a new link in a chain so long it was to give me a freedom of which I had never heard or dreamed.

'I'd leave the boots for a day or two,' Vitelli told me, in a voice so gentle it moved me to pity. 'That sludge on the floor is rank and dangerous, it will cause infection if you get it anywhere near your grazes. Dry them off and let the boots be until those two are convalescent.'

'They are would-be deserters,' I told him, in my thick dialect, and he smiled, repeating the word in his own strange tongue in a way that was quite similar.

'No one in here would want to leave their boots off – bare feet are the forerunners of the firing squad, bare feet in here feel unlucky. However, soldier, you have shown today that you are favoured by the gods. You have risked death and survived it, so perhaps you can afford to risk bare feet and let what little air there is get to your grazes.'

Vitelli talked and talked, cradling me in his monologue, rocking me with the fine soft tones of his voice, ferrying me from the land of dull silence to the shores of a new world. He talked me through its geography, mapping out its terrain. It was as though our dark cell had become filled with stars and my master, in one of his rare expansive moods, had been remade in a younger and more elegant form, his voice softened from its gravelly croak to take up teaching me with the urgency of a dying man. I was no longer prodded into the darkness and left there trembling to find for myself and plunder for another an unknown tomb.

Although we were only nineteen links away from each other, I had never noticed until my return that Vitelli lived on an island within our squalid cell. His possessions numbered more not only than those of any other of us, but more than I had ever seen: more than my master's tools and more than my mother's dowry. He also kept the space around him, small as it was, both clean and tidy. Again, I hadn't noticed how once a day a gaoler took away a soiled bundle of twigs from around Vitelli's feet and replaced it with a fresh mat of strewn lavender and rosemary twigs, vetch or grass.

His books and ornaments and instruments were ranged around him as round a shrine. His place, I saw too, was under the one small window, not by accident but by design. I shared his air by good fortune, but it was his fortune that earned him, and later us, many minor privileges in that cell. Vitelli, it seemed, had refused to be ransomed. This had enraged our captors, who had briefly abused their noble prisoner. They had relieved him of his signet ring, his gold chain, and all the more valuable of his personal possessions, leaving him a skeleton of comfort in the books and instruments that they deemed worthless and he held indispensable to his survival.

It didn't take them long, though, to realize that, perhaps, the prisoner Vitelli could be converted into gold. They must, therefore, mistreat him sufficiently to make his present stay so uncomfortable that he would relent and sue for ransom. Yet they knew that such discomfort must not lead to his death, for to lose his person would be to lose their reward. To this fine balance, Vitelli owed the aromatic herbs under his feet, his straw pillow, his wedge of crude soap, his occasional pail of almost fresh water, and the unannounced addition of potatoes, carrots and the odd chicken wing to his bowl of cabbage broth. From the day of my return from the death yard, Vitelli shared not only words with me but also his petty privileges and, eventually, his store of possessions.

For a year, Vitelli tutored me and said he made more headway than he had ever dared hope. The certainty of death had left me hungry for knowledge and new tastes, experience and an understanding of life. It left me desperate to learn. My master of stone had often called me a halfwit and a dreamer; each time he caught me moonstruck by the beauty of a carved face or hand, or the intricate work of a wing tip or a tracery vault, he would clip me around the ear with the flat of his callused hand with such application that, to this day, I have a tenderness on that side, and sleep for preference lying on my left. So convinced was my master of my dullness that I concurred with his judgement.

My Zio Luciano, unique in our family, could tally and write his own name. My mother always maintained that the devil had given him this gift of numbers in return for his soul. As proof she showed his unhappiness and his inability to sit down and relax with anyone from the time he left our valley and took up trading and tallying in the city.

'Poor Luciano,' she would lament, 'he's sold his soul to the devil and it's bringing him nothing but misery!' On her monthly washing days she dwelt on his wealth, defection, and unhappiness. As she pounded the ashes and boiling water on her linen sheet, my father's two shirts and our other meagre rags, the wooden dolly would pound with a savagery that I always felt might have abated had Zio Luciano only brought a little less of his melancholy to our homestead and a little more of his ill-gotten gold. But Zio Luciano was mean. My mother said he had a scorpion in his pocket and was afraid to put his hand in for coins for fear of being stung. When my father was out in the woods or the fields, my mother said a lot about Zio Luciano. They were not words to say to his face, though, because the hope of his doing something for me never went away, and such a hope should not be spoilt by sharp words. Even when my uncle did something for me, and my mother was so beside herself with rage that she pounded my little sister's dress into a pulp in the washing pot, nothing was said to Zio Luciano's pitted face.

It was a day of grief in our household when it became known that my uncle had taught me to tally. Had the devil himself singed a cloven hoofmark on my forehead my mother could not have been more upset. Long after I was in bed, head to toe with my brothers and sisters in our iron crate, my legs tingling still from the thrashing my mother had given me for having started on what she called the path of no return, I could feel the cold come up through the loft floor as below she turned the room to ice with her tears. My father sat up with her, trying to comfort her for this loss of a son. Between her stifled sobs I heard her mutter, 'He's ruined for the fields now, lost to us, he's taken the bread from our mouths.'

Those numbers, which I later learnt from Vitelli came from Arabia and carried all the mystery of the cabal and the very secrets of the stars, were my first conscious bite from the fruit of the tree of knowledge. No fig has ever tasted as sweet to me as the numbers in my mouth as I went to sleep that night, set apart from my entire family and, if my mother was right, from Christendom itself. Lost as I was, after that, and condemned to some new trade or service, I played with the numbers that had outlawed me and took pleasure in them. I counted the leaves on trees and the blackberries in the hedges. I counted the twigs in bundles of faggots, the stones on the path to the wood and the stones on the path to the river. I counted and subtracted, added and multiplied until I was as drunk on numbers as my father was on wine when he stumbled home after a feast at the monastery.

Later, I learned more with my master than ever I could with my Zio Luciano, but my master never allowed me to be intoxicated by learning. He never allowed me my pride. So I learnt and he laughed at my ignorance. And he taught me reluctantly, as though time spent on my improvement was time wasted unless it had to do directly with the carving of stone. Reading and writing I gleaned despite him, and a smattering of Latin came from the churches where we worked. For the rest the trueness of my hand, my eye and the purity of form were all I needed to know from him.

Vitelli was the suit of golden armour for which I had been sent so many times to search. He was the chalice and the jewel. He was the tree of knowledge, sweeter than the scent of quince blossoms, sweeter to me than my own mother. Through Vitelli I ran along the paths of no return and gathered such a stock of learning that it left my mind for ever a hungry sponge needing to absorb more and more understanding of life.

We studied French and Latin, Italian and etiquette, poetry, myths, mathematics, botany and even, with the help of the insects and mice that infested our cell, biology. He plucked a vetch flower from the grating above us and showed me the stalk and the sepals, petals, stamen and pollen and linked that little mauve flower to a greater pattern. To the one slice of light that edged into our cell, he added his own light and made me as though by the taking of his own rib.

I disappointed my mother and I disappointed my master, and, although he never showed it, I know that I also disappointed Vitelli, because there were times when, for all his light, I descended into darkness. A dying of the mind. When it came upon me, there was nothing Vitelli could do or say to dispel the black shroud that smothered me.

I was nothing in the darkness, not a man in transition or even a man at all. I was not a boy or a prisoner shackled to another. I was nothing, and that absence of being terrified me. I was less than the lice that scuttled across the filthy floor, less than the slime. Flesh turns to slime and leaves only bones, but I had neither. Thoughts so inspired by Vitelli were numb – more numb than my feet. I was nothing. Only the darkness had being and it was everywhere.

Coming in and out of this melancholy, it seemed that only if I could make my mark in stone and hold it could I stay sane. During the long winter nights, with the cold creeping up my shins, Vitelli recited poetry to me and passages from the Bible. He led me many times through Dante's hell, hoping perhaps to give me some insight into my own. There were no faces in my hell though, and there were no definitions, no circles, nothing tangible. When the blackness took me it was as random as the sea taking a sailor. I tried to carve an angel in my mind, a beacon of light to guide me back from the underworld. I tried to reshape the serenity of Donna Donatella. I lost her, though, and neither her memory nor her image would come to me.

Only the long-beaked priest was there, before the nothingness began, before even his hooked face disappeared and left me adrift in the night.

Vitelli's voice would become a droning soon to be silenced by the black miasma, or he would sleep and be as lost to me as death itself. On the outskirts of lunacy, in its rambling suburbs, before being prodded into a state where nothing was recognizable, I grasped at light.

One night, as the full moon began to wane, it sent a shaft of ghostly light into our cell and, catching the small silver clasp of Vitelli's Bible, it was reflected on to the barrel vault of our low ceiling, hovering strangely on the stone as though anxious to chip away some of the grey granite of our dungeon. Then the mason in me began to help the moonlight, chiselling out to the four compass points to raise the vault and trace a pattern as the moonbeam shifted over my head.

That was the start of the palace. That was the inner vault of the cupola on the tower of the west façade. It began slowly and then gathered speed, like a coursing hare, to run from vault to vault and room to room. It grew and kept its shape even in the darkness. It forced the nothingness out of our cell and out of my brain and put in its place a labyrinthine plan. As the months dragged by, the nights of mindless fear lost their power and the dread of losing my mind waned as the building grew and lived in my stead. Roofs were changed, wings demolished, towers lowered, windows altered, niches added, arches subtracted, halls divided, stairways balustraded, cantilevered and spiralled. It was both solid and fluid. It took over every night, filled my waking hours and my dreams. I carved a frieze of angels, each with the still beauty of Donna Donatella and each placed on high along the north façade, shaded from the sun of Castello as they added majesty to my vision.

So, from being nothing, I became a man possessed, and where once only Vitelli could teach and inspire me while I remained as raw clay in his hands to mould into something finer, now I was able to repay a fraction of what he gave me by sharing my dream and taking him through its many chambers.

⊶ III ⊶

Who knows how many other cells there were like ours along the hooped tunnel that led into the yard? Vitelli and I knew only that there were prisoners either side of us; we heard their grunts and their laments. At slop time, doors banged and keys turned, but we didn't know how many. Someone in a neighbouring cell told jokes endlessly, and someone else laughed. And someone else sang forlorn couplets in a tortured wail. The words never filtered through the thick stone, but I knew from my childhood that the lyrics of these ballads were all the same: life is hard and then you die.

The flies and mosquitoes gathered a balletic corps and choreographed a campaign against us so incisive that every lesson had to include a macabre dance of shackled victims trying to fight back. Even Vitelli flailed and jumped when the delicate gingery horseflies chose his freckled skin for target practice, dancing in his goatee. He and I buoyed each other's spirits, but the voyages of discovery that our cellmates were making were not of a kind to cheer them.

The brothers who had turned the corner by the iron door into their private ghetto, and who whispered prayers and curses, had come to be as much a part of the cell as the small grid of air and the cess pail, died together of the flux. Their gaunt grey faces, almost hidden under matching bushes of bristly hair, had watched Vitelli and me as a loyal audience. The cell was a theatre, Vitelli and I, the play. During my written lessons, the brothers slumped in unhappy resignation on their stone ledge, but during etiquette, personal hygiene, deportment and table manners, they watched with glee, slapping each other with childish excitement. Their favourite, though, was dancing. Apart from the twice-daily clank and shuffle to the cess pail, nothing had ever moved the brothers from their mouldy stone ledge.

In the early days, during the Reign of Terror, when the guards came round to weed out fodder for the firing squad, the brothers acquired the immobility of stone. Their grey-flecked faces held like two petrified chameleons against the grey-flecked wall. They suspended their breathing until each time the studded iron door clanged shut on us once again. Then each man let out a wheeze of relief as loud and as long as the outburst of air from a pig's-bladder balloon.

Months passed, and the executions ceased, but the brothers remained transfixed in their places. Only the dancing could bring them to their feet. The sight of two men, chained to each other by their ankles and nineteen links of wrought iron, holding each other close as they struggled and swayed through polkas and waltzes drew them from their camouflage. We were a meagre seven in our cell, but even the brothers rose and stared, snorting and wheezing ovations.

Sloppy food was delivered and left. In the beginning, prisoners were delivered and left, the cess pail was delivered and left, emptied and left; and on random mornings, before dawn, men were condemned to die. The dead men left their boots and unpredictable bundles of treasures. After they were led away, I found myself missing, with a keen sense of loss, men I had scarcely known by seeing and touching the things that they had held dear. Some were so poor that their treasures consisted of an acorn, an inch of stained ribbon, a twist of hair, the handle of a porcelain tea cup, a butterfly's wing, a desiccated orange as shrivelled as a shrunken head but scented like spice. One had a tinder box, one the imprint of a child's hand on paper. One had a baby's lace shoe and one the remains of a linnet's egg.

When alive, those men, steeped in their own filth (we, too, were filthy, but there was a hierarchy of dirt), half covered in rags, wild-eyed or dull-eyed, but always overgrown with hair, had mostly been shadows to me. Yet, from the moment the carbines ceased to fire and their bodies ceased to be, I felt a closeness to and a sadness for them: a belated responsibility.

The two brothers, who had so successfully hidden themselves from the guards' attention, would have been horrified to see all the attention lavished on them from that quarter after the flux carried them off. They died in the night, silently, and it was some hours before we noticed they were dead. Vitelli, dragging me behind him, banged on the door and summoned up the surly drunken guard. The brothers were big, they were heavy, and two guards could not move their corpses. They hit and slapped them, kicked and shoved, threatened and swore, but the brothers seemed glued to their ledge. After the cadavers had finally been hauled away, it was days before we were rid of the traces of their flux.

That night, the cell seemed lonely without them. Once it had been so crowded we could only stand, then we had been reduced to seven, then five with the brothers and Captain del Campo. The firing squad claimed Captain del Campo after only three weeks. He was the last of the condemned men, an afterthought, perhaps. He had not gone quietly. Del Campo had been a talker, who prattled through the nights to keep his courage up.

He described his boyhood as a ward of guardians he loathed and of the elation of coming of age. He boasted that he had squandered his inheritance in less than a year to spite them. Each time a guard asked him if there was no one to ransom him, it triggered off a rambling diatribe against their meanness. 'Even my cousins would let me rot,' he complained. 'I have offended the family piety. Even my mistresses were paid for. But I'd have done things differently with a bit more time.' He spoke of all the plans he had for after the war. He never mentioned death, although at all times he and we felt its closeness with us. All night he talked, muttering even in his short sleep as though through talking he could keep his executioners at bay. When the guards came for him, he was still talking, telling a complicated story I had long since ceased to follow. As they led him away he talked on. I heard his voice across the yard, chatty and unmoved as he talked on, to be stopped only by the salvo of bullets he had known would be the conclusion to his anecdotes.

Without Captain del Campo or the brothers, Vitelli and I were alone, alone in the cell, alone in the world. Only muffled sounds joined us, and insects, rats, mice and the occasional bat.

There were many days when I was happy in our cell; happier, I think, than I had ever been. The absence of any other prisoner not only gave Vitelli and me the freedom to discuss and debate, recite and read uninhibited, it also meant no more cell mates to lose to the firing squad. No more men to miss. From now on, if the guards came back before dawn, it would be for me. At night I dwelt sometimes on such a possibility, fought with the strange moods it engendered, added an entire wing to my palace, a dower house, a stable block, a Gothic banqueting hall and minstrels' galleries to quell the sad panic brought me by the thought of dying. All I could find in death's favour, arguing rationally as Vitelli had taught me, was that if I were forced to quit life now, I would have an inkling of what it was, and if my chip of stone were removed from the human mosaic, then someone would notice, someone would care.

My nerves, my thoughts, my hopes all turned towards Vitelli. He described our friendship as an affinity. Before I knew the word, I would have called it love. I saw in him a man made to perfection: the essence of harmony. I studied his small-printed lexicon to find superlatives with which to praise him. I have always craved praise. I am a performing dog. And I was vain. When Vitelli cut my hair, taught me to shave properly, to grow whiskers, to wash and manicure my hands, to look as courtly as I could, I was nearly struck dumb by the handsome blade who peered back at me from the silver clasp of Vitelli's Bible.

Vitelli was not vain, though – perhaps a little about his beard. He spoilt his goatee in the attention he gave it. He trimmed and stroked and caressed it – only, it is true, when he thought no one was looking. But where was the privacy in a stone room twenty shuffles long and fifteen wide? No, Vitelli was not vain, but I am, and maybe I have never been more so than I was as I dandied in that fetid boudoir. With one of Vitelli's silk cravats and my hands well tended – cuticles, a signet finger, clean emeried fingernails – and a walk that floundered somewhere between a slouch and a strut and the inevitable prison shuffle, I thought myself magnificent.

The guards began to notice me. They smirked, they stared, and when, finally, they gave me tokens of the respect they gave to Colonel Vitelli, I was convinced that they, too, saw me as magnificent. I was a butterfly emerging under their eyes from my drab chrysalis. I was a miracle of nature.

My only looking glass was the Bible clasp, yet because it was on the Bible, I felt it could not lie.

I was full of confidence in our cell. Full of love for Donna Donatella – and longing for anything that moved in a skirt. I see now that Vitelli's patience with my absurd clowning was yet another instance of his goodness. One word from him and I would have sunk back into the mire, but he kept me on his island of sweet-smelling herbs and infused me with his designs. Just as my old master trained me to do his work, to take his place in life, so Vitelli trained me to take his. I didn't know it then. I know it now.

The only curb Vitelli put upon my new character was in the cult of himself.

'Never think that I am perfect,' he said. 'The Musselmen say that only Allah, their god, is perfect and no man is or may be. That's why they always weave a flaw into the exquisite rugs they make, to prove that they do not even aspire to divinity. Don't think that because I am kind to you that I am kind, or because I am good to you that I am good. You don't know what I've done in my life, or where I've been.'

Since I measured myself against Vitelli, I didn't like to hear his self-denigration. He had said himself, not long before, that all things are relative. So, if he were bad – my saint – where would that leave me? If he were bad, then I must be a monster of depravity. He saw my dismay.

'I am not a bad man and I am not a good man, that is all. I am human, and I try to be good. Life does not always present us with the opportunities we need to show our better side, so we have to try to make or take them.'

I shrugged.

'Look, one day, we'll be out of here, and you'll have your life to live. You'll make of it what you want. You've seen yourself how short a life can be. All I'm saying is, don't take anything for granted . . . or anyone.'

'How can I think of you as anything other than good? And why would you want me to? What have you taught me that could be construed as wrong?' I asked.

'Some people would say that knowledge is a mixed blessing, and others that it is pure evil. You'll never be the same now as you were. You cannot go back. You have no choice but to go on. So I'm giving you a future, but I have stolen your past.'

I reminded him then that I had wished for my discipleship in the yard, of the emptiness that had invaded me then before the firing squad, and my awakening. His plans had met my own desires, so he had stolen nothing. I told him how my mother had outlawed me from home for learning to tally.

'Hmm,' he said, with the finality of an amen.

It was raining outside, in a desultory way, and had been all morning. We both sat and watched stray raindrops trickling down the wall. A flash of lightning burst into our cell, and with no further warning a storm broke. Our talk ended for a few frenzied minutes as we stripped off our shirts and boots and stumbled into a position under the grid to take a god-given bath. Storms with an easterly wind flooded into our cell, cascading through the grid, allowing us to wash ourselves, our clothes and finally the putrid floor. When we had finished sweeping it with bundles of grass and vetch, and our clothes were wrung out and draped over jutting stones, our hair was sleek and our skin clean and raw, Vitelli said, 'Everyone, from the woman you marry to the child you sire to your best friend will be flawed. Of course, there are greater and lesser vices, but if you love someone, you must love them with their faults and blemishes. Some people do not know what their faults are, which makes them dangerous. I will tell you mine, and since I have shared so much with you, from our daily necessities in that loathsome pail to all the ideas I hold most dear, I shall share it with you.

'I am a gambler. I gamble at cards. I was never ashamed of it before I came here, but I am ashamed of it now. It is not the minor vice I used to see it as.

'Beyond the walls of this prison, I gambled with lives, soldiers' lives: boys like you and the ones who have been shot out there. I lost. That is why I will not be ransomed. I gambled and lost, and what I lost was more precious than any pouch of gold. One day I shall pay a heavier penance than these leg irons and this cell. Meanwhile, I am rotting away in this twilight, and but for you and all you have come to mean to me, I don't know if I would even want to see the free world again . . . And here endeth the ninth lesson, young man. The tenth will be how to make our cards. Gaoler! Gaoler!' he shouted, jumping up and shuffling to the door, forcing me to lurch behind him. 'Gaoler, I need some flour, as much as fits in the cup of your hand.'

The guard had come scuttling to the cell. A call could mean a ransom, capitulation and gold. Cheated, he stood behind the iron grille and showed no signs of scuttling away to do as he was told.

'Flour, bread flour, bring me some.'

The guard stared and stayed put.

'Bring me some, and you shall have a trinket of value.'

'What?'

'A trinket.'

'What trinket?'

'The cornelian counterweight from my timepiece.'

The guard no more knew what such a counterweight might be than he would have known how to counterbalance the Leaning Tower of Pisa.

'You can sell it for gold – the rim is gold.'

'How much?'

The transaction was finally concluded and the cornelian was bartered for a half-gourd of weevily flour.

➻ IV ➻

✛ It was raining hard with a dull patter on the cobblestones in the yard. Somewhere, a thrush was chipping
a small shell on stone. Although we had not a drop of wine
in our cell, Vitelli seemed feverish with drink.

'A book must go. Which shall it be? We need paper.
You must help me choose – it hurts to sacrifice my library.
Which one? Not Dante, not the lexicon, not La Rochefou-
cauld, not Virgil, not my Bible, of course; not—'

'There are four Bibles,' I reminded him. 'There's Captain del Campo's, and Cut Cheeks', and Grazzini's and that
one that was embedded in the floor when I arrived.'

Vitelli frowned. 'That would be sacrilege.'

'It reeks of piss.'

'It's a holy book.'

'We're in a holy gaol. It would be a shame to lose one of
the few books you have. Besides which, all my lessons are
written between the lines.'

Vitelli frowned again, but less, I thought.

'I'll do it,' I said, and pulled him over to the far side of
the cell, took the book from its hiding place and pulled it
apart.

'Under the circumstances, it would be mere superstition

for me to cross myself. Take heed, though, that I could have stopped you and I didn't: such is my love of briscola.'

For the next several days, the brothers' newly vacated ledge became a workbench. Vitelli mixed up a paste of flour and water, and layer upon layer of Bible leaves were stuck together to fashion thirty-six small boards. When they were dry, the cards were numbered and a knave, a queen and a king were drawn – by me – in the four suits of spades, denari, coppe and bastoni. Four aces were made, each with an angel's face, and four threes bound into fasces. It was the first chance I had had to show my teacher my drawing, the fruit of twelve years' apprenticeship.

The deck of cards took us no further than Genesis, Exodus and a chapter of Leviticus, leaving hundreds of pages on which I could sketch my palace. These were my first drawings of my dream. Until then, they had been meticulously stored in my head. I have them still, those early details and ground plans; elevations and cross-sections. I keep them in a tin chest, because although the smell of urine has faded, it has never died away.

Vitelli was true to his word. He was an insatiable gambler. He loved to play game after game after game. The best of three, the best of thirty, the best of three hundred and three: it didn't matter to him so long as there was always a winner and a loser, and something to win or lose.

Behind each of the delicate drawings and the arabic numerals of the playing cards there was the fine print of the Bible. Certain pages took on a new significance for me, and as the cards returned time and again to my hands, it seemed to be more than coincidence that I should so often see Genesis 2:4: 'And they said, Go to, let us build us a city and a tower whose top may reach unto heaven; and let us make us a name, lest we be scattered abroad upon the face of the whole earth', and Genesis 32:30: 'And Jacob called the name of the place Pen–i–el: for I have seen God face to face, and my life is preserved.'

The queen of denari's face was superimposed over a prison text:

> and they continued a season in ward . . . And they dreamed a dream both of them, each man his dream in one night, each man according to the interpretation of his dream, the butler and the baker of the king of Egypt, which were bound in the prison.
> 6 And Joseph came in unto them in the morning, and looked upon them, and behold, they were sad.
> 7 And he asked Pharaoh's officers that were with him in the ward of his lord's house, saying, Wherefore look ye so sadly today?
> 8 And they said unto him, 'We have dreamed a dream and there is no interpreter of it.'

There were lucky and unlucky texts. Sometimes the words themselves were an omen of misfortune, sometimes a card became unlucky and dragged down its text through usage: if the five of bastoni fell into Vitelli's hands, he was sure to lose. The words from Exodus were no more an exultation of victory, but a menacing threat:

> Then sang Moses and the children of Israel this song unto the Lord, and spake, saying, I will sing unto the Lord, for he hath triumphed gloriously: the horse and the rider hath he thrown into the sea.

First Vitelli, and then I, grew uneasy holding the drowned horse and its rider. That it continued, 'The Lord is my strength and song, and he is become my salvation: he is my God and I will prepare him an habitation; my father's God, and I will exalt him. The Lord is a man of war: the Lord is his name' was irrelevant.

The outsize cards with their texts and omens were unwieldy to hold, and they exuded an essence of concentrated urine.

We had grown used to the stale smell of our cell, but we did our best to reduce both the smells and their sources, not only for reasons of fastidiousness but also for health. Thus the cell passed through many phases and degrees of fragrance, but as the months crept by, and as it emptied, we extended our efforts to sluice it and sanitize it and the stench had been reduced. Once the brothers had departed, with their damp sweaty vapours and their flux, our space was clean enough for my nose to grow particular.

'Very good, very good, you are becoming a true gentleman: fastidious and a connoisseur of scents. I must introduce you to essence of lime, bay rum, rose water, frangipani and—'

'And orange flowers and jasmines, wisteria and violets,' I butted in. 'Even peasants have noses.'

'Hmm,' he said, eyeing me slyly as he did on the rare occasions when he found himself lacking in tact.

But Vitelli was so fond of playing briscola that he pretended not to notice the odour of our cards. He held his three as though they were a delicate fan of rose-scented wafers. It irked me to feel the urine ingrained in my newly cleansed fingers and I sniffed at the sting of it.

'It is uric acid,' Vitelli announced, 'and it won't go away by your inhaling it. The olfactory nerve is a creature of habit.'

The cards turned the tables on us. Teacher and pupil reversed roles. I won most of the games and gained power. Vitelli lost and strained to learn by what alchemy my hand invariably turned trumps. That summer, with its wet beginning and baking end, we played all night, lit only by a handful of fireflies in a jar. Sometimes Vitelli dozed by day, exhausted from the strain.

I won all his possessions from him: the books, his instruments, his quill pens, his seal with its bull's head, his mother-of-pearl-handled fruit knife, his writing box and the cambric shirt off his back. I didn't want his things, but it was a hard task to contrive to turn the tide and let him win them back. In the end, we played for forfeits, incorporating the gambling into our lessons. I learnt more that way, I think, than in our earlier classes. Vitelli recited with passion when he lost, canto after canto, verse after verse, chapter after chapter, battle upon battle.

Twice, Vitelli refused to play. Each time he justified himself by saying, 'You have to know when to stop. Gambling is a disease. It can kill. You can grow rich from gaming, but you must know when to stop.'

And once, when I refused to play to match his advice, he chided me: 'Gaming is an addiction, an obsession. You are not in her thrall. There is no merit in your stopping now. I mean later, later you must know when to stop and go home.'

'Home,' I echoed, thinking that I did not have one.

'Yes, home. Your palace will be your home ... Now deal.'

According to Vitelli, we had been in prison for a year and five months when the unthinkable occurred. Our cell was relatively clean, it was tidy, our rations had improved and, as the dungeons emptied, increased. We studied and talked and we played innumerable games of cards. My palace covered the entire Old Testament as far as the Book of Joel. Our clothes were threadbare and our boots rotting, but our leg irons were finally removed. We were free to roam our damp cell. At first, I felt as helpless as a swaddled baby without my guide shackled to my side. We were so used to the chains that it took weeks not to rise instinctively when the other did, and longer still to remember not to shuffle.

The prison filled with November fog, so dense we woke sometimes blanketed in clouds. It was on such a misty day that I was woken early by an unusual commotion in the yard. We had spent the night discussing the idea of true love. I argued that my love for Donna Donatella was as much a part of me as my own blood. Vitelli spoke of *transfusions*. I argued that it was my heart. Vitelli spoke of strokes and haemorrhages, and cardiac arrests.

'What of Dante and Beatrice?'

'Would he have loved her so if he had married her?' Vitelli asked. 'Would that love have lasted? Can love last at such a pitch?' I kept him awake till dawn. I had to: without Donna Donatella neither I nor the palace could exist. Vitelli challenged my claim that my love and the idea of her would sustain me all my life. At first light, he fell into a deep sleep, stretched out in the luxury of his own ledge. With the coming of autumn, Vitelli had moved to the brothers' shelf, away from the biting wind that crept in through the open grille. I was not yet gentleman enough to have shaken off my years of sleeping under hedges with my old master not to enjoy the blasts of chill air, so I slept on what used to be our shared granite bunk.

Wrapped in his blanket, as in a shroud, Vitelli slept undisturbed by the apparent riot in the yard. Boots tramped past the grid and boots returned. After a while, I detected a pattern in the noise. Cell doors were flung open and prisoners were unceremoniously dragged away. The firing squad, which had been silent for so many months, was rattling out rapid deaths upon that most cold-blooded of words, 'Fire!'

I let Vitelli sleep on and waited while the pattern intensified. One, two, three executions had summarily taken place across the yard and against the pock-marked wall. To calm my fear, I sat on my shelf with Vitelli's mahogany writing box upon my knee, and with his best quill pen I drew a courtyard of my own with a pillared loggia and a honeycomb of vaults with a fountain in its centre.

I was poised thus, wearing Vitelli's embroidered smoking cap to keep up my courage, when a guard I had never seen before banged open the door of our cell.

'Are you the nobleman?' he mumbled in the dialect (I noticed with a spark of pleasure) of Urbino. My silence told him neither yes or no.

'Are you the traitor Vitelli?' he demanded, more clearly and more angrily as he lurched towards me.

'I am,' I told him proudly, and he pulled me away, out into the barrel-vaulted passageway, past cells with their doors gaping open (there were eight on that side) and past the guard room and its stink of sour black wine. He pulled me out into the light of day, out for the first time since I had cheated the firing squad.

In the cobbled yard, under haloes of grey mist, three soldiers in their Vatican uniforms were sitting at a table. A group of Vatican officers, in slightly dishevelled gilded pomp, had been herded up beside it and were held at bayonet point. They had been stripped of their arms, but waved their gloved hands in outrage. They were offering death, court-martials, excommunication and eternal hell-fire to any soldier who dared hurt a hair of their heads.

'Don't aim at their hair, boys,' my guard called out, and the drunken soldiers around him laughed.

'Sign here!' one of the three at the table ordered, half rising as he did so to prod the captain opposite him in the chest.

'Sign here, aristocratic scum. We'll wear the cockades now, and you and your sort can go to hell!'

'I absolutely refuse to sign,' the prodded officer lisped. 'This is an illegal procedure. You have no authority.'

'Shoot him,' the soldier barked out. My guard did.

'Sign here.'

The excitement, tension and a fog of wine gathered into a distinct rhythm. The shot, lisping officer folded at the knees, and his uniform sank to the ground in slow motion, as though his skeleton and the dying body itself were made of cloth. Kneeling, he stayed propped against the worm-eaten table leg. His speech slurred but continued to trickle out of his mouth. 'I refuse to sign,' he whispered. A thin stripe of blood continued to flow after his mouth had been silenced. All around him, the puddles shimmered like broken mirrors.

All around him, the shouting and confusion crescendoed in a savage drum-roll of voices, and the beat of my own blood in my ears became the *da da da dum, da da dum* of the long drums of Gubbio, the frenzied rhythm of the Ceri: the ancient festival of candles that was the city and ruled the city. I am in Piazza Grande witnessing the charging and discharging of pure energy, the superhuman manifestation of the human spirit. The artisanry who carry the gigantic *ceri* are called *ceraioli*, they are the gods of Gubbio, the gods of the moment; and life itself distils into one moment, one day when the *ceraioli* overcome both fear and courage, pitting each man against himself in the death race through the walled city. All year the Eugubini await that day, the fifteenth of May – they live and die for it. It is the dream of every Eugubino to carry the colossal *ceri*, and it is the dream of every stonemason to be the *capitano* and conductor of that festival.

Every human emotion boiled in the glorious cauldron of the carrying and the racing of the *ceri*. They were the great wonder of my boyhood. For the nine years of my childhood, I had watched them every year, wearing the golden triangle of Sant' Ubaldo round my neck as all my family did, yearning to be man enough to carry the candles myself one day. The greatest disillusion of my growing up was to discover that I could never be a *ceraiolo*, that I, who felt as Eugubino as all the other boys I knew, was banished from birth from that moment of glory. Because I was born beyond the boundaries of the three quarters of Gubbio, I was exiled from my destiny. I could never be a *ceraiolo*, and the crowd would never cheer and chant for me.

Vitelli's frayed silk cravat was the pale yellow of Sant' Ubaldo, the patron saint of Gubbio and patron of one of the three quarters. My family had always supported him, we were yellowites, rivalling the blue of St George and the red of St Anthony. A gaggle of drunken prison guards had shifted towards the gates and stood in enclave, fumbling to tie red triangles round their necks but finding their fingers less willing to turn coat than they. Yellow, red and blue: these were the colours. But in Gubbio, there were never winners and losers, there were the winners and what we called the fallen.

Within the walled precinct of the prison yard, I watched the fallen slumped in their own blood; I moved towards them, slowly, straining. I confronted myself and felt the excruciating weight of Sant' Ubaldo's great wooden candle pressing down on me as surely as if the statue of the good saint himself were capping the beech-planked carapace. I offered my life in a torment of pain and exertion, in homage to all I loved, tilting the *ceri* in obeisance now to Vitelli, then on through the narrow lanes to bow to my mother, my master and on towards Donna Donatella while the drums and screams, the stampeding feet of the crowd and the other *ceraioli* ran on with me in sublimated agony, running on stone, running on air.

I looked at the soldiers around me, trapped in the tension, unable to move as the great procession raced by. Although I was running so hard towards the destiny shared by all the true Eugubini, when I paused for a split second, lost my nerve, then I seemed not to have passed the table of soldiers or the shot officer or come any nearer to the pock-marked wall, and the crowd was not the townsfolk and the villagers of Gubbio, cheering ecstatically, but a group of mutinous soldiers baying for blood. So I ran, carrying and then becoming the essence of life.

Three hundred and sixty-four days of the year are days of rigorous preparation for the one day that counts, for the moment of glory and unanimous euphoria. My life had been one of rigorous preparation, and the teaching of Vitelli had been an initiation ceremony. I had become worthy. I carried the candle.

Vitelli had said that every man needs a sense of purpose, a reason to be beyond mere survival. The Eugubini are blessed among men. They have their reason in the Ceri.

It was in my blood. It was a shard of stone from the Palazzo dei Consoli lodged in my veins that gave me my mastery of matter and an insight into the orchestrated hysteria, the ecstasy, of the Ceri.

As I waited to die, I lived a moment of intense joy, sharing in the weight of my patron saint, enlightened by my sudden conquest of fear. I felt my spirit pause and bow to a new-found courage, harness it and run on in slow motion over the pockets of mist.

'Sign here,' the soldier in charge repeated to the remaining officers and myself, then sat down and scratched his lip. 'Sign here, and you, and you. Garibaldi is at the gates with his Red Shirts. See what the Pope can make of them!' Each startled officer signed his supposed confession. Even an astonished pot-bellied general, trembling in the grip of apoplexy, signed. Two at a time they were led across the cobblestones I knew so well.

It was my turn.

'Sign here.'

Two at a time they died on 'Fire!'

The straggling vetch had died against the wall.

I signed, Colonel Imolo Vitelli di Santa Rosa, Marchese di Borbon and Count of Gravina.

'Fire!'

Rough voices were singing somewhere behind me, but I did not turn. I could not – no *ceraiolo* can. The words were blurred, I tried to catch them, to take them in to steady my feet.

The ink dried on my writing. The crowd was closing in. Were they singing the hymn to Sant' Ubaldo? Out of the roar the mist caught phrases and gave them like votive offerings to my ear. Bursts of blasphemy suddenly became clear. There was always blasphemy at the Ceri. Then the music came out of me,

> *'Oh lume della fede*
> *Della Chiesa splendore*
> *Sostegno d'ogni cuore*
> *Ubaldo santo—'*

I surged forward into a rival chant to the same tune as our Ubaldini anthem

> *'Perché non sei venuto?*
> *Perché non ho potuto*
> *San Giorgio caduto—'*

'Move the piles of shit along. Keep the signatures,' the leader ordered. 'You never know, in times like these, we might run into problems from the Garibaldini and his Red Shirts for this. But even Red Shirts shoot their confessed traitors. Yes, keep the confessions.'

Red shirts, red scarves of Sant' Antonio, red skirts of village girls, red eyes of the *ceraioli*.

Sweat salted my eyes. Ahead, two officers stood by the wall. One was peeling the kid gloves off his fingers as calmly as though he were peeling an orange at a ball. The other was holding his plumed hat, turning it now this way and now that, scanning the scarred wall for somewhere to hang it. He moved his feet like a woman dancing, avoiding the pools of shattered glass.

'Fire!'

The guns rattled out their tattoo. The two officers slumped, one after the other, one clutching an ivory kid glove, the other his feathered hat. Behind them, the pock-marked wall was frescoed with their blood, vermilion, haematite and red jasper layered over rose madder, red lead, red ochre and the iron oxide and sepia of earlier deaths. They signed the stucco so vividly it would sink in, like a true fresco, to the very stone.

A hand pulled at my elbow, jostling me towards the plumes of cordite and the one last officer, twinning me with him to walk to the wall. Hands always jostled the *ceraioli*, caressing, touching for luck, shoving on. The air was a vapour of wine. My feet had the rhythm of victory: *da da da dum*, *da da da dum*. Words flooded my mind. Words played on my neck, *da da da dum*; words pressed on my head, they were my words, my last words; they were the profane lyrics of the *ceraioli* and the crowd, they were my prayers:

> '. . . *Balleremo diverse quadriglie*
> *puttana la mamma con tutte le fije—*'

And I ran on and on. I couldn't stop, no *ceraiolo* can.

'Wait,' a soldier shouted, grabbing my right elbow.

'What?' my escort shouted back, clawing at my sleeve. I was pulled each way but I struggled on. I had to. *Da da da dum, da da da dum*, I searched for words in the rhythm but they were as elusive as the mist.

'What's he doing here?'

'Who?'

'Him.'

'Who's him?'

'*Dio buono*! Him! He's not one of them. That boy's not a nobleman.' The soldier with the sheaf of confessions peered at the names.

'It's Colonel Imolo Vitelli di—'

'It bloody isn't. He's an impostor. It's that nutcase peasant monkey Vitelli shacks up with.'

I was nearly there, nearly at the wall, nearly at the Basilica of Sant' Ubaldo. I kept running, I had to.

Beyond the prison walls, I could hear fireworks. Inside, I felt my ear explode as a rain of fists and gun-butts attacked my head.

The next hour was related to me by Vitelli. He told me how he had been slapped awake and dragged, bootless, along the passageway. 'There was madness in the yard, pandemonium, the noise had a wild momentum to it. I cannot explain—'

Twenty-seven drums, ten horns, the bells of nine churches and three thousand voices hoarse from cheering and jeering. If we Eugubini are mad, then that is the sound of madness and its rhythm is the rhythm of running feet and the *da da da dum* which rises to TUM-tata, TUM-tata, TUM TUM, TUM TUM.

'There was a delay while a scrawled confession was drawn up for me. That delay saved my life, you know. You saved my life,' Vitelli told me, over and over again. 'And the gates were rammed open by the Red Shirts. A few shots were fired—' TUM-tata, TUM TUM.

The guards surrendered. The Red Shirts poured in in

such numbers it was like a village festival. I was liberated, still half asleep and bootless.

'I christened you as you lay at my feet: Captain Annibale Gabriele Matteucci del Campo.

'Now the war is over, del Campo. The war is won. The Vatican State of Umbria will no more be a vassal of the Pope. This is day one, del Campo, of a new life.'

My friend had brought me round from my beating most tenderly, cradling my head while applying a tin cup of coffee laced with brandy to my lips. It was a heavenly concoction that burnt my tongue.

As he spoke to me, I heard his voice with one ear, while in the other I heard the tattoo of twenty-seven drums.

❧ V ❧

The stones of Venice were green with slime. They were as dank and close as the cell I had just left. I arrived in the city only to spend my first days like a rat creeping along the edges of that network of grandiose sewers. My disguise was still new to me, it felt untested and I unsure. It seemed that at every turn of an alleyway someone would challenge me. Where the city echoed with its own mysterious orchestra of voices and water, for me it seemed to contain the constant threat of mocking laughter. Clothed in the fopperies I had bought and stolen along the way, I felt more naked than in my own skin.

Every fishwife and urchin, but mostly every soldier who passed me, turned me from a man into a cold-blooded animal, a reptile, a crawling thing, transfixed by fear to the dank stone. I was sure they could recognize my fine breeches for what they were, stolen from the corpse of a slain soldier in a ditch outside Forlì. And the hose and boots that I had been so pleased to find on his dead legs, surely they sighed out supernatural messages in the dark, signalling their origin. The concealed bloodstain on the toe of my right foot, that darkness calling out from the leather, did it not tell of desecration?

During my first weeks in that watery city, every time a priest passed me, nursing the hem of his dark robes over the oozing filth, I was ready to sink to my knees and confess to both my fraud and theft. But these priests were always hurrying. They took no interest in me and my raw soul. There was an outbreak of ague in the city. The rich were buried by day and the poor by night. It was said that there were scarcely enough hours in the day to bury the dead and that the cemetery island of San Michele had coffins piled up on its shores.

The fascination of the city was that, there, all things were pretence; the place itself was a master craftsman of disguises. I had heard that the purchase of a small white mask, an expressionless face called a *bautta*, made of paste and many layers of paper, would enable me to move around the city in anonymity. Not, of course, that anyone could have known me there, but my own face was like a mask I did not yet know how to wear. I had planned to keep on this Venetian mask for all my waking hours, thus arousing neither suspicion nor comment since it was the fashion to do so.

Alas, I had heard gossip of days gone by: the masks were no longer allowed. As the days passed, though, I saw fantastic costumes emerge and the city gave itself over to a remarkable frenzy. These costumes had been forbidden by the Austrians and flaunted every day by the wealthier citizens. In shops along the *Frezzeria* I saw the beak-nosed masks of the plague doctor, pale traps of the priest's nose following me, probing my sores.

I had heard speak of the wealth and decadence of Venice: I knew that entire noble families had ruined themselves with cards. This gambling, too, was illegal, but I had heard that there were secret dens where a man might make or lose a fortune. I had nothing to lose and much to make. All my lessons with Vitelli had made me seem like a gentleman, within the confines of our cramped cell, but they could not gain me admittance to Donna Donatella nor would they build for me the palace I had dreamed. So I moved cautiously through the dark labyrinth: an unmasked man in a masked city, fearing to ask for that which I had come, but trusting that luck would lead me to it on her own. I thought in those days that luck was like a falling star. I thought that I had only to hold out my hands and catch it.

I had heard of a gambling club owned by a lame army captain who called himself Bastoni. I had gambled *en route* to this open replica of my vaulted cell. While my Emilian winnings lasted, fear kept me from seeking him. Once they ran out I knew I would be driven to him. Bastoni: the name augured well for me, bastoni was my lucky suit in cards. If bastoni were trumps, I won.

My father had taught me to watch the stars, and my master in Urbino had instructed me in the geography of constellations. He was reluctant to share with me any secrets beyond our trade, but sometimes he would relent and sweep me the dust of what he knew. My master had studied under the Jesuits and was a learned man. His body was shrivelled and his tongue harsh but he kept a lively interest in life, translating it into stone. From the age of ten, when my Zio Luciano sold me to him, my master and I set out before dawn on our way to the quarry of *pietra serena*, to a graveyard or a chapel, a castle or a church. Most of his work was for the Curia. With our slings of tools we set out to traverse the Umbrian tracks and roads under the guidance of the moon and the stars. When the mood took him, he shared them with me.

My master was an old man, but his step was quick. I struggled to keep up with him. Sleep nagged at my eyelids. My master's ears were deaf from the blasts of stone. He had served his own apprenticeship in the quarries of the Grand Duchy, and the noise of gunpowder had taken his hearing, he said, had trapped it in a great cube of marble. He claimed that his hearing hovered in St Peter's itself, lured there by Cardinal Ettore Consalvi in a block of pink travertine destined for the Holy See. My master used to say, 'Take heed of the Northern Star, boy, be guided by its light which is the only true light. It comes from the polar regions. If you ignore it, it will freeze your heart and leave your carcass for the sun to thaw and the wolves to chew.'

So I grew to respect and fear the stars and their Jesuitical power and vengeful wrath. When Colonel Vitelli told me that my own great star shone on me and me alone, the idea filled me with dread. Then the dread turned to ambition and the lifeblood of ambition is greed. The great star that saved me would make me rich. This wealth would be like gold, molten in the fire of my dreams, which would shape the precious metal into my palace. My master had sent me down those times, when his mind wandered and work was scarce, to turn Etruscan bones into gold. He spoke often of a chalice. He spoke with awe. My palace was to be a golden cup which love would fill for me. Such miracles had occurred around my prison cell that I began to believe not only in the star, my star, but in its alchemy. More, though, than any northern light or any real or imagined star of my own. I had been guided by Vitelli. Away from him, although I was farther north than I had ever been, the great star of which he had spoken seemed indeed to shine for me. Yet without his light and guidance, I felt lost. The fog from the lagoon wrapped me in its smothering darkness and the maze of alleyways filled me with anxiety. Many a time I thought to flee the city. I eyed the provenance of every set of clothes askance and I studied other gentlemen with misgiving. My attire had seemed outlandish when I first donned it, yet in Venice, when I cautiously paraded it along the mildewed streets and across the chilled harlequin arcades, it seemed modest by comparison to the weird and fantastic dresses of other citizens. My own costume spelt sacrilege and stealth and I tried to imagine what degree of crime lay under such brazen flaunting.

Under the sinister mists of Venice there was a layer of immunity. There were other layers, as many as in the strata of a rock, but at first I was too nervous to look at them. There was the olive-green water of the lagoon, the stone, the brick and the fog; beyond that I was afraid to go, not knowing what putrefying layers I would discover in between. Had it not been for my appointment with Vitelli, I would most certainly have fled. My only link with him was a future date: the equinox of spring at Florian's *caffè* in St Mark's Square, in the front room at the table opposite the window.

I would have surely died without the hope of seeing my friend and mentor again. I arrived in Venice in January, on the 21st, and then I counted the days and sometimes the hours until that appointment should fall due. The rendez-vous was a fashionable place where dandies and grandees gathered. It was the only place where Venetians and Austrians sat together – the rest of social life was strictly segregated. The Austrians were mostly despised and this was another disadvantage to my own disguise. How could I pass one of the occupying Austrian soldiers and sleight him, I, who still jumped at my own shadow and instinctively bowed to my own reflection?

How that city teased me! Inside and out, there was nothing but reflections. I was steered through the sluggish waters along with hundreds of other foreigners in the city. The authorities were on the look-out for spies. I took up residence in Rialto and in my second week the Austrian secret police took some interest in me. They must have decided that I posed no threat, for in the three years that I subsequently dwelt in Venice, I was never troubled by them again.

THE PALACE *49*

How cold that city was: a great watery tomb submerged in its stinking finery. Venice had all the opalescent sheen of a fish's scales. The sickly winter sun shone through this bright transparency to the rotting flesh of the severed head inside. The sheen was a fake armour. Yet how proud they were of their sinking apparition! Before Giovanni entered my service, when words failed me the subject of the miraculous beauty of the city saved me. The speech was fast and strange, a barbaric sing-song that lingered in my ear like licked-over whispers with slurred lost meanings. I learned to exchange a litany of praises. It seemed a lexicon of wonder had been handed down from generation to generation. Even the illiterate mud-pickers knew how to enumerate the treasures of St Mark's. These things impressed me more than the fantasies of Carnival.

> '*O Venezia benedetta*
> *Non le vogio più lasar!*'

they sang as they nursed their torn fishing nets and their lobster pots and their chilblains. I learned their refrains because I was like a parrot repeating what I heard with no notion of its meaning.

My affection for the place its inhabitants called the Empress of the Adriatic was feigned. It formed another rung on the ladder of lies that I climbed to become a gentleman. Yet, like so many of the other trappings, what began as a sham ended by being sincere. For, guided by Giovanni, my mathematical gondolier, I grew fond of that gloomy floating mausoleum. I grew to love the resonance of its empty halls, to look lovingly on the green knap of slime that coated the pediments of even the finest palaces. I grew to enjoy the false glitter and the prisms of cut crystal, the crocodile tears of blown Murano glass that dripped from every chandelier. Lulled by Giovanni's garrulous indolence, I became an admirer of Venice. I drifted along canals, steered by Giovanni Contarini. Giovanni, as was the custom, bore the name of the family his family had once worked for, which gave rise to endless stories of illegitimate daughters and sons of great noblemen of the city, together with whispered claims of their great fortunes.

I think the poorer citizens enjoyed the company of us outsiders. We were their captive audience. They had us prone in their funereal gondolas, adrift and at their mercy as they spilt out their secrets and their fantasies. It didn't matter whether one believed them or not, they enjoyed telling the tale; that was enough. Giovanni proved no exception: every journey we made, he contrived to pass by the pink and white wedding cake of the Ca' Contarini, the better to tell of his own claims.

✢ I had three reasons for coming to Venice, of which
the principal was to meet up with my friend Vitelli;
the secondary to take advantage of the city's illicit
gambling dens to make my fortune under the light of
my lucky star, and the third concerned the nature of the
city. I could say it was geographical; it reflected, as all
things Venetian do, something else. It reflected my fear of
horses.

As a boy, I rarely saw a horse, and when I did, it was
usually from a distance. On those occasions when my
master's work took us into town, I saw these beasts from
closer quarters. I knew that a kick could kill. I had heard of
a boy who had been felled by a hoof in the head. I saw for
myself the slavering mouth, the foaming lips yawning to
show a jaw big enough to swallow my entire head and teeth
so massive they could have bitten through my neck as
lightly as through the stalk of an apricot. From as wide a
berth as I could give such a beast, given the narrow streets
of our towns and my master's angry chiding, I observed the
look of evil intention in a horse's eye, the impatience to
wreak havoc. My master threatened me with wolves and
bears if I dawdled in the woods or by the wayside as we

walked to work. He could have made me run if he had known my dread of horses.

Neither a peasant boy nor a stonemason's apprentice has much use for horses. In the fields around my father's hut oxen were used to draw the plough. When they were unavailable, a team of young men took the halter and dragged it through the mud. I had seen mules balancing loads of wood on their backs and sacks of corn. Later, I saw mules and oxen again, hauling stone from the quarries. I saw mules pulling the long lever of the olive press round and round with their eyes bandaged against their lot. Even then I was afraid but, since no one asked me to approach them, I had no need to admit my fear to anyone but myself.

However, when I began to wrap myself like an earthworm in the cocoon of a silk moth, when I began to spurn mud in favour of the succulent mulberry, I was forced to recognize that gentlemen rode horses. From within the squalid recesses of my prison cell, this eventuality had been so remote that I did not consider it. It was only upon our mutual release, when Vitelli instructed me to make my way north, purchasing a horse *en route* and then to rendezvous in Venice, that it became real.

'What?' I asked him. 'Me, get on a horse and ride into Venice?'

'Not into the city, Gabriele, how could you do that? Venice is built on water. The Venetians get around in boats or they walk like crabs down their wet alleyways.'

I decided that, until fate should find me another, Venice would be my home.

I learnt as much about manners in the next eight weeks, covering up my mistakes and learning as I went along, as I had in all my time in gaol. Taking bread and peccorino and a jug of hot milk at a taverna not above three miles from our gaol, I found myself the butt of ridicule and speculation: I passed a wretched evening on my first night of freedom.

It was not until well after dark, when I stopped worrying and began to observe my fellow travellers, that I discovered the scorn and suspicion had been attributable to my failure to tip. Upon seeing others do so, I called the insolent waiter across to me, took a coin out of my meagre stock and by a social alchemy made a friend out of an enemy, transforming his surly disdain to open flattery. A second jug of sheep's milk was brought, unasked for, to my table and put down with a handful of almond biscuits 'for the gentleman'. I had seen that gentlemen don't dip their bread in their milk and suck it, or embrace the waiter, or sit on the stairs. Neither do they take off their hats to ostlers or pedlars, bow their heads, or lower their eyes when spoken to by other gentlemen. They do not cross themselves before each shrine with a peasant's ostentation. Such things I could not have learnt in my cell and yet, by glancing around me, I saw them to be so.

I passed muster in Reggion Emilia despite my blunders, thanks only to the chaos that reigned. A province recently torn by war is like a broken ant-hill: everyone is so busy running and repairing and gathering casualties that there is little time to spare for an itinerant officer. I had had many months to learn to talk, to walk, to eat, to speak a little French, to learn the niceties of a drawing room. I could move, fence and write like a gentleman, so long as I was not required to do any of these things to a high standard or for too long. Hardest of all, though, was the name I had assumed. It was so new that I had difficulty pronouncing it, let alone allowing it to roll off my tongue with a haughty indifference.

I realized too late that I should have chosen someone who died a long time ago rather than snatching the identity of Captain del Campo. It had appealed to me because I was born in the fields and I was of the fields and the name of that meaning belonged to me a little more than any other might. Vitelli volunteered to retire me officially and sort out my paperwork, and he handed me a time-piece that the real del Campo had given him as the guards had led him out of our cell to the firing squad. Yet, however much I recited that name, Captain Annibale Gabriele Matteucci del Campo, I was bound to stumble on it.

By Ravenna I had dropped both the 'Captain' and the 'Annibale'. Roman history had taken over the name. I had enjoyed my history lessons as much as any and memorized the names of all the generals. With freedom, I jumped from prime student to dunce, instead of Annibale I kept saying the names of his generals and I realized that however successfully my historical namesake had been at crossing the Alps, I would fare badly on my own journey north with such an inner confusion. I kept 'Gabriele' for myself and was able, vainly, to associate with an archangel. In Rovigo I bumped into a Matteucci lover who offered to introduce me to one of my clan, so by Padua I had become simply Gabriele del Campo, a name I have kept all my life, neither owning nor deserving it. I am the ghost of a shot officer.

On my first days in Venice I slunk around the Castellani side hardly daring to raise my head. The city had as many priests as vermin, each scurrying to the dying in their warrens. I remembered the last rites that I, too, had received and I remembered how grudgingly they had been given. That memory strengthened me in my endeavours. The lanes were full of bustle and jostle but they had too much life in them for a cautious ghost like me. I often took refuge in the freezing churches. The austere, vaulted tombs suited my mood. These churches were, in turn, haunted by my mother. The mere sight of an altar filled my eyes with tears.

My mother never had a great grasp of doctrine. She went to mass on the first Sunday of every month, regardless of the weather, walking the two miles to Sant' Angelo. She could whisper her Ave Marias and her Credo and her Paternoster with the rest of us, never understanding what they meant and never wanting to. She knew that there was life and death, heaven, hell and limbo and she strove towards Paradise on the inevitable trek towards death. I thought of her a lot in Venice, of her cracked red hands, her hooded eyes and her wide smile of broken teeth.

Paradise for her would be to be reunited with my dead elder brother, and perhaps to ease her weight from the bulging mottled veins of her legs. The Church offered her this possibility and through its dourness helped to calcify her bitterness. My father was a slow man and mostly silent. He came to life each year for the Ceri, ran wild and then retired into his shell. He toiled and hid, bearing the brunt of my mother's bitterness. His children left him to his own devices, an unknown shadow whose tired eyes avoided ours. I never even tried to understand my father: I tried so hard to please my mother I had no time for him. But no matter how hard I tried I could never appease her. All I could do was conform to outward forms.

I wondered what she would say if she could see me now as I had become: a man transformed and left in limbo. I had justified all her worst fears for me. I would never be able to return to the labours of the fields and so often I felt unable to attain the goal of being a gentleman. She would cross herself and whisper and make the sign of the evil eye. She would see me as a ruined man, not just lost to her but lost. I know she would pray for my release from purgatory, lest my state might affect her own. But she would be afraid to take me back. She would see my perdition as contagious. I, who had nothing to inherit from my family but their meagre love and warmth, would be disinherited.

It was so cold in Venice, so cold in those churches. It crept into the marrow of my bones. It crawled along my body and arched my back, digging its fist into the base of my spine like an icy shard of glass. My clammy black Venetian cloak was lined with damp. It covered me like a wet winding sheet. Around my cloak, the mist smothered me. The alleyways were traversed by dark tunnels so low I had to crouch. Anxiety was an unwelcome lodger inside my shirt. It wove in and out of the thick mists with me, collecting echoing footsteps, conjuring up thin grasping fingers from the peeling walls to apprehend me. Strange boys chased after me, hurling boxes and trolleys at me as I scuttled along. The fat rats that shared the alleyways stared into my eyes, twitching their whiskers with a confidence that disturbed me. Slops were dropped on my head. The city knew that I carried cowardice in each of the corners of my tricorn hat.

The homely boots that my master had ordered for me from the shoemaker at Miraduolo where we were employed to restore the Chapel of Our Lady had seemed like iron clogs to me when new. Every two years he ordered me a new pair of cowhide boots as big as boats for my wide peasant's feet to grow into. At first, I would slip and slide inside the stiff leather. By the time I grew out of them, they would bend my toes into shapes the bones could hardly turn to. So my boyhood shoes seldom fitted me. I thought I knew all there was to know about foot pains and cramps.

My mother had looked at me with grave suspicion when I went home to see her with shoes on my feet. It was not their size that shocked her, it was their existence. She kicked ash over the brittle toes as though to cover up the tracks of her maternity. With the ash she let me go, a dwarf Zio Luciano in her mind: a hybrid, useful but sterile. I was eleven years old when my shoes came between us, leaving me an outcast from her sinewy arms.

In Venice I realized I was not the connoisseur of shoe torture I had thought. From Emilia, where I found the offending boots, until Padua, I had alternated the stolen ones with my own worn-in and truly battered pair. I told myself that this was necessary to remove the bloodstain on one toe. During those weeks, the stolen boots lured me with a sense of false comfort. Worn only for an hour at a time, they seemed to augur a lifetime of luxury. Just outside Padua, I abandoned my old boots in a ditch, hoping in some way to repay my earlier theft.

Crushed chilblains, grated corns, blisters, with them I diluted the original bloodstain with new ones of my own. I do not know what ached the most, my conscience or my feet. Yet my feet ached entirely, while my conscience limited itself to intermittent remorse. My fear of discovery was far greater than my repentance.

At first, hobbling and shuffling along the narrow alley-ways of San Lio, too unsure of the water to get back into a boat, I followed the flow of the crowd. Swept backwards and forwards like a human pendulum on those noisy tides. The crowd rushed into the funnel of La Merceria, pushed in and out of St Mark's Square as though by the breathing of a giant fish. Then the crowd was sucked and pushed back under the stately arcades and out towards Rialto. I clung to the bridges and tried to hide in angles of walls clinging to chimney flues as the waves of people swept along chattering and shrieking all the way. Sometimes I found myself trapped all day in that inane sway, rushing and pushing, receiving a hundred sharp elbows an hour in my swaddled ribs. Sometimes I would take refuge in the church of San Lio, and sometimes I would escape the crowd and seek sanctuary in San Zanipolo.

I had been in San Zanipolo many times, cringing to make myself invisible in one of the dark pews, resting my feet and cursing Napoleon for his many abolitions, when I first spied the tomb of Bragadino. Being a stonemason I was well used to tombs and graveyards. I had sat on many a tomb-stone in my time and chipped away at a Latin inscription or worked on a headstone. I was not one to be unduly worried by the dead. I suppose the ease with which I debagged an officer will testify to this. I paid scant attention to the plaques of the churches I sheltered in. I could not help casting a professional eye at the carving and sometimes, despite my grim mood, I could not help marvelling at the beauty and workmanship that went into that city.

One day, when there was a storm of razor-edged sleet to add to the usual horrors of the street, I sat in Zanipolo and cast my eyes at the bust of this Bragadino with a dark fresco above him of a violent nature that I could not discern. Staring up into the faded pigments, I was accosted by a monk who talked through a large gap in his mouth whence the stumps of his missing teeth seemed threatening to fall. By a series of loud sucking manoeuvres, he kept his palate intact.

'I see you are thinking about Admiral Bragadino,' he said, sucking for all he was worth. 'Would you like to see his skin?' The question was delivered together with a shower of viscous spittle. I began to back away. The disappointed monk followed me.

'Flayed off his back,' he sucked, 'as soft as a glove and folded neatly with nothing to fear.'

Outside the church doors the sleet slanted on to my own skin, flaying my cheeks. I found a wine shop and sat down among a rough crowd of men. For once, I didn't mind being out of place. I cursed Napoleon Bonaparte for forbidding the use of masks, leaving me to finish my transformation as skinless as a flayed man.

I would have died, gladly, in those early days, had it not been for my dream. I had invented a palace and the sight of all the palaces of Venice merely confirmed me in the knowledge that such dreams could come true. And it was my duty to become worthy of Donna Donatella. Whether or not she would ever love me was a matter I dared hardly think of, but she must grow to notice and admire me. I saw clearly that, to that end, I would suffer any amount of flaying or pain and that my insect-like transition would eventually end.

⇻ VII ⇺

✛ I had found myself apprenticed to many things, but
it was in Venice that I served my apprenticeship to
wine. It was a new and powerful master. As a boy I had
savoured the *vin santo* of Communion and tried, like all the
others, to gulp down more than the proffered sip. Its sweet
raisiny taste always went straight to my head. I would like
to tell that I learnt to drink as easily as I had learnt my
other lessons, but I did not become a connoisseur, I became
a drunk. I didn't trust myself to drink in wine shops, since
I knew I might talk rashly and I knew that I would be sick,
so I spent whole days lolling around in my room in a
drunken stupor. Between jugs, I was overcome with unworthiness, be it to Donna Donatella, to myself or to Vitelli.
They were the three people I missed most.

I did not succeed in drinking myself into such oblivion
that I could ignore the fact of my money running out. A
real nobleman could afford to be penniless; I could not.
The time was upon me to seek out Bastoni's. I didn't feel
ready for it in my soul, but my pocket insisted. I knew too
much about it to go there lightly.

It was a gambling club, run strictly to Captain Bastoni's
own perverse rules. Infringements were settled swiftly,

piratical style, in which, it was rumoured, he had first made his wealth. I heard it suggested that some of the sacks dropped out towards Sant' Ariano no more contained the victims of malaria than they contained the biscuits or the coal of La Befana. It was said that Bastoni had no need of the famed Venetian assassins with their glass stilettos; he settled his accounts himself. I had heard these warnings and clues to his character from as far away as Ravenna. The field of his ruin was as wide as the vast plain of Santa Maria degli Angeli. I had thought, foolishly, that a man so famous and so feared would be easy to find. But nothing is easy to find in Venice. I exhausted myself like a clockwork toy. I was down to my last francs. My lodgings in Rialto had not been paid since the end of January; if I paid my landlord I would be beggared. My clothes were wearing thin, and my raw feet were howling for a new pair of boots. The threat of poverty, which should have acted as a goad, sapped the last of my energy.

A bad wind and a high tide had flooded the streets. Everything from St Mark's to Rialto was awash. Cold seawater had lapped in over the top of my boots, freezing my ankles while sending salty stains up my legs, and I decided to cross the Rialto bridge and wandered through Santa Croce to San Stae.

Upon my arrival in Venice, I had been directed to my lodgings by the boatman who had rowed me in. The landlord was a big red-faced bossy man with strong ideas. When I enquired of Bastoni, I was told with great vehemence, and much shaking of the head, 'You don't want to go there, not there. Best not even to say the name. I'll pretend I haven't heard you. There we are.'

He presented me with the same blank welcoming face of my arrival with all traces of disgust and disapproval wiped off as though with a towel.

Another day, seeing me set off in the opposite direction

to my habitual one, he demanded, 'Where are you off to, signor?'

Was it my imagination that he added the 'signor' as an afterthought? Had this man seen through me?

'I have a mind to explore the other side of the Bridge.'

Mine host let out a theatrical splutter, followed by a solemn gasp and a ferocious shaking of his grey mane; then he crossed himself, looked anxiously to either side, then leant forward as though to whisper and shouted in my ear, 'Never! Never go there, signor. The bridge is a whore, signor. The fairest bridge in the world, set there to lure you to the other side. Don't do it, signor. Don't do it, I tell you. That bridge is limbo, oh yes, it divides heaven and hell. If you cross that bridge, I'll ask you to settle your bill for I may not be seeing you again. Am I clear?'

This message rang in my ears for hours after it was delivered. During my early weeks, I had heeded it, but now that the water rolled right into the hallway of my hotel I took advantage of the confusion to cross over the brazen bridge. I took myself into a maze of tiny streets so dark and narrow and draped with washing that I could hardly navigate my way out into some fresh air. When I turned back, it was only to get more lost and more deeply entrenched in lanes of hovels and dirt. The vapours and the dark cobwebby feel of those tunnel-like streets made me feel faint. I sat for a time on a small hump-backed foot-bridge, clinging to its railings to keep my head from falling down. When I came to, I found myself staring through black patterned iron down a vista of water with houses leaning in on either side. These are views to be had all over Venice, yet I had never paused to look. I was struck by the stillness of that watery street and again by the simplicity of the Gothic arches of the ironwork which, together with a base of roundels, made as pleasant a balustrade as I had ever seen. I did not realize then but I was halfway to being cured of my apathy. I had begun again to amass details, stockpiling ideas for the palace.

By degrees, I made my way to a dead end: an open quay of slabbed marble in front of the pillared portico of San Stae. There was nowhere to sit but on the ground, so I sat there by the water steps like a package awaiting collection. I wrapped my wool cloak more tightly around me and dangled my aching feet over the edge of the Grand Canal. It was there that my gondolier and future confidant, Giovanni Contarini, found me, sleeping, as he so often reminded me, like an abandoned baby swaddled in black. When he offered me his services for the remainder of the day, I had little choice but to accept him. I shuddered at the thought of the stinking labyrinth behind me and, unlike the English lord who had left such a mark on the city's imagination, I could not swim.

'Where are you going, milord?' Giovanni asked me, with gently mocking flattery.

'Take me to Bastoni's,' I told him, with as much authority as I had been able to use in the last seven weeks put together, 'and a bit less of the milord, do you hear?'

Giovanni smiled and puckered his mouth into a Cupid pout. Later he told me that this was something he had practised and refined to an art. He claimed that he would have long since starved or succumbed to the fever had it not been for his thick chestnut curls and the sensuality of his mouth. 'The ladies love it, and sometimes, you know, there are gentlemen who have their fancies too. Winter is very long and not easy for a gondolier. We have to fish and that again is not easy for a boy who has spent so long learning to fish compliments, eh?' he said, and smiled so broadly that I felt myself forced to join him.

'Look,' he said, once he had settled me on to the damp cushions of his barque, 'Giovanni knows where Bastoni plays his games. But you cannot get in without a mask. The house rules are very important at Bastoni's.' He stooped to cross his thumbnail over his throat, momentarily upsetting the rhythm of his oar.

'You understand?' he asked me, suddenly worried that he might have offended me and lost his day's trade.

I nodded, somewhat indifferently. The slow rocking of the gondola was encouraging me to sleep.

'Giovanni could take you to a nice place to play cards, if you like.'

I nodded again then closed my eyes. Although it was still light, the winter evening was on its way. Soon the sky would be full of stars. I imagined no better place than the one I had to watch them. I saw Orion and the Milky Way, the Great Bear and the North Star.

'Take heed of the Northern Star, boy!' Rocking in the gondola I thought of my master, of the tricks I had played on him, the tools I had hidden; the scalpel I threw away. He had worked so hard and worked me so hard too. By the time he bought me he lived in fear of his old age and incapacity. I was to have been his insurance against disaster. Sometimes, it seemed that he taught me with a frenzy, making my fingers ache with his flurries of slaps and my mind futile with all his demands. No sooner would I finish a piece of carving than he would cast it aside as flawed and worthless and have me start again. His eyes burnt when I damaged a stone and he warmed willow withies on my back. I see now that he was anxious to teach me all he knew, to make me competent to fulfil his commissions in the event of his sickness. The sickness was in him, even then, corroding his peace.

The water by night was so peaceful, though, that my master soon slipped from my mind. As I glided along the canals, interrupted in my thoughts only by the occasional seabird cries of Giovanni as he turned blind corners, a calm seeped over me, lulling my fears away. The water rocked me with the gentleness of a mother. I forgot that I was a fugitive from my past and from myself, I forgot that I was an impostor. I even forgot that I was an Eugubino, a landlocked Umbrian with an inborn horror of water. Every time I opened my eyes, I saw palaces, bits of palaces, which I began to store away in my mind for future use on my own. For the first time since my arrival, darkness fell without any accompanying sinister feelings. I felt safe with Giovanni, which shows both how foolish and how lucky I was. He had steered me into a part of the city I did not know and he moored at the head of an unlit alleyway. Then he guided me, lantern in hand, to a battered, nameless doorway and knocked out what must have been a code. I was pulled and shoved through an equally dark courtyard, encouraged up some steps, then led into a small rank room where a group of cut-throats and ruffians was drunkenly playing cards. Fear arose only when I looked round and saw that Giovanni had gone.

'Giovanni?' I demanded.

'Keep the riff-raff outside,' I was told gruffly.

I was supplied with a pink glass of hot spiced wine, which was welcome on that cold night. There was little heating in the room which, despite its high ceiling, had only a brazier of hot ashes in the corner.

'I understand you want to play cards.'

'Maybe,' I answered, with a coolness that I by no means felt.

'Here it's yes or no. This is a serious establishment,' I was told by a man with a bulbous nose and eyes like two black currants soaked in brine. His voice was as cold and sharp as a stalactite hovering in the air, unstable and dangerous. He rubbed his hands together, cracking his knuckles inside the half-gloves he wore.

'Maybe,' I replied again, looking now at the three tables with their players.

There was a pause in the general conversation, if such I can call the ribald shouting match I found there, as the company summed me up. The long silence was broken by one of the players calling across to me, 'What do you play?'

'Briscola,' I called back, although the size of the room scarcely warranted it. Then the hubbub began again, starting with its full volume as though sliced by a knife and then respliced.

'Shall we?' the same man called to me, motioning to the place across his table which was at present occupied by a soldier swaying in his cups. My opponent dealt, handing me the pack to cut. Three cards each and bastoni for trumps. I knew I would win as soon as I saw the queen of bastoni slide under the pack. I had sixty francs left in my pocket and in the world. I bet fifty and won. I could have beaten him a second time, but I needed a lot more than a hundred francs to keep me going in Venice. I let my opponent win the second game, giving him back his lost fifty francs. I had decided to keep on Giovanni for the remainder of my stay. It would be infinitely less lonely with him. He could show me around, guide me through his puzzling home town. I decided to get him to take me to a bootmaker. I'd get some boots made to fit my feet. By not concentrating, I nearly lost my third game, then the huntsman's instinct took me over. I followed and chased my prey. I must have played him down to nearly his last coin because he was sweating and his eyes had a desperate look in them that I recognized from my own. I decided to leave him wounded but not slain. He begged me to play again, double or quits. When I would not, he toyed with a dagger that I saw he had partly concealed under his jacket. Again there was a hovering silence. Then the invisible conductor struck his baton and the orchestra played on.

I left, expecting to feel the sharp edge of his blade in my back. All down the steps I anticipated the traditional

Venetian treatment for runaways, the thin blade of a glass dagger in the back or side, thrust in and broken at the hilt. Through the curling fog I saw Giovanni waiting for me and he led me safely back to his gondola.

'Where do you live, signor?'

I told him and he whistled with scorn. 'In God's name, why do you live there?'

I shrugged and told him I was a stranger.

'Tomorrow at ten o'clock I will come for you. You will see my gondola waiting by the bridge. I will find you decent lodgings and a servant.'

'What servant?' I asked.

'Me,' he said, smiling in such a way that all his face exuded pleasure. I tried to pay him, but he said, 'Tomorrow,' and pushed away my money.

That night I dreamt of a room full of silks folded and stacked. A circle of women was stitching the edges of the silk together making a pool like rippling water between their knees. Then the room became a garden, fragrant with May flowers, and Donna Donatella walked by in a gown made of stitched petals. She was holding a small purse in her hand; as she passed, a waft of orange flower passed with her. She turned and spoke to me. 'See what a sweet scent it has,' she said, holding out the purse for me to smell. I dropped to one knee and sniffed it. Her wrist had the scent of orange flowers, but the purse burst open and out of it fell the skin of Admiral Bragadino. I started back, and she laughed, flipping the skin back into her purse as quickly as the flick of a serpent's tongue.

All night the canal water rustled like blown silk outside my hotel window, licking the pavement with its high tide.

⊰ VIII ⊱

✚ I am like a mule. I cannot move forward without a goad. My ideas travel from my mind to my mouth and then stick in my throat and choke me. I attribute this to my native clumsiness. My master may have turned me into a mason, and Vitelli may have transformed me into something between a gentleman and a buffoon, but I was born a peasant. I have the wide hands and splayed feet of a *contadino*. My feet are weighted with mud, weighted with stone. Some things cannot change as easily as others. I am ashamed to relate to what extent the advent of Giovanni Contarini changed my life in Venice. He moved me to San Lio, opposite the Campo della Guerra. He struck a deal for a risible sum of money to rent the first floor of the residence of a Signor Paccagnella. This comprised a long drawing room, which my landlord insisted was universally known as the Peacock Salon, with nine rooms leading from it. Both the landlord and Giovanni apologized profusely for the dilapidated state of the furnishings, whose richness, to my eye, surpassed anything I had imagined. The landlord wished for a year's rent in advance, which would have seemed ridiculous had it not been such a paltry sum as to make no difference. I had not the least intention of staying in Venice beyond the spring.

I believe the first serious doubt Giovanni had as to my origins came when he saw my one small case and opened it to find only a Bible, a silver knife and fork and a half-hunter watch rattling inside. I caught his suspicion and threw it back to him. 'The war,' I said, intimating that it had stripped me down to this sorry state.

Giovanni shrugged, unable to deny that there had indeed been a war recent enough to have so denuded me. He stood by a tall window overlooking a courtyard of statues and oleanders; his lips were moving and muttering what sounded like whispered imprecations but were actually calculations. Giovanni in his twentieth year could not read a word, but he knew his numbers and had such a head for figures that he delighted in equations. He had studied prices and he carried the knack of trading in his blood. No matter how indolent he might seem, one eye was eternally open for a bargain. He husbanded my own meagre fortune with the care of a market gardener tending his onions and asparagus on the island of Sant' Erasmo. In some ways, I became like a mannequin in his hands. It would be hard at times to say who ruled whom. In those early days I took him up, and he took me in hand. It did not matter to me that Giovanni occasionally had the upper hand: I knew his hand to be temporarily surer than my own. I had only to look at my fingers to see they were palsied with doubts.

The reign of the Galantuomo had begun all over Italy; only Venice and Rome were still immune to his manners and his charm. The new king set the tone for the new age. I was like a pensioner waiting in a dark antechamber to be let into his light. My initiation into society was so close I could smell the trail of bergamot and rosewater it left in its wake. I came from a different tribe; at some point I had to step into the painted, paraded society that moved all around me with its measured steps. I had to dare to join them. The Venetians referred proudly to their square as the drawing room of Europe; but I was still uninitiated, no matter how many times I crossed that vast and misty drawing room. One day soon I would have to go inside those palaces and run the gauntlet of society's stares, test my disguise for its real worth and Vitelli's experiment for its true value. Meanwhile, Giovanni helped to equip me for this ordeal. He escorted me to a shoemaker beside San Tomà and to a Jewish tailor who made two suits, shirts and four cravats, two of silk and two of satin, that transformed my appearance within the week. Giovanni insisted that I indulge in waistcoats to wear under my new frock-coat; he made me buy gloves in the *Frezzeria* and a cane from a shop in the Campo San Bartolomeo.

'I never really thought you were a milord,' Giovanni confided in me, 'but now . . . we shall see. Perhaps you will be surprised to find yourself catching a milady if you hold out your net.'

My first clothes had aroused little comment, my new ones even less. Venice held a magnifying mirror to herself so closely that she had no time for outsiders. Like an ornate and slightly shabby theatre set, she occasionally opened her heavy velvet curtains to swallow up an interesting and eligible visitor. This fading beauty had simple tastes in food and would only pretend to try exotic dishes, nothing that might further damage her already clogged veins or her pock-marked complexion. Small, plain, unthreatening morsels were gobbled up and spat out as picked bones for the ossuary. For the rest there was an air of resignation and gloom which pervaded the city. The occupation of the Austrian army and the inherent defeat that those foreign soldiers signified brought the feeling of a lingering disease to the already endemic melancholy of the lagoon.

The heart was dying, the lungs wheezed, the blood oozed round the ancient body. Where the mud and the sewage blocked veins completely, life began to stagnate.

The ague victims were lowered from windows and bundled into boats. By day there was the sweet-sickly smell of gangrene in the air; by night, under the shrouding mists of Venice, there was a layer of immunity. By day, the robust tunes of Austrian orchestras played in various parts of the city, sending their clear notes out into the wintry haze. This music was ignored with the same resentful silence as greeted everything else that hailed from Vienna. By night the grim silence was punctuated by the splash of disappearing bodies and rebellious bells. Wooden poles, stone, bones, mud, slime and water were but a few of the layers, the archaeology of the city's soul was as rich as its coffers. Byzantine arches crowded against Gothic turrets, Renaissance doorways were squeezed between medieval pillars with wooden huts on stilts overlapping Roman columns. There was gold, mould, mosaics and polished stone, blocks and rotting planks all askew, and all afloat appearing now like a brilliant smile and now like a grotesquely broken and mended mouth. Style had run riot for so many centuries. It was a carcass of antiquities, a tray of slops from a prince's table.

After Giovanni took me under his wing, I still drifted up and down the arcade outside Florian's *caffè* like a lost ship rocked by a restless wave. The brightly lit lamps, the plum-coloured velvets of the seats and chairs, the quaintly painted frescos and the liveried waiters dancing attendance all looked ridiculously small. I saw them like the miniature doll's-house interiors that the craftsmen of Santo Stefano made. I knew that if I went in and sat on one of the rickety little chairs it would snap and break. I would be unable to get my huge hands around the tiny coffee cups. It was another world in there, an alien world that I watched from the outside, like a continual puppet show.

When the time came, however, I would walk in through the thin double doors and take my place, splintering that wonderland to keep my appointment with Vitelli. I would have walked through the gates of hell for him – this might have been easier, if anything, than the doors of Florian's. But, then, had not Dante copied his hell from Venice itself, from the furnaces of the Arsenale? Venice is unique, if only in the perversity of her splendour. Inside and out, there was nothing but reflections. Was there ever such a vain face as that of Venice? Art, artifice and nature had all conspired to flatter her. Whole islands reflected each other in their architecture, mirroring tower for tower in ghostly games across the lagoon. The canals reflected each façade, catching them up and folding and knotting them like the gnarled twists of wisteria. Windows mirrored windows and the water threw back their light, glinting and dancing on internal glasses and more mirrors like a network of spies. Giovanni steered me through the sluggish waters, cutting through the constant illusions with his skilfully managed, but slightly unstable, barque. His service transposed me from sewer rat to one of many hundreds of visitors to the city doing what all foreigners must, gliding along the Grand Canal to the strains of accordion music.

Giovanni gave me a persona; I existed because I was his master. People would ask him, 'Who is that man, so nervous and silent?'

And Giovanni would calm their curiosity by saying, 'Why, he is my master. He lives in the Paccagnelli Palazzo on the Rio della Guerra.'

'Ah,' the enquirer would nod sagely, and partially satisfied. 'I see.' And the air of grim mystery that had hitherto surrounded my surreptitious meanderings began to fade.

Although there was no contract between us, Giovanni became my factotum, my man. He did for me all that needed doing. In some fields, his skill and efficiency bordered on genius; in others, he had a negative excellence. He did nothing by half-measures. In the kitchen he became a dangerous weapon. He managed to combine ambition with an ineptitude so great that his failures were not only inedible, their smell lingered in all nine rooms of my house. Thus, upon my suggestion, we began to eat out in local taverns and wine shops where hot food was served.

When I was a boy, I thought the rich ate all my favourite foods in great abundance and I often envied them for it. As my master and I chewed stale bread with a raw onion, the sounds of banquets served in noble halls had made my mouth water. Had I known that even in eating a man must serve an apprenticeship, I could have saved myself those early envious thoughts. Fine food is poison. It can be as bitter as antimony and bitter almonds and as repulsive as swallowing live toads. Like the poison the emperor took every day to stop himself being poisoned, fine food must be taken daily until the system becomes immune to its ravages and the tastebuds beaten and abused to the point where they not only accept but savour every vile concoction under the sun.

My gut took over from my feet as the chief victim of this stage of my apprenticeship. I ate things in that city of an unnatural nature. I ate fish that crawled out of the sea on their own legs; intermediary creatures with goggle eyes and glassy skins through which one could see their inner anatomy. I ate things that any member of my family would have run away from, had they been confronted with the like in Gubbio.

And all the while, to add insult to injury, as the legs and fingers, eyes and whiskers tickled my throat to make me sick, I was bombarded by Venetian pride. As soon as my mouth was full, someone would be deputized to molest me.

'So, what do you think of Venice? Beautiful, eh?'

I wondered again how every waiter, vagrant and half-starved pedlar knew of such matters. Where was the fragrance in their miserable lives, truncated by ague and hardship? How could the otherwise ignorant be so erudite? I myself knew a little of the towers and churches of Gubbio, I had seen *The Madonna of the Pomegranate* painted by Pier Francesco Fiorentino and other treasures of the city, but I had been ten years apprenticed to a master mason and two more years working in his studio as a stone-carver myself. I had been forced to see certain things. My master beat me with a leather thong if I failed to observe the statues and the pictures in the churches we worked in. He trained my hand and my eye, but who trained the eyes and imaginations of all those ragged courtiers?

> *O Venezia benedetta,*
> *Non le vogio più lasar!*

Every few days I wiped the mineral salts that exuded from the walls of my apartments with the same nonchalant care that a mother might wipe her baby's face. I ceased to see everything in terms of decay; the city converted me. I succumbed to her delusion. Despite the evidence of her sinking, I saw her very existence as a proud refusal to die. I concentrated not on the dead tips of her body with their decomposing remains, but on the miracle of the continued life of the bits of the great skeleton that still lived.

Lulled by Giovanni's garrulous indolence, I became an admirer of Venice. I viewed her first as a stranger might view an ageing courtesan and then discover gradually that, despite the garish paint and the peeling make-up, the shredding silk of her gown and the musty smell of her ancient flesh, she still had more wit and spirit than many a pretty girl and that she had a perfume of her own, an essential oil of sensuality which was lost in the artifice unless you were very near.

As we drifted along the canals taking what Giovanni laughingly called 'a breath of fresh air' he told me about his family. There were two parts to it, which Giovanni kept segregated in his mind, bringing them out in strict rotation. There was his immediate family, his widowed mother and his three sisters and a great many cousins all bearing the name Maria – to differentiate between them, he referred to them as Maria of this or Maria of that, Maria of Giacomo or Maria of San Lorenzo. It took me many years to follow these family ties, not least because the second part of Giovanni's family seemed to include the entire history of Venice, from her founding in 421 by his ancestors, to the seizure of the body of St Mark from the Muslims and its immersion in a barrel of pork, to the explosion of one of his forebears from overeating. These details would be told to me with a passionate pride. Every time some new occurrence was relayed, Giovanni would pause in his lanky rowing and thump himself tearfully on the chest.

'My family, Signor Gabriele, my ancestors,' he would say, threatening to capsize the gondola with his emotion and his desire to be believed. There was scarcely a family in Venice that was not woven into the tapestry of Giovanni's past. He spoke of the fifteenth century as though it were but last week. All the great houses of all the great Contarini were as familiar in Giovanni's speech as dear aunts and uncles. Not content with this, he was also closely, 'but closely, Signor Gabriele,' related to the Baffo, Balbi and Benzon families, and the Dondolo, Foscari and Loredano, also the Marcello, Queriai, Tron and Vendramin. 'But everyone,' he would burst out, unable to keep up his lists, 'really,' he would insist, forestalling any possible disbelief, 'really everyone.' And he would turn so red in the face that he would seem about to explode in imitation of, and homage to, his favourite ancestor. I was his captive audience, prone in his funereal gondola with its chipped black paint on the edges where it had grazed against rival boats. I listened and learnt a strange garbled history of the city. Our routes were random, except that Giovanni still always contrived to pass the pink and white marble of the Ca' Contarini at least once a day like a Muhammadan turning to Mecca with his prayers.

Giovanni unwound me like a tangled ball of string, which he ravelled into a presentable skein. Whenever I asked him why he refused to guide me to Bastoni's club he always replied, 'I can still see your nerves, signor. You know you need to be steady to play cards with professionals. I have found myself a pretty job. I don't want to lose it yet.'

This presumption angered me. I remonstrated several times with him, and at last I shouted at him and berated him so roundly that he took me back to San Lio in sulky silence and then rowed away. When he returned, twenty-four hours later, I was so pleased to see him I could have kissed his curly lips. I had reverted into a creature of shadows and darkness, had not dared leave the house for fear of missing him, and inside the palatial rooms I felt a loneliness that convinced me I would never give way to my temper again. When at last he came, he was neither apologetic nor resentful. He took up his position as valet and jack-of-all-trades with a boyish ease I envied him.

Giovanni loved secrets. He had tried many times to make me unfold my own needs and desires to him so that we might share the complicity of my endeavours. It pleased him that I was a gambler. Like a crab who finds a crustacean changing shells, he thrived on my vulnerability. He would have liked to have known all my weaknesses so as to gloat over them, but more than that so as to be the general in charge of the strategic protection of my fallibilities. He had often offered to procure a pretty girl to spend an occasional evening with me. I found myself refusing, out of shyness and a sudden prudishness. It seemed that Vitelli would never have allowed his valet to pimp for him and I felt honour bound to emulate my idol.

On the other hand, my chaste dreams of Donna Donatella had given way to sensual explorations of her hair and hands, her neck and feet, her breasts, shoulders, back, thighs, her skin, her breath and her secret places. In my dreams I kissed her so passionately that our two heads fused and our tongues lived in each other's mouth for days on end. There was no part of her body I had not imagined, touched, stroked, caressed and kissed. I loved her more than ever before. I lived beside her warmth, drowning in her fragrance of orange flowers, smothered by her hair and her limbs.

There had been times in prison when I found myself envying the *castrati* in the choirs. I didn't know for sure if such half-men existed any more, but my uncle Luciano always threatened us boys with having our balls cut off if we didn't behave and then being forced to sing in the choir. I had heard some boys in the choir at Gubbio, singing with voices so high and so sweet they made me feel dizzy. I had asked my master if these were *castrati* and he had told me they were. I also knew that Domenico Venturini had been gored in the groin by a mad bull and his voice had a strangled quality that made people both laugh behind his back and pity him. After the first six months in prison, my yearning quietened. I didn't know if I could bear another such time. I sometimes felt aroused at the most grossly unattractive spectacles. I began to look on statues and pictures in a lustful way. I found I could no longer trust myself to visit churches. I fancied that the chaste virgins on their tombs were flesh and blood and came to me in my truckle bed naked but veiled. I buried myself inside them with the ferocity of a snorting bull. I watched, from afar, the courtesans on the lagoon, each with a coloured lantern, each as alluring to me as life itself. When Giovanni left, I spent the entire night pacing the Peacock Salon lusting after them. My love for Donna Donatella was unabated. I loved her with all my soul, but my body mutinied daily and demanded satisfaction.

Giovanni invited me back into his gondola. I stepped down into its dark cushions with the emotions of a reprieved man. We rocked with the rhythm of gentle lovemaking. I had only missed a day, but it had seemed infinitely longer.

'So, what now, Signor Gabriele? Tell me something nice.' I understood that I was to tell him something salacious or demeaning to myself. I toyed with the idea of confessing to my fear of horses. As a boy of the lagoon he might sympathize with me, but I had to be careful not to give away too much about my origins so I compromised and pleased us both by admitting to my lust.

'You have made me a happy man,' he announced, grinning in a way that was scarcely decent and made me fear for a moment that his infernal dialect had come between me and my meaning.

'No, really, you have made me a happy man.'

I waited, apprehensively.

'My cousin, Maria of San Polo, is waiting for this news. She has been standing by from the first evening we met. She keeps accusing me of not mentioning how pretty and how very clean she is. Let's go,' he said, racing back towards Rialto with a speed worthy of the regatta.

Over the years of our acquaintanceship, Giovanni often took it upon himself to procure girls for me with as little success as he brought to his cooking. However, in this first instance, his descriptions of his cousin Maria of San Polo were, if anything, modest. She was a tall, pale girl with thick chestnut hair that she wore loose but not tangled, and she had the grey-green eyes of the Adriatic. In fact, her eyes had such a trusting, innocent air that I found myself reluctant to take advantage of her. This scruple was no more than skin deep, and since she had some of the ebullient character of her cousin Giovanni, we had soon made more use of the apartment at San Lio than it was likely to see again for some time. Each of the nine rooms, including Giovanni's modest abode, was christened by our lust. The marquetry floor of the Peacock Salon marked both her back and mine. I drank the soapy sweat from her skin, following the contours of her bones with my tongue. It was not a hurried, bungled tumble under a bush; it was hours of repressed passion drawn out like the taut string of a violin until fine music flowed. We pleased each other, ravished each other, turning again and again for more. Only Maria of San Polo's face, so pretty, I know, blurred when we were close so that she became faceless, mysterious. I wanted her so much, but I wanted her to be another woman. My first impression of innocence had been an illusion, but Maria's sweetness was real, and the next three days did more to unravel my nervous system than all Giovanni's measured rowing. On the third day Maria announced that she must depart. She dressed, named her price and accepted her payment with a demure curtsy. Giovanni escorted her home, returning with a white mask and the intention to lead me to Bastoni's. It seemed that when I was a naked soul I could not wear a mask, but now that I had graduated to being a man of confidence I had to mask my power.

⇥ IX ⇤

Under cover of night Giovanni led me to the gambling den. I knew the city fairly well now, thanks to his exertions. There were many canals and lesser *rii* that I recognized as he rowed me from the Rio della Guerra into Santa Maria, and San Severo and across to San Lorenzo. That night I made a point of memorizing the landmarks along the route, so as to be able to find my own way to Bastoni's in future should the necessity arise. We passed the Questura and moved into the foul-smelling capillaries of Arsenale. When we finally moored, it was outside the squalid gaming room to which Giovanni had first taken me.

'This is not it,' I told him in a gritted whisper. I knew a little about Bastoni's from Vitelli. It was he who had first described the club to me. He said that he had frequented it during a phase of dissipation and disillusion after the defeat of the Piedmontese at Navarra and the subsequent peace, which left him with nowhere to go but Venice or Rome. When Rome fell to the French, only Venice remained a safe haven for exiles such as himself.

'We began gambling to raise money for a new republic. In 1849 we used the vice for a noble cause. Then time passed and it had entered our blood, my blood. I became a slave to the cards. At first I laughed it off as a show of affection for my Venetian grandmother. You see, I have Alvise blood on my mother's side. But it was more than that, more than a habit, it was a disease, a fever that burned me.

'Mazzini says we all have our own devils. If that is so, gambling is mine. I have had to fight it. I still fight it, even now, six years at least since I last touched a pack of cards, I still fight my urge to play.

'Bastoni ran his club like an aquarium. He kept a strange assortment of creatures there. Some of his guests went dressed as animals, but the strangest creatures of all were the drugged slaves who worked for him. These were rumoured to be men he had broken at the gaming tables whose lives he had spared in return for their servitude. It was said that these henchmen were his executioners, although I have also heard tell that it was Bastoni himself who dispatched any troublesome or insolvent players. There are those who claim that he relished the task. Be that as it may, his staff dispose of the bodies. One of these servants is said to be an English lord who gambled his entire estate away at Bastoni's.'

Like pieces of a jigsaw puzzle, Vitelli had built up a picture for me of the club. He told me that the enslaved minions all wore black velvet doublets and hose, black masks and black ostrich plumes in their tricorn hats. He told me that they never spoke. It was rumoured that their tongues had been cut out as part of the bargain. All that he told me of that murderous place, he told me to warn me away from its snapping jaws. Men who were led there in good faith were later carried away in sacks. At one point, seeing my morbid fascination for that evil den, he paused in his descriptions and took my hand.

'Swear to me that you won't go there. Swear to me on

your honour that you will never put yourself at the mercy of that bloodthirsty pirate.'

'Colonel,' I assured him, finding it hard as usual to use his name, 'you may rest assured that I will never put myself at the mercy of this Bastoni, but as to promises, it is too soon for me to start swearing on an honour that I have not yet earned. What use are the promises of a worm, a maggot? Let me grow out of this larva first. I don't even know who I am.'

He apologized and calmed down. I suppose the apology should have been mine. I had made my first use of his lessons on the duplicity of language. It was he who had taught me to manage words in a courtly way and already the words had turned round to bite the hand that spelt them. In truth, I had no intention of putting myself at the mercy of the ruthless Bastoni: I intended to win.

Before all the angels I have carved, and all the love I have given and by all that I have held dear, by my very dreams, I ask: How can I praise a god who gives us wisdom only in our old age? How can I praise the god who gives us the vision to see our mistakes when it is too late to correct them? What irony is that? What justice is there to the human heart in such unloving guidance? I know that I must first tell how my cup filled before I grieve for its curdling. Suffice it to say that I no longer pity the luckless man who is forced to fall back on thought.

Sometimes my mind grows confused. My memory silts. Giovanni tells me it is old age, but neither I nor he are old men. I always had a clear head when I gambled. I always concentrated and stayed calm. Playing cards for wealth or death, you lay your heart on the table. I was not ready then to admit to the whole nature of my love. I hid it until through a passion of gambling, I had served my apprentice-ship to love. While I played, I gave myself entirely to the game. Moment by moment I possessed it. For all her sweet sensuality, I know that I didn't, wouldn't, ever love Maria of San Polo. I needed her. I delighted in her and I grew fond of her but love was in my fan of cards, and, once the veil lifted, it had to be for Donna Donatella. I have taken to gambling again to keep my head clear. I gamble medicinally. Sometimes I miss the element of danger. As Vitelli pointed out, it was part of the attraction of Bastoni's that one risked death by going there.

Giovanni Contarini was a true Venetian in his nature. He rarely offered more than passive resistance to any plan, it was in his blood to flow with the tide. He gossiped because he loved to gossip, but he rarely passed judgement on anyone or anything. Whenever I was displeased with him I thought his mind was like a muddy channel trapping all that passed in its bed of slime. Usually, I found his qualities attractive, even his continual gathering of information. I saw this trait as like a walled orchard catching all the seeds and fruits and pips of fading flowers. On good days, Giovanni had a mind like the pomegranate garden behind the villa at Castello where Donna Donatella had walked in the morning sun, framed by the scarlet blooms that sat in the pomegranate trees like exotic butterflies. It was never Giovanni's wish to stop me from going to Bastoni's, but it was his fervent desire that I should not be killed there. His last passenger still hadn't come out.

'I waited a week for him, going backwards and forwards to eat and then keeping guard at the place he had told me. He never appeared. I saw a big man and a dwarf, both dressed in black costumes with feathered hats, take a sack away on the third day after he had gone in.

'I could be very useful to you, signor, and ... well, you could be very useful to me. Giovanni thinks that even if the signor has nothing to do, it would be better to do it in one piece. Bastoni's is a place for desperate men. Everyone knows it is the haunt of assassins and thieves. Even the authorities know this, but they let the desperadoes kill each other – it saves paying for their trials.

'If I may speak plainly, for some things the signor is very knowing, but for others, it seems he is still a child.' Thus spoke my keeper.

'Don't ever think I have nothing to do,' I told him, ignoring most of what he had said. 'I have so much to do there will scarcely be years in my life sufficient to do it.'

Giovanni smiled politely with an encouraging look which combined both disbelief and faint praise.

'Don't give me that condescending look. I tell you I have a mission in my life.'

There was a further disinterested silence.

'It's true. I am going to build a palace.'

Giovanni continued to row, striding backwards and forwards along the prow as he did so, pulling the oar to him with long even strokes. I felt my secret dream splash, like a drop of water into the canal. On either side of us, palaces rose up majestically from the murky water, lit from within by hundreds of candle flames. We turned the corner into the wider Rio di San Lorenzo and another vista of yet more palaces.

'Half of the palaces of Venice are empty or used only as warehouses, you could buy one easily.'

'I don't want to buy one, Giovanni, I want to build one.'

'I see,' he said, puzzled.

'I have designed one in my head and I want to take it to a hill somewhere and build it standing in its own gardens.'

He shrugged and rowed on past façade after façade of pillars and balconies and inlaid marble, towering over us in the moonlight. The more he eyed me from his disapproving silence, staring down at me as though I had just escaped from the asylum on San Servolo, the more I felt obliged to explain my project to him. I had run through the construction of several wings of my palace when he interrupted me. 'Why? Why do this?'

'I am in love, Giovanni.'

'Dear God,' he said, with such relief that he nearly toppled into the muddy channel he was navigating, 'you had me worried. Eh, now I understand: you want to make a summer villa for your bride.'

'Perhaps.'

'You see, a palace is in a city, a villa is in the country. You cannot have a palace in the country. It is not possible. Palazzo Contarini degli Scringi, Palazzo Contarini Fasan, Palazzo Contarini Angaran, those are palaces.'

It began to rain in a fine drizzle over the city, bringing with it swirls of fog like bunched voile. I slumped back under the awning, gathering the soiled and misunderstood bits of my ideas back to me like lost chicks under my wing.

I realized I didn't have enough balconies on my plans. I would have to add more, and a pillared loggia on the first floor with these Venetian pillars, patterned in ways I had never seen before. Not even my master, I thought, would have known these Eastern designs. He would have been astonished by the carvings here. I would buy some charcoal on the following morning and begin to draw these oriental capitols, also the balustrades ...

'Here we are,' Giovanni called in under my sheltering *felze*. Looking out into the grey mist, I saw that he had tricked me. It was the same place in which I had first gambled.

'This is not it.'

'Surely the signor needs more than half a roll of gold pieces tonight.'

I wanted to tell him to row on. I wanted to explain that it was never lucky to gamble in two different places: if I won here, I risked losing where it mattered most. Before I had a chance to speak coherently, the water doors opened and a cloaked figure leant out. To speak now would be to make Giovanni lose face, and to do that was to risk losing him, or so it felt that night. The gondola was moored now to a rotting pole, and for a moment I sat and he stood, both locked in our stubbornness.

'What is this?' a voice demanded suspiciously from the opened door.

'A customer,' I told him and got out.

Once more I was jostled through a swampy courtyard and up some steps. This time the moon illuminated the squalor that on the previous occasion I had only imagined. My pride was already nettled and I did not take kindly to being pushed by the attendant.

'I have no need of your assistance to walk, thank you. I do not have a wooden leg.' The attendant sprang back from me as though stung by a hornet. It was well known that Bastoni had a carved limb – his name was probably just a reference to his peg-leg.

Once again it was cold and damp in the gaming room. This time I noticed that the walls were greasy and dis-coloured. The floor was heavily stained and scattered with a token layer of sawdust. Six men were standing around: two were blond sailors who looked like brothers, with pale parboiled eyes bloodshot by drink. They were propping each other up in a corner, nodding from time to time at each other and the room at large. There was a smell in the room of old wine and vomit superimposed on the usual odour of mould, which moved like an undercurrent through most Venetian houses. A third man, older and with a purple-veined face and swollen nose, was drinking on his own, staring morosely into his wine, as though it had just tried to cheat him. The remaining three were all dressed similarly to myself, although their clothes were less new and their buttons less polished than my own. Two tables stood empty, each waiting with a pack of cards pressed like a stigmata in its open palm. The third table was taken up by four grimly silent players at a game of poker.

'What do you play?' one of the three fellows asked, feigning as much boredom as his natural avarice would allow.

'Briscola,' I told him.

The tips of his thin moustache twitched in disappointment. He had a handsome face and fashionably sad eyes, but his pale wintry skin was pimply. One of his friends drawled from behind his back, 'We play poker here.'

'Congratulations. I play briscola. If there is to be no game I'll be on my way.' I turned to leave. They changed their minds, and we played my game. It was mine from the first hand. I picked the three of them as clean as a bleached fishbone. Their companion was a foreigner. He might even have been Austrian, but he seemed too nervous for that. I thought perhaps he was Russian. We played game after game and in each one I beat them. I was sure they had been intending to cheat. It is hard to cheat at briscola. They offered me a foursome but I trusted none of them enough. When we had finished, or rather when I had finished them and they no longer had a stake between them, the pimply one said, 'Now we'll play poker.'

'I don't play poker,' I told him.

From what I had seen of the game, it seemed to be a game of lies and bluff. Luck didn't seem to play much part in it. Vitelli hadn't shown me how to play poker but he had shown me my luck and the fragility of it. Briscola is a simple game; it doesn't require much luck to win, nor much skill. But poker is all about bluffing.

So I didn't play, but tried their tactics, gathering up my winnings into a leather pouch Giovanni had given me that night. The foreigner stayed my hand on the table. I pulled my fingers free.

'What if we do not want you to leave?'

He was looking straight at me. I stood up and took a step back from the table.

'Then I'll kill you,' I said, as matter-of-factly as I could.

'We are more than you,' one of his companions volunteered.

'Then a wooden leg will get the ones I miss,' I said, and turned to leave, exposing my back to their poisonous looks and any weapons they may have drawn. I did not look back. I opened the door and made my way through a passageway to another door and the outside stairs. I left a shudder in the room behind me like frozen fog. I was learning the politics of fear.

I was a mere ten days away from my meeting with Vitelli. I could take my purse of ten- and twenty-franc pieces and my pile of gold coins and go back to the Campo della Guerra and wait for him. I could go out in the morning and buy some more books and read them and be ready to please my tutor with my studies. I could save this money, each coin of which was more than my entire family ever saw at one time, and send enough of it to ease my mother's old age. 'Mother,' I called inside my head. 'Mother, look at your son now, squatting like a fat toad on the water. Listen to him croaking, gloating. Look at him wasting his life and other people's fortunes. Look at him squandering his luck.'

Giovanni steered me on, gliding through the moonlight reflections on the rippling water like a throw of shattered glass.

My mother would have been afraid of so much money. She would have seen the devil's hoofprint in it. I resolved to find a way of sending her ten francs a month. This would be enough to protect her and not too much to alarm her. Ten francs and a new linen sheet.

'Signor,' Giovanni whispered through the rain.

I looked out and saw a tall dark wall like the side of a prison or an orphanage.

'I'll wait for you,' he whispered again.

'What, for a week?'

Giovanni crossed himself and grimaced. He looked genuinely afraid. He called in a low gull-like voice, '*Sta lì*.'

His bird cry was met with silence. He handed me my white paste mask and I fumbled with it, trying to tie the ribbons behind my head. I had never been good at bows in the prison, they seemed a very cumbersome way to join two laces; however, Vitelli had insisted that I persist and eventually I found a laborious way of tying laces. This clumsy method did not rise to tying bows behind my head in the dark on a rocking boat outside a den of cut-throats. In the end I settled for a knot and had scarcely time to return the tricorn to my sweating head before Giovanni signalled to me to stand up.

I was led through a hall darker than the moonlit night outside. I hoped that the gaming room would be in true Venetian style, full of mirrors so that I might see myself again and regain my confidence. I needed to be strong to win. I had found pleasure in the arms of another woman. Had I betrayed Donna Donatella? A mirror would set my mind at rest. I had kept her image. I slapped my handmade boots across the wet marble floor repeating all my recent sins in my head: lust, greed, sloth, vanity. They were all the vices I had aspired to. There was no trace of the *contadino* in me as I traversed the vast labyrinth. The mask had finally brought me out of my chrysalis and I was drunk with power.

I had thought my guide was a child, his short legs scarcely bridged the stairs, but when he turned round ushering me abruptly into a lit salon I saw that he was a dwarf. His hands were deformed, cut off halfway down the fingers leaving truncated stumps that made him look amphibian, an impression enhanced by a black mask with a crested face. I knew he was a dwarf only by his eyes, which peered out of the appropriate holes in his mask showing clusters of wrinkles in the sickly green skin underneath and an expression of ancient scorn. The salon was a bottle green with yellow veins crudely painted on to give the sense of marble. The furniture had been upholstered in a watered green silk to match the walls, but between the fading of one and the peeling of the other there were only chance meetings of colour. A great many animals were sprawled across the chairs and sofas in this room. Later I saw that many were stuffed, although a number of slavering hounds were real enough. The centre of this room was bare except for an octagonal table, with drawers all round it. Upon it were several firearms, daggers and a rawhide whip. Although brightly lit, the salon seemed to be exclusively for the animals.

From that green room, that portal of the underworld, I was led from one communicating drawing room to the next, each a different colour both in walls and in furnishing. All these rooms were empty of human beings.

After four or five such chambers, we came upon a malodorous room where about a dozen black-costumed figures were pacing. Their masks were all fantastic, drawn from mythology and creatures from the sea-bed. One was so tall I felt sure he must be wearing stilts or the extravagantly platformed shoes worn by the gentlewomen of Venice to prevent their fine silks from trailing in the mire. The atmosphere was tense, made worse by the pacing, but thick and charged with vice. There were mirrors, tarnished and speckled with age and flecked with what either was or was meant to look like blood. I assumed that these creatures were the drugged slaves of Bastoni. I saw my own reflection in the once gaudy mirrors, but my earlier pride had evaporated, had been taken over by curiosity to study the bizarre masquerade around me. I was also eager to see Bastoni himself.

I believed that Bastoni really did have a remorseless savage streak in him, a cruel vein to which he gave vent whenever he had the chance, but I saw, too, that he must be a vain man who wallowed in his own reputation. When he stood out of the throng of servants, I knew him not by a limp but by its absence. He walked with perfect equilibrium – so perfect, indeed, that it hinted at the hidden wooden leg, carved, it was said, to the exact shape and weight of a real leg by a wood carver near the Accademia whose main trade was the carving of the gondolas' *forcola*. It was said that a man's amputated leg was delivered to the workshop one night and left there until the morning so that the master carpenter might take its every measurement and gauge the exact weight required, carving even the swelling of the onset of gangrene. Bastoni walked with the unerring step of a drunkard trying to look sober. He had a presence about him easily discernible from the cringing of his minions but also from some innate quality in himself. A frizz of black beard escaped from under the edge of his black sea monster's mask.

He was a tall man, as tall as me, and he stood close up to me for some seconds, trying to intimidate me. As I have said, I did not feel afraid.

'We pay a hundred francs here,' he said, in a deep melodious voice that jarred with his appearance.

I took the money from my purse. Behind his mask his eyes darted down to look into that leather pouch. He had Venetian eyes of a grey brown as clear as the pebbles on a beach and as limpid and changing in their colours as seawater rolling across rocks. Had I not known who he was, I would have said that he had honest eyes. Perhaps they were honest in their ruthlessness.

'What do you play?' he asked me, taking my money and handing it to a boy swaddled in a black silk costume that showed up his ribs like a bivalve fan.

'Briscola,' I told him.

'That we shall see,' he replied, tapping the floor with his wooden leg. As we spoke, I realized that all the past minutes from the time of my entry had been spent in silence. I remembered what Vitelli had told me about the tongueless losers. Perhaps I should have been more intimidated by the nuances of his game but, alas, the nuances were lost on me. I had neither the education nor the upbringing to feel fear at his elaborate stage play. Instead I felt faintly exhilarated to be allowed into some of the Carnival I thought I had missed. Safe behind my own mask, I was intoxicated by the spectacle of such orchestrated fantasy.

Then Bastoni led me into a salon of despair. After the rich but faded furnishings of the other rooms, this chamber had a grim, judicial air. In a corner, across an inlaid marble floor in black and grey, a huddle of semi-human shapes seemed to have locked into an embrace and died. Upon closer inspection, I saw that it was a knot of some five emaciated boys clothed in the regulation tight black costumes. They all wore strings of pearls, like the eyes of so many drowned sailors. Their heads were entirely encased in masks and, although they were faintly breathing, they were either asleep or unconscious. From a distance, I saw them as a giant spider or a great black crab. Along either wall on plain parallel wooden benches a number of despondent men waited like petitioners at a court of last appeal. One, who struck me under his disguise as a man far older than myself and somehow of great respectability, was holding his two cupped hands to his face, nursing, I supposed, a bleeding nose. His oyster gloves were stained to the wrists and his shoulders were shaking with a silent pain. At either door, at each end of this long narrow chamber a half-naked attendant stood with black dye ingrained in his skin and with a shiny mask consisting mostly of teeth and jagged edges. Each wielded a long whip held tightly in hands so large they could have cracked a human skull.

I began to realize a little more of what Vitelli had tried to warn me against: here was a place far more insidious than a mere gambling den. Bastoni held a court of vice, he dealt humiliation with his cards and ruin was the least of the concerns of the losers. At the time, I was ignorant of the great merchants of vice and perversion: I had never heard of the exploits of Gilles de Rais. With hindsight, I think that Bastoni had studied the French tormentor closely. The sense of artifice and imitation was everywhere. Yet centuries of state records and archives, and savagely enforced laws and rules, had left their seal even on the macabre farce of Bastoni's den of assassins. There were rules and laws in that gambling club: just as the medieval doge had been forced to sign a list of all his possessions from his position of absolute power. This list was read to him once a year to remind him of the unrivalled oppression of tradition in Venice. Thus, by a series of cruel reminders, the losers at the gaming tables knew exactly what gruesome fate awaited them. What had appeared to be a court of appeal was, in fact, just that. From there, a player had one last chance to win or to disappear.

Though the atmosphere of this last salon was full of gloom, I could hear strains of music coming from its far doors. An aria from *La Traviata* was being played on violins and there was a muffled din of voices. I was growing hot under the *papier mâché* of my mask. The lower half of the face jutted out into a mouthless beak, forcing me to breathe through the small space underneath. I felt my face run with perspiration. I saw that more experienced masqueraders had pierced their masks with two holes at the nostrils. As we approached the second formidable porter, my guide and host, Bastoni, stepped aside.

'Viva Verdi,' the undersea porter intoned.

I was so surprised to hear him speak at all that I reverted to my first Venetian fears and spoke without thinking, parroting his phrase. 'Viva Verdi.'

That one moment of fear proved fortunate. I learned later that whoever failed to repeat this password was taught the words with the lash of a whip. I knew the significance of the password; Giovanni had told me that all patriotic Venetians shouted 'Viva Verdi' whenever they could, since the name stood for the slogan 'Victor Emmanuel, King of Italy'.

It seemed that the tests of entry were easy; the hard part was getting out again. Double doors creaked open to a glittering display of masked dandies, one of whom wore the crested head of a seahorse. Panelled into the walls were strips of raw pink coral, ready to impale whoever flagged and leant against their jagged reefs. I sensed Bastoni move behind me. I tensed, wondering if by some trick I had been discovered. This was no place for peasants. His lavish entertainments were designed for noblemen only. I felt like a man hiding under a skirt to enter a sultan's harem. Behind me, someone approached. It seemed that I must remain calm no matter what occurred or surely spend the rest of my days weighted somewhere at the bottom of the Canale Orfano where the judicious killings of the State once took place by cover of night and where no man would fish even though the pickings are rich in that turbid stretch of water. Giovanni said there was a foul smell of rotting flesh around that part of the lagoon; it was haunted by its fetid secrets.

In front of me I had the glare of hundreds of dripping candles. Despite the damp chill of all the preceding rooms, this last one was as hot as an opera box. The room was full of exquisitely dressed men and women, all masked, and, it seemed, all talking at once. Behind me, like a reminder of the halls I had just travelled through, a foul gust of sewage vapours wrapped around the back of my head and reached in under my mask, lingering there, trapped in that airless prison with my face. On entering the room and heading towards all the card tables that lined its edges so discreetly that one would scarcely have known that they were the purpose of the ball, I saw that the loser with the bleeding face had followed me in. He was close behind me, so close that his blood nearly fell on my clothes, and so close that I learnt that the poisonous stench was erupting from his breath.

I stood at a distance from the players, eyeing their games from the neutrality of centre floor. An amphibian waiter brought me a glass of sparkling wine, which could have been an Asti or perhaps champagne. I have always found the two similar, although Vitelli assured me that this was not so and that the Italian wine was less ephemeral and altogether more satisfying and better. A number of games were being played of which I recognized poker, rummy, 151, briscola and bezique. I knew that I would opt for briscola because it was the only card game that I know well. I had brought it with me, together with my naked body and my dreams, but little else from my transition. Each year, at Capodanno, and again for the *festa* of the Madonna I had played briscola as a boy. My Zio Luciano brought the game back from Castello with him, a city game that was to be the first bud of city life grafted on to my own. My parents had found him hard to deal with ever since he had caught his foot in a web of prosperity. He was a man of means, but, even so, Zio Luciano never gambled money and I never owned any to gamble until I was in my twentieth year. He would sit outside my father's stone croft on the summer evenings preceding the *festa*, with a plank of wood across his knees, and we would play briscola while the fireflies hovered in the warm twilight. The holes in his pitted face seemed to tighten in irritation every time he lost a game, which was strange because he always lost. His bad luck never stopped him from coming, though. I suppose that, compared to the kind of fortunes I grew to deal with, he was just another poor peasant like us, but from the greater poverty of our smoke-grimed, windowless kitchen, he was a tycoon. He was always a little embarrassed by his prosperity yet he was too mean to help any of the children but too fond of his past to relinquish it. I think he thought the blatant evidence of his misfortune at cards would mitigate other circumstances, such as his growing paunch and the bought cotton of his trousers. My mother saw him as a skinflint who came round to gloat and diminish our already precarious larder with his indecently large appetite, but she was afraid to offend him, lest he repented and left something in his will. Zio Luciano had no children of his own and my father, his brother, was convinced that Luciano would eventually cough up something to help us. He regarded our card-playing with indulgence, almost indifference. He was an unlit candle. During the Ceri, my father spoke of an imagined proximity to the avuncular pot of gold. Little ever occurred to my father, and not even my mother realized that cards could be serious – but, then, it never occurred to me either until Vitelli spoke of men making fortunes at the gaming tables of Venice.

I had learned to play other games, dice and morra, but I never felt comfortable with them. Briscola was a smuggled part of my childhood mixed with excitement. Even in the dour context of my infancy, it had been briscola that provided a respite from my chores and briscola that mingled the hopes of food and fuel every winter. My Zio Luciano never left me his cards; he was averse to giving any kind of present. It was as though to give something would be to set a precedent. He told me that there was a tax on cards, that a pack was worth a great sum of money. Once, he dropped a seven of bastoni in the long grass that grew outside our croft. I found it after he had left. We had been sent in summarily mid-game by a sudden storm. As soon as it abated, he took his mule and left. I found the dropped card and I kept it with me until he came back. It was mine for two weeks. I knew that a seven was lucky.

At night, squeezed in between my sisters in our sleeping crate, I kissed and licked that card. In fact, it suffered badly in the fortnight that I owned it. I took it to work in the fields and I kept it in my trousers while I chopped wood for the kitchen fire. When my uncle returned, I gave him the crumpled, chipped seven back again.

'What good is that?' he asked me, and screwed it up under his powerful knuckles and put what was left of it in his pocket.

'How can we play without it?' I asked, watching anxiously as he dealt out the rest of the pack. When I picked up my own three cards, as though by a miracle the seven of bastoni was there, made new and healed of all its cracks.

'Look, Uncle,' I said, unable to keep the usual rules of secrecy. 'Look at that. How did you do it? How was it possible?'

I could not conceive of two packs. It was years and years later that I discovered that each card I stroked and fingered was not unique. In Bastoni's card hall in Venice I was impressed by the glut of cards. There were piles of fresh decks. There were packs of briscola cards and Neapolitan cards, there were the faces of as many different kings as the Doge's Palace itself must have attracted in the heyday of the city states.

A woman in a sumptuous gown with scarlet ribbons hanging from the waist came and took my hand in her gloved fingers. She wore the small black mask of *la moretta*. Her face was powdered, dusted with marble. She had tight pretty ringlets the yellowy beige of baled hay. The sight of her brought the taste of Maria of San Polo back to my tongue. I licked the corner of my mouth, resavouring her juices. A flickering of sensation reminded my groin of all the favours it had so recently taken. Under the rising furnace of my mask, I smiled to myself to think that had this masked damsel appeared to me but four days earlier, it would have taken every ounce of restraint in my aching body to refrain from pouncing on her. Despite the heat, I congratulated myself. I would have done so doubly had I known at the time what I came to know later. Most of the women in that room were men. Maybe they all were, I do not know, I was there to make money and to stay alive; the secondary pursuits of the club I ignored. Our masks kept our eyes free and our ears open but, like most of the other players, I chose to blinker and muffle those senses in the pursuit of my fortune.

Like a man entranced, I allowed myself to be led through Gothic halls. I built my church neither on sand nor stone. I built my church on bones. Under the palace there lies an invisible ossuary, the dust that cements the foundations together are powdered bones. It is the sea of black coral, the reef of despair, the scupperers of fortunes.

Sometimes in my sleep I see those drowning faces of Bastoni's losers. Sometimes in my sleep I fancy that I am walking underwater with webbed feet, the claws of which catch in the strands of hair that float up like filigree seaweed from skulls immersed in the mud.

Scholars write the history of nations and the history of kings, but think what histories lie on every piece of gold. Think of the lies that wrap around coins like fingerprints. Think of the deaths recorded on each *denaro*. You see, I have become a complacent thinker. Now that I have finally finished behaving like a Venetian pirate or a Napoleonic legionary, robbing antiquities for the embellishment of a new civilization, I have developed what Vitelli would have tagged a moral tone. I take to my imaginary pulpit now and

I preach the goodness of the milk of human kindness with the fervour of a dairy farmer trying to sell his gallons of milk before they turn sour. Giovanni chides me; he says that nothing is built of regrets. It is not so much regret as surprise that I want to express. There is an element of the former, but it is cursory, an acknowledgement of the baseness of human nature rather than regret at my own. I am surprised at the lengths to which a man will go to achieve his goals. I am surprised by the unscrupulousness of obsession. I am a tomb robber. I stand back like an anthropologist and observe these phenomena; that the man is myself does not alter my clinical interest in his behaviour. I regard him as a specimen pinned to a board. The dandies at Bastoni's were no different; they were neither more nor less than a collection of butterflies pinned to a board stuck through the heart or the groin or the head to a particular pattern of behaviour.

I was, I confess, a great deal less analytical on my début at the club. No one there seemed the sort to sit and listen to an improving lecture. I was anxious to play, dangling on the hook of avarice. The assembled company took me in without making any fuss, a new piece of bait, a fat worm to swallow. Bastoni signalled to someone at the other end of the room. 'Shall we play?' he asked, in a most courteous voice, at the same time bowing low in a fake gesture of respect. He had removed his hat and as his head swept down I saw that his black curls were interrupted at the crown by a tonsure with a small cross carved in scars across the skin.

I took my place at a delicate cherrywood table where I was quickly joined by a man in pale blue silk with the large mask of a lion from which greedy brown eyes were staring not at me but at the hovering Bastoni.

I knew that I had to win and I knew that it was written in the stars that I would do so. It did not occur to me then that every man in that room held the same conviction. What gambler ever feels he's going to lose? I lost my first game and my second. I was a hundred francs down. If Giovanni could have seen me, he would have said it was as well I had taken my extra money, but I knew that I played better with an edge, a push of fate breathing down my neck. I had too much gold in my purse, and my neighbour of the foul breath and the bloodied gloves was standing so close to me I could hardly concentrate. I pushed my elbows out irritably. We were playing too slowly for my taste. The expression in my opponent's eyes changed. Perhaps he was preparing for the kill, getting ready to deliver up a new treat for his host.

I played a third game and lost through my own choice. I could have won, but thought I would make more money if I presented myself as a potential victim. Such was my arrogance that I never imagined any danger to myself. I could not believe that destiny had dragged me twice from the jaws of death only to drop me into a watery grave somewhere out in the grey lagoon.

'Three games,' Bastoñi called, announcing the count like a croupier.

'Double the bets,' he ordered.

My hot mask hid my smile. Like a chisel tapped into a vein I streaked through the evening, winning and doubling, winning and doubling until the whole room paused and paid attention to my game. I think my luck must have been contagious that night, for the loser with the bad breath whose elbow was practically buried in my ribcage was pulled away to the table in front of mine where he, too, won, recouping, as I was later to discover, enough to save his life. Like a harlot with a price on her virginity I never played so well again or won so wildly. Vitelli told me that gambling was in his blood like poison; it was in my blood like a drug carrying me to a greater understanding. It was a current. I had a palace in my bloodstream, a huge cumbersome breathtakingly beautiful palace to lay in homage at the feet of my love; there was no room left for any other obsession unless it carried me on. My brain was fragmented into rooms and corridors – even as I wandered through Bastoni's halls, my mind was registering details, noticing a certain shade of silk or a particularly elegant door handle. The strange events of my life were mere furnishings for my dream, windowed on to that one and only internal courtyard of my thoughts.

➤➤ XI ➤➤

✠ Three times I returned to Bastoni's before the spring equinox, and each time I was rowed away slowly in an overladen barque by a proud and relieved Giovanni. I would have played there four times before the end of March but for the club closing, like any little draper's shop or trinket stall, on Mondays. By the end of my third visit, I had accumulated such stacks of coins that Giovanni was afraid to keep it in the house. He tried to persuade me to lodge it in a bank. After much explaining, I gradually understood what banks were and what they stood for. I was lost in admiration for the entrepreneur who had first devised the scheme. I had heard of pirates and bandits, but these bankers were more brazen and more dangerous, it seemed, gambling with other people's stakes then either growing immensely rich or closing down with much regret, depending on their luck. Despite recognizing the genius of such trickery, neither Giovanni nor anyone else could ever persuade me to deposit my own infant wealth there. Not that my money was hard earned; the only sweat from my brow shed over it had been due to the unnatural heat behind my mask on account of the excess of candles in the gaming salon. It was easy money in its gaining but I would have rather gambled it all away myself and lost it down to the last cent rather than take it where I could not even see it and where I would have to ask permission to spend it.

Giovanni was fascinated by banks and finance. He loved to count my fortune and to calculate hypothetical rates of interest on my money. He had the instinct of centuries of merchants, and it hurt him to think of money lying fallow when it could be used for further gain. Paper money offended him. After his failure to interest me in the national banking system or in Venice's own financial miasma, Giovanni began to hanker for other forms of investment.

'What if Venice again becomes the pawn of nations?' he would wheedle, starting in the early morning over my first cup of coffee. 'What if all your coins become worthless?'

I would shrug. The early morning was not my favourite time. Despite my liberation both from the cornfields and my intransigent master, dawn was still redolent of hard labour and fatigue. Balanced against this was the memory of my dawn encounter with death, which gave that hour a sombre feeling that fitted ill with Giovanni's sing-song nagging.

'What if the old coins should be confiscated by a new state? Who knows when Venice will form part of a united Italy . . . and then? And then what? Signor, I said "and then what"?'

Giovanni was like a child sometimes. He demanded to be answered, a shrug was not enough to satisfy him; he had to have words and a show of attention.

'In God's name, Giovanni, let me rise in peace will you!'

'But what will we do if the coin is changed?'

'Well, I shall be a poorer man.'

Giovanni had a string of imprecations and saints' names, like a string of dried fish, which he kept for moments of emergency. He pulled them out now, muttering under his breath a bestiary linked to the names of dozens of local churches. He had done this once or twice before, and I knew that it was as useless to try to interrupt him in this blasphemous flow as it was to interrupt a monk at prayer. Most of the words that surfaced from his invective were animals, of which pig, wild dog and wild boar were the most popular, recurring after every invocation of the Madonna as the only punctuation in this verbal fit.

It was now only a few days until Vitelli was due. I did not want him to find me struggling to keep house on my own. I wanted to invite him back as my guest to clean, well-ordered rooms. I wanted him to see how well I was managing my transition. I would confess to my earlier difficulties but only in jest as we glided from place to place, safe in the hands of the faithful Giovanni. Thus my valet's hysteria, coupled with a probable prolonged fit of sulking, did not suit me. When he had finished, before he could skulk out of the room, I called to his retreating figure.

'Tell me another solution, then, for these coins. I will not use your banks, Giovanni, but if there is some other way of avoiding being murdered in our beds then maybe I'll agree.'

'Oh, signor, you are so good and accommodating.'

'I said maybe; I have agreed to nothing more. First tell me your plan and then I'll see.'

Giovanni's business sense was sound, far more so than my own. He explained to me that a great many families in Venice lived on the brink of ruin. The palaces stuffed with art treasures were no indication of the state of the average Venetian nobleman's pocketbook. 'It is true that the city has been sapped by gambling, but a lot of gentlemen gamble to pay their grocer's bills. What is the good of ancient coffers and painted walls when there is no food on the table? There are a great many antiquarians here in the city, signor, and you may wonder why the great families do not sell an occasional precious object. But can you imagine the shame of having your Renaissance candlesticks displayed in a shop window on La Merceria for all to see? Guests who sat by its light in your drawing room one week must not see it up for sale another.' He shuddered, sharing the plight of the beggared aristocrat to such a degree that his cheek muscles sagged momentarily, giving him a pinched and hungry look. 'It is true, there are hundreds of tourists, many of whom would take a diamond diadem or a ruby brooch and pay more than its actual value for the pleasure of knowing that it had been handed down from mother to daughter by princesses since the times of the Fourth Crusade. But could these same American tourists be trusted not to flaunt their newly acquired trophies here in the city centre or at a ball in Padua or Treviso where gloating aunts could pounce on such a proof of penury?

'There are very few clients, signor, and very few servants loyal enough to be entrusted with such sales. Because of the clandestine nature of such transactions, the prices are low. Objects that must disappear into private collections only can never reach their market value.'

Giovanni manoeuvred a dramatic pause before getting to the crux of his discourse. 'I have cousins, signor, in high places. Instead of stacks of idle coins you could be collecting priceless treasures and helping gentlemen in distress as well.'

Whenever Giovanni wanted something, he nagged so persistently that he would usually achieve his aim, if only in the name of peace. He was armed with enormous amounts of information about unorthodox trading practices. When it came to illicit dealing he could always quote a handful of instances, permitted or decreed by the State, which made his own minor infringements of law or decency seem heroic by comparison. That most of the usages he cited had not taken place since the fifteenth century, or had been abolished by Napoleon in 1797, was, to him, irrelevant. He moved as though through known channels in treacherous waters. It was enough that someone else had charted that particular stretch of the lagoon before him for him to venture into its muddy embrace. If the *bricole* were still there in place marking the navigable channels, so much the better, but if all that was left was a ripple where an outpost had once been sunk, its absence did not deter him.

Thus he quoted to me the laws of immunity extended to the city's bandits, whereby the simple murder of one of their colleagues, with adequate proof to verify the deed, released the assassin from further convictions.

'Eh, signor,' Giovanni would tell me when he thought me sluggish in my praise of his financial machinations, 'how would we have the body of St Mark, the most holy relic of all our city, if two brave captains had not stolen it in 829?'

I, who was a peasant and had received scarcely more education than Giovanni, and certainly knew fewer facts and considerably fewer numbers, used to tease him. 'How do you know these dates, Giovanni, when you cannot read? Would it make any difference if the body had arrived in 827 or 828?'

Giovanni never rose to my bait. He would gaze at me askance, with a sly, knowing look, as though to remind me that numbers were sacred and beyond the reach of jokes or the realm of controversy. He knew what he did because all Venetians knew it. He deigned to explain this to me only once. 'Look, Signor Gabriele,' he said, with condescending patience as though to an obtuse eight-year-old. He pointed back towards the city, turning his gondola round with his usual precarious skill. We had been on our way to the Lido to meet yet another cousin of his who thought he might have some information about my friend Vitelli.

'Look,' he repeated, wagging his finger perhaps to imply that I had already wantonly forgotten the direction of his argument, 'St Mark's body was returned to Venice in a shipment of pork in 829. Venice first married the sea in 997. In 1202 there was the Fourth Crusade – which was profitable to us. In 1355 Doge Faliers was beheaded, and my father said when they opened his vault that the skeleton of the Doge was still there with his skull jammed between his leg bones, and in 1846 the railway causeway was built by the Austrians – to our great shame and the detriment of boatmen like myself. I did not invent these dates, signor. These dates are known to everyone. I will prove it.'

At this point another gondola was steering silently towards us. The lagoon was doused in mist and there was a sepulchral hush into which Giovanni's voice had rung incongruously.

'*Eooo,*' he screeched, startling the passengers of the approaching gondola to such an extent that a glove was dropped on the steely surface of the water. A ruffled man struggled to retrieve it, further upsetting the delicate balance of the boat. The neighbouring gondolier, who shared none of Giovanni's grace or youthful good looks, lunged across the laps of his two passengers, retrieved the glove and delivered it dripping into the gentleman's lap, then ignored their foreign remonstrances while Giovanni yelled across the five feet of water that divided us in a voice worthy of a foghorn, '*Eooo,* when was the Fourth Crusade?'

'1202,' his colleague screamed back to him.

'You're telling me!' Giovanni laughed, gleefully and then added, 'How's it going? How's life treating you, Beppe?'

'Eh, here I am,' a portly red-faced Beppe yelled back, and then, looking out across the grey blur to the Riva Degli Schiavoni in the far distance, he seemed to recall where he was and where he had stranded his protesting passengers and began to scythe the sea, gliding into the swallowing fog.

Giovanni smiled at me, his point proved. He took this

one confirmation as a seal of approval and official stamp on everything else he had either told me in the past or intended to tell me in the future. His smile reflected the degree of licence that this entailed.

I suppose I should have just accepted Giovanni in the carefree spirit of a liberated age. Sometimes, though, our spirits clashed, not least because he was determined to mould me into a model dandy. He detected, quite rightly, that I was a man in an unfinished state. Like an amateur sculptor he rose to the challenge. In many ways this suited me, yet, having come so far towards achieving my goal, I could not be diverted by anyone, no matter how charming or dedicated to me. I never felt articulate enough to explain how much I appreciated his sharing his strangely gleaned education with me. He gave me a sense of identity, a retrospective past. His endless lectures might have irritated another man, but I found them as effective as plates of armour, fishes' scales that built up to cover a nakedness that no clothes could disguise. While I lived in Venice, I never passed for a Venetian, but after I left, thanks to Giovanni, I was able to imply it, without admitting to Venetian origins, thus avoiding undue excavations of my nebulous history.

The thirty-first of March had been and gone. I had an appointment with Vitelli at four o'clock in Florian's. I had been up since dawn chattering like a child at the Ceri, following Giovanni from end to end of the Peacock Salon telling him anecdotes at such a pace that, for once, he couldn't get a word in edgeways. At three o'clock, I picked my way through the pigeons in the square and climbed the marble steps with such a pounding in my heart that my ears rang and my hands were numb. It was my first ever entry into that *caffè*. Later, I would spend some hours of every day idly watching the tourists saunter past while swapping gossip with fellow gamblers. However, my meeting with Vitelli was the circumstance that first lured me through its doors. I felt absurdly proud, so proud that I hardly paused to feel intimidated by the miniature décor of that élite establishment. I took up my position on a bench opposite the central window. I had determined not to sit on any of the chairs. The little room seemed miraculously larger on the inside than out and, far from taking up the entire space I had once feared, I saw that I was just another presence among a host of English, German and American tourists.

As I walked in, blinded by emotion, I had hoped to open my eyes and see my dear friend and cell mate already at the table. This was despite my having checked before going in, but I longed to see him with a desire so strong that rational thought had little place in my head. All through the afternoon as the bells of the Campanile and the clock tower tolled their quarters, I found excuses for Vitelli's lateness. I drank a thick purple liquid, which stuck to the roof of my mouth, and I drank coffee and more coffee, and an infusion of hot water which was served with great ceremony but tasted of nothing. The purple paste, which the waiter called chocolate, and which Giovanni later confirmed as a fashionable choice, was my favourite. The coffee was served a mere drop at a time – in fact, it seemed that the waiter had forgotten to serve it at all with my first cup, which contained just a wipe of black slime around the bottom.

At first, I felt convinced that Vitelli had been delayed and that he would appear at any moment. Then, as the hours dragged by, underlined and framed by the relentless bells, I began to worry that some trouble might have been the cause of this delay. I waited the more impatiently after my fears for him were aroused. If he needed money, he could have all I owned and I would work every card game in the city to get him more, if more he needed. If I could pit my strength against any importunity that plagued him, I would do so.

Looking out on to the pink light of the square with the last of the crowd straggling back to their indifferent dinners, I vowed to myself to help him in whatever way I could. I would nurse him if he were sick, protect, assist or accompany him to wherever he needed to go. I was his creation; he was my maker and I worshipped him. By ten o'clock I had begun to feel resentful for my lack of opportunity to demonstrate this allegiance. By midnight, the puzzled and weary waiters were beginning to prepare the *caffè* for closing time. The shutters were battened down and lights were dead and I stood outside alone in the vast and eerie square. There was no sign of Vitelli. I had eaten nothing all day. It was beginning to rain. I had drunk at least a dozen cups of gelatinous hot chocolate. I walked towards the clock tower and the archway that would lead me back to the Rio della Guerra. The clock struck one; a bronze giant hammered on his bell. The sky on the clock was lapis lazuli, the stars were of solid gold, the signs of the zodiac spun round the hours. The sky was lost in fog, a cold, clammy, strangling finger wrapped around my throat and I was violently sick. I returned home alone and too tired to explain to the anxiously waiting Giovanni why my friend the Colonel was not with me, nor why my boots were coated in porphyritic sludge.

⤖ XII ⥆

✠ The doors of Florian's opened at eight o'clock and
closed again at any time in the small hours of the
morning. For an entire month after my appointment with
Vitelli, I waited there, still hoping that he would turn up. I
had no other way to contact him. I didn't even know his
regiment, and in troubled times I was sure that he would
not welcome enquiries from someone who in themselves
could bear little close inspection. All through those days,
when my mind was not on Vitelli, it hovered around my
love for Donna Donatella. I had thought that only she
could wound my heart in such a way as to make my life a
slave to her whim. When first I saw her, walking in her
orchard, I felt my life touched as though by a vision. The
light she cast on me, a poor apprentice cleaning a marble
angel in her father's garden, was ethereal. It was the light
of holy scripture made real in her flesh. No moment has
ever had the transfixing brilliance of that first sight of her
wandering through pomegranate trees. Like poetry, in
times of intense emotion, the image returns to me. Like
poetry, it stroked my soul and, by turns, lulled and stoked
my senses. She had a beauty as pure and as powerful as the
moon and her phases.

I heard the rustle of her gown and the rustle of her slippers in the grass. I heard the rustle of her petticoats in Giovanni's oar as it stroked the water and the sound of dry leaves blowing across an empty *campo*. I heard her presence everywhere in Venice; that first time, though, I had turned to look at her, thus changing all my life, and she had walked on, unaware of my presence. Neither acknowledging nor consciously ignoring me, she had just walked on as though I was not there. That night, years on, lying on old sacks beside my master, I writhed with fever. It lasted several days, delaying the work on the broken angels. My master nursed me, complaining bitterly. There was an epidemic of cholera in Castello and some fifty people had died during the early summer. My master believed neither in doctors nor hospitals, and he kept me hidden, not wanting to lose five precious years of teaching to a fever ward. Work had been slack for months; the Curia had taken to commissioning statues and fonts that it then found ways of not paying for. My master had been to a friend, in Assisi, and to the new Bishop of Castello. He complained that his friend in Assisi had died before settling the accounts, and Monsignor Letterio Turchi, the new Bishop, had promised him much but given him nothing. It took him many months to galvanize his courage to complain and he was sadly disappointed when nothing came of his petition. Our presence in Castello had been part of his secular rebellion. He was using his skill for work not destined for the Church. He had sacrificed his whole life to the glorification of God. I think I took my paranoia from him. He was convinced that the Pope and all his cardinals would find him out and reinstitute the Inquisition expressly to punish him for his desertion. When I fell ill, he saw my fever as judgement. Had he known that it had been caused by the sight of a beautiful noblewoman, who had failed to notice me kneeling in adoration by her path, he would probably have maimed me with the beating he would have administered. As it was, there was cholera in Castello, and he nursed me with a tenderness I never knew he owned. I was the key to his old age. I was the stock in his larder that he was hoarding against disaster; I was to be his nurse. Knowing these things, he mothered me back to health.

I recovered, but the sweet poison from that first arrow stayed in my flesh, a love dart lodged for ever in my brain. It was the pin that pierces the seed of the pomegranate. With each new day that passed still bringing no news of Vitelli, Giovanni struggled to understand my grief and to combat my decline. I fell into a fever. I dreamed that I was asleep prone in a slow black gondola and my gondolier was the ferryman of the underworld carrying me across the Lethe to my death. All around me more funereal boatmen rowed their limp passengers, leaving nothing in their wake, not even the cries of gulls. In each hand I held a gold *denaro*; as the mist thickened, I placed the chill coins on my eyes ready to pay the boatman. Once my hands were empty, I groped around me. The gondola was full of chickens' feet. They began to walk across my shins and then to crawl and scrabble over my thighs, working at my groin. All the feet were severed at the puff of feathers around their legs. The scaly claws multiplied and became the platformed shoes of Venetian women. They were heavy, they pressed me to the ribs of the boat. They became a gaggle of courtesans. Each brought an offering to a shrine. The shrine was my mouth, they curtsied and pushed a chicken's toe and a tuft of pubic hair in my throat before straddling me. They smelt of honey and seashells. The gondola glided on; the river grew wider. The whores rode me, squeezing the seed from me one at a time. When my mouth was so full of hair I could neither breathe nor vomit, they sang to me in a *castrato*'s voice: 'Do you love me?' The boatman held his oar to my ear and I spoke through it as through a long trumpet:

'Which of these chickens' feet is Colonel Vitelli's?' The *castrato* voice sang again: 'Me, me, me,' so high the boat pole shattered into glass fragments, which stood up on the water. Over the jagged edges Donna Donatella walked towards me. She was naked except for a garland of pomegranates round her neck. She approached on tiptoe across the broken glass. I tipped up the gondola and all the chickens' feet and the courtesans fell into the water. Then Donna Donatella straddled me, sliding my member into her. She said, 'Do you love me?' I cried out to her and choked on her hair. Then she came to my side and shook me, 'Signore, signore.'

Giovanni nursed me both patiently and impatiently. Once my fever gave way to apathy he began to pester me for some explanation and gave me no peace until I invented a reason for my despair.

'Unless I meet up with Colonel Vitelli, I may never see the woman I love again. He is my link to her,' I lied, and Giovanni was satisfied.

In my native Umbria I would never have had to resort to such falsehoods. I was born in a scattered hamlet close enough to the ancient city of Gubbio to be termed an Eugubino. Everybody in Umbria knows that the Eugubini are mad. The most ignorant woodsman, the stupidest ploughboy, even the charcoal-burners who live like animals in the woods and never see the light of day unfiltered by trees know that the people of Gubbio are mad. Within the city we are proud of our reputation; we attribute it to the arcane rites of the Ceri. On the day of the Ceri, outsiders look on in wonder, but their admiration is tainted with envy and fear. The servants in Castello told me that the Eugubini were mad because the Romans had built an asylum for the insane there, and all lunatics from the Roman Empire were sent to Gubbio where they were free to roam and streets, contaminating the entire population with their sickness.

My master told me this was not true. He said, 'If all the mad Romans had been sent to Gubbio, it would have been a city bigger than Rome or Byzantium. The madness that is spoken of is merely the wisdom of millennia. It is what has saved our city from destruction. The whole world and its follies, its hopes and its triumphs are reflected in Gubbio. The city will live for as long as life exists.'

My master was a wise man: when he was a boy he had helped to run the monumental wax *ceri* of the tree of St George. He often talked about those days, describing the five pieces of cod and the fifty glasses of wine of the vigil, and the euphoria of the race, run in apparent madness, but calculated to the last detail. He ran his life in a similar fashion, though more slowly and more decorously in homage to his employer. Every detail was foreseen and every difficulty covered.

My master taught me to enter material and bring out its soul. He married me to stone, mated me to it, sending me in as to a sexual encounter, to chisel and scrape at porphyry, Piedmontese granite, grey basalt, Carrara marble and quartz, until I found life in the dead matter. He taught me with fanatical devotion and with an obsessive harshness, not forgiving my mistakes and allowing no slacking.

When I was a boy, I never questioned his methods. My life at home had been hard, and my mother had been harsh. When I failed to see the logic of his treatment, I merely smiled, knowing that my master was an Eugubino. He came from a race of people who defied logic, who mocked even the laws of gravity. I was accustomed to madness: I had been born near the shadow of its great stone walls. I had grown up hearing the bells chime from its impossibly high tower. I had not been born in the city, so its slate grey stones would always be mysterious and superior to me, but I was tainted by its reputation. I could never share in her secrets or carry her candles or even jump over the dying fires, yet I had a right to her licence. When I did eccentric or strange things, it would always suffice to say, 'I am Eugubino,' and my neighbours would laugh and understand that I was touched by the millennial madness.

Alas, the fame of Gubbio had not travelled to the lagoon. Giovanni knew nothing of my native place, and even if he had, birth was now another skin that I had shed. So I told Giovanni that all my anguish and distemper was due to a sudden thwarting of my love plans. I thought I lied to him, and yet fate was mocking me, jeering like a cruel spectator at a lunatic asylum. Instinct had kept me from ever naming Donna Donatella's surname to Vitelli. I imagined that if I pronounced her name in front of the man who was reshaping me in his own image, he might somehow force with his human alchemy the pure flame of my love to gutter. My instinct tricked me, though, and continued to lead me a merry dance until, under all manner of misapprehensions, I had wrought a fair degree of havoc. Then Fate chose one of her favourite mantels, a cape of ermine and spite, and showed me what I had done and introduced me formally to Colonel Imolo Vitelli, Marquis of Borbon, onetime visitor to the very villa in Castello where I had restored an avenue of broken angels, and cousin to the daughter of that house, Donna Donatella.

In many ways, it is fitting that my fortune was in games of chance. My life has been lived and twisted by continual coincidences: chance meetings, overheard words and words withheld. When Monsignor Moreschi rose in the splendour of his purple robes to preach in the Cathedral of Castello, did he know about the God of malice, and did he believe in him? Did his same maker of heaven and earth really have the time to dedicate to tormenting the likes of me, Vitelli and Giovanni? Was Monsignor Moreschi's God a scientist, and did he plait the destinies of disparate people, using their passions for mere experiments? I tackled the Bishop once on the subject and he replied, 'You Venetians have more churches than anyone else in Italy, but you are an arrogant and irreligious lot, you have bribed so many popes that you think all things can be bought, and when you cannot bribe destiny to favour you, you feel slighted and start blaming God.

'Make a donation to the orphanage, Gabriele, and finish your port wine, and somewhere between the two you may find your mind easier.'

What use was there in adopting one language if all that its words could do was unpick the tapestry of our union? I thought then, as I grazed on the modelled marzipans in a dish before me, if a man were to set down a record of his life, readers would be surprised to see how great a part of it is captured and held to ransom by the petty side of destiny. The Etruscans, the Greeks and the Romans had believed and appeased many gods. Life is, in itself, like a temple built with innumerable bricks and inside the clay and straw of every brick there is concealed a wisp of irony. The gods were hungry, they bayed for blood as loudly as Vitelli's hunting dogs on the trail of a deer, and they yapped for attention and a chance at the entrails like the pack of mongrels the peasants kept, tied to a post against their thick walls. The gods were hungry and I failed not only to see it, but also to recognize it for what it was. Once, I refused my blindfold (out of cowardice, I admit) and I stared my ultimate destiny in the face. Why then have I been so blind, so myopic until now?

⇽ XIII ⇾

✠ I was thirteen when the shortages of 1849 had occurred. My eldest sister sent word to me in the city that two of my brothers had died and my mother was laid low with a fever. My master refused to let me go to her. Perhaps I have never hated him or anyone else as much as I hated him in those few days. He locked me into his studio for the first night, and then he took me away to work on a tomb in Umbertide. He said, 'You will thank me later, boy. This apprenticeship is of more use to your mother than your presence there would be now. Besides, you, too, might catch the fever.'

He had a horror of fevers. He was right in many things, but when it came to comforting my mother, he was dealing in long-term plans without taking into account the capricious intervention of fate. I should have held my mother's emaciated body in my arms then trapped blackbirds and thrushes and sparrows for her to eat in broth. It might have been my one and only chance to please her. I missed it. When the famine of '54 came, ruining harvests far and wide, chewing up the Indian corn and rotting the potatoes underground, desiccating the barley on its stalks and shrivelling up the wheat, I went home. My master remonstrated, but he was growing daily weaker, and I was a big man of eighteen with nine years of service and experience behind me. He needed me more than I needed him. I could have set out as a journeyman, repairing tombs as I went. He needed me to fulfil his commissions from the Curia. I had few holidays: half a day for the fires of St Joseph, the whole of 15 May, of course, for the Ceri, half of midsummer's day and then the Epiphany. I was allowed two more days a year, by law, but sometimes my master failed to give me these and, one year, I failed to take them. In '54, I took a week to spend with my mother. I deserted: in the army, I could have been shot, as an apprentice I could have gone to prison or been whipped, or both, and my Zio Luciano would have had to pay back the francs he had been paid to have me taken on.

Somehow I knew that there would be recriminations on my return to Cagli, but I was sure that my master would not involve the authorities. He had a choleric temper, and the blood flew to his face whenever he felt the world conspired against him, but he did not want me in prison, he wanted me in his workshop; and although he was already ill and much weakened by a palsy in his arms, I knew that on my return he would rather beat me himself than risk losing me. The hardship was general: on either side of the Via Flaminia, the fields looked as though they had been laid waste by a conquering army. It took me nine hours to walk home from Cagli, where my master had been commissioned to restore some Gothic masonry in the Church of Sant' Angelo in Maiano. We had taken lodgings in the town in an alleyway behind the *palazzo communale*. I had saved what I could for my family. I had been saving for several months. I made no bones about it to my master. I told him that one of my sisters would come for my hoarded provisions. He told me, 'If you have food to spare for your family, then I must be giving you too much.'

I was no longer a child; I was no longer afraid of him. Even his beatings were like the ineffectual pummelling of a girl. The palsy was eating his body as surely as the famine was consuming the flesh of the peasants who came in from the outlying villages. We saw them in the town. There were women who came to beg with their babies strapped to their shrivelled chests. In Cagli the cobbled streets were full of whimpering and wheedling. There were severe shortages in the town. The Church didn't seem to suffer – in fact, it came into its own, administering charity from its engorged coffers. The Benedictines and the Franciscans vied with each other to ladle out their thin broth. I thought Don Giorgio, our local priest, might at last be able to do up his buttoned soutane, which gaped over his bulging paunch, but his belly maintained its fat. My master's work was unaffected too and the music of my chisel and hammer continued to fill the cellar of a stonemason who shared his bench with us. My master watched me angrily as I packed a sack with the victuals I had put aside. His limbs were trembling more than usual, his eyes were bloodshot and popping and the words were trapped in his throat. I could see that he wanted to forbid me again, but his malady plagued him with its own trickeries: sometimes he could not speak at all, and sometimes he spluttered over some garbled nonsense while his eyelids made long blinks to rest his frustrated and beseeching eyes. I had lived for nine years with my master; he was already closer to me than my family. None the less, I missed my dead brothers and my living sisters. I did not remember my father well, but I missed the idea of him and I dredged my memory for incidents other than his resigned grunts and his annual ignition at the Ceri. I missed my Zio Luciano and our games of cards. As a mark of rebellion Gubbio had defied the Pope, and to avoid his taxes on tobacco and cards, their use had been forsworn. Zio Luciano and I had thus been partners in crime. Far more than anyone else in all the plain of Santa Maria degli Angeli, I missed my mother. I wanted to be with her, to cosset her, to learn how to draw the spirit from her calcified heart. She was to me like yellow quartz, dulled but full of secret veins that a skilled hand could light and make glitter. I dreamt of smoothing her rough edges, of filing down her rage.

My walk through the fields and lanes that day sickened me. Hunger had stretched out its hand and taken all the *contadini* of the surrounding valleys and pinched their cheeks and honed their noses. These were the lands of the wax worshippers like myself. These were the supposedly fertile plains where Vatican corn was grown. The ashen leaves of the olive trees had fallen into the baked mud, plucked like stiff feathers from a giant fowl. Beyond the walls of the big estates, the fields were singed and fruits had dried on their stems. Farms that I remembered in the days of their plenty were dying. They worked on *mezzadria*: half of everything was for the farmer and half for the *padrone*. My family looked in awe at such farms; they were the easy way of putting polenta on the table every day. Now even the *mezzadrie* must know the sour taste of hunger. They would be entitled to half of nothing. The day labourers like my father, who hired themselves out like daily serfs, must have been the first to suffer, where there were never any supplies from one season to the next. The harvest of 1853 had failed and now it was the year of Our Lady of 1854 and the corn had withered on its stalks. It was bent and burnt and the fields had all been pounded with pigments of a gruel so thin that no amount of stirring could thicken it to polenta, and the itinerant labourers were reduced to begging. Whey-faced children stared up at me from the scorched grass beside the road; their faces were narrowed, their shoulders turned stiffly on the hinges of their backbones. They clawed up to me for a crust of bread.

The sack on my back was leaden. I felt the hessian stretch and weigh down on my shoulders like a sack of stones. I had five pounds of flour, a small sack of potatoes, a pound of barley for my mother to toast and make coffee with. I had half a peccorino cheese and three salt fish and a five-pound sack of beans. I even had the end of a salami, as priceless as a pile of coins. I was carrying a feast on my back, a banquet and enough food to tide my family over for at least a month, maybe more. I looked down on the decrepit huddles of children and I felt like a thief, stealing the food from their mouths. They were like so many sacks of bones when my own was weighted with flesh. Time and again I was tempted to distribute my provisions *en route*. I saw old women so thin they were hanging together like washing sluggishly stirred by the wind. Starvation was stretching skin like metres and metres of finely spun cloth across the arms and faces of the peasants, then the sun was burning it the golden yellow of ripe corn, and the crows were hovering in their own states of famine, waiting for something to die so that they too could eat. The drought's palette was of raw sienna and yellow ochre, raw umber and burnt umber and beige. Pinches of red and yellow oxide had been scattered everywhere, staining even the brackish pools of once lively springs. Wherever I walked drifts of acacia fluff had settled under the dust. There was a smell of ash and dry dung and a staleness of dried sweat. Most of the fields were deserted: the labourers were too weak to work the land, and the land was too blighted and too parched to merit any more efforts until the sun relented.

As I approached Monte Ignano, the high hill of Gubbio, I felt elated despite the groups of peasants who sat around their huts in stunned silence. Some had lain down, their bones cast on the ground in an oracle of ill-omen. I felt the food in my sack burn into my back. I thought of my family, of my brothers who had died in the last crop failure, withered like grapes on a vine, and my mother whose tendrils had gnarled after their loss. I thought of my thin sisters and my emaciated mother with no one to help them and I walked on, determined to carry my booty to them and them alone. They could be dying, for all I knew.

All the road was familiar to me, even though it looked as though lines of stonemasons had plied their craft along its way, coating everything with white dust. The willows and brambles, the bulrushes and the grass were as white as my master's eyebrows after a day's work. Each leaf was laden along the stark dust road. Even the old oak tree at the crossroads with its ivy girdle full of blackbirds, a prey to boys' catapults, was powdered, its leaves already russet and falling, having mistaken the long drought for another season. The colours and smells of rotting crops and scorched insect-chewed grain blotted the otherwise familiar landscape. I was used to moving through this world of ochres and umbers crowned with evergreen woods of oak and pine. I was used to the skirting oakwoods that never lost their leaves until a new spring supplied them with a new set of foliage, forcing the stiff orange shavings off their stems like reluctant dowagers evicted from their homes. I knew the few olive groves in the neighbourhood, and the many chestnut and walnut woods. When the chestnuts ripened, there would be enough nuts to poach and roast for the winter. Chestnuts were the woodman's flour. Meanwhile, entire peasant families were trying to reverse the seasons, attempting to hibernate, to expend as little energy as possible, to stay alive until the autumn when another cycle of hardship and drudgery would help them, like blinkered mules, on their way.

The steep track to our croft was rutted and baked, littered in places by desiccated beetles and grasshoppers. It was a landscape in mourning, sprinkled with ash. The dogs that would once have barked me up the track had gone.

The croft of our neighbours, the Poesini, was abandoned and gutted. Even its roof had gone. The only trace of Taddeo, my boyhood friend, was a pyramid of frail birds' bones and the feathers we had plucked from them together in the corner of their vegetable plot. Three wood pigeons' feathers fanned out of the top of the pile. That would have meant, 'Meet me in the woods after work.' Had he left the sign for me? He'd gone and I sensed that I would never see him again and never know.

I delivered the food and I stayed a week, as I had intended, poaching in the woods for whatever songbirds had survived the drought and their frenzied persecution. There were not many birds left, that year, and those I found seemed to know my purpose. I had little success with my nets. I caught a skinny pheasant and we ate it after burning all the feathers in the kitchen grate. Both my parents were afraid of my temerity: they could have lost their croft and gone to prison for the theft of such a bird. They found my city ways disconcerting, and I don't think they enjoyed the roasted bird eaten with the bolts drawn on the door and the little shutter of the loft window barricaded against discovery. There was a fine balance in their serfdom: they had managed to scrape enough to survive on gruel by means of their careful *mezzadria* of the year before. They had a strip of land and a palisade with old hens and a walnut tree. Come November they would gather the nuts and with their 40 per cent they were confident of swapping enough flour to see them through. The *padrone* was a generous man and no families had yet been turned off his estate despite the disastrous harvest. I had already abandoned them. I could have kept my head, never learned to tally, stayed and helped farm the strip of land, maybe even taken on an extra strip. Instead I had gone off to the city to play at living. My brothers had died, no thanks to me, and I had not even had the decency to carry their coffins to the cemetery. My father's big bovine face stared at me from across the smoky table. I imagined that these were but some of the thoughts he was thinking. This surprised me; I had never thought of my father thinking before. My mother also took quick birdlike glances at me. She didn't recognize me. A part of her refused me and a stubborn voice seemed to ask inside her, 'Why should we risk starvation for a stranger?' The sack of provisions had been accepted and hidden like stolen goods. I disturbed my parents. They seemed to have joined forces to oust a cuckoo from their already precarious nest.

While my father was about, I respected his silence; when he went out to poke around in his ruined strip of corn, I tried to approach my mother. Everything I said to her seemed simultaneously to translate into a single threatening 'cuckoo'. My two sisters, however, Luisella and Clara, showered me with attention. I had brought them both a coloured wooden comb for their hair. I could see that they would have rather had one comb and shared it and been given some other exotic city thing, like a ribbon, for their second present, but they were happy nevertheless with their prize and seemed genuinely glad to see me. Despite their isolation, they had gleaned more knowledge of city life, from their annual pilgrimages to the Ceri, than I had. Their curiosity was so insatiable that I found myself inventing details just to satisfy their thirst. All through that late August week, the sun beat down as though administering a savage punishment to an unforgivably perverse offender. It showed no mercy. It dried the marsh at the bottom of our hill to a prickly carpet whose bog flowers turned to powder at the slightest touch. It dried the stream that irrigated the fields and it reduced the spring of fresh water, blessed in my father's childhood by a bishop, to an unsteady yellow trickle. The famine began to move towards us like a travelling wind. It scattered its bleak and desolate dust across the land, settling in a patina of despair. During the week I stayed with my parents, the walnuts on the tree fell off their shrivelled stalks prematurely, foetuses miscarried by a severed cord. My mother registered the violence done to her hopes and sat all evening on her doorstep shaking her head in a disbelieving stupor. Luisella explained to her that my sack of stores would tide them over. My mother refused to be comforted. Her eyes flashed out an occasional message. I saw it and I remember it still: it was the face of hunger remembered and abhorred. As I left, I promised my father that I would return before the winter was over; I promised to bring more food. When I spoke of returning, my father looked away from me and made the sign of the evil eye. I wondered if my mother also thought the walnuts had fallen because of me. I could not tell. She showed no more interest in me. I had wanted to tell her about Donna Donatella; but in the end I had thought it better to keep my counsel. Luisella hugged and kissed me and warmed my heart. She promised to visit me in Cagli. She was fifteen and pretty in her way, with thick black hair, like a gypsy's, and the oval face and dreamy eyes of a Madonna. If she didn't smile, her prematurely broken mouth did not let her down. It occurred to me that it would be dangerous for her to travel alone, but she looked at me as if to say she would welcome any danger rather than that of a winter steeped in want.

In that calamitous year of '54 I saw many faces of famine. It looked out from every skull like a walnut cracked open and emptied by a parasite. I saw that face from every angle but the inside; I should have recognized it.

⇢ XIV ⇠

✠ March had turned to April, and April turned to May and yet my friend Vitelli neither arrived nor sent word to me. I have heard that, next to humans, the best mothers are bears, that they suckle their young for years and tend them with a care so loving and so intense that the cubs grow entirely dependent on them. Whenever there is danger, the mother bear teaches her young to climb a tree and wait for her until she returns to rescue them. Sometimes she leaves them there all night; one or two trusting cubs waiting for their redeemer. For three years, the mother never lets them down. Then, after three years, the cubs are weaned and trained in every way but in the breaking of the emotional maternal bond. The mother sends her cubs up a tree. She gives them no warning of her intent, and then she leaves them. Days go by and the cubs suffer thirst, hunger and acute anxiety. At some point, usually about a week after their desertion, their natural instinct to survive gets the better of them and sends their racked and famished frames back down the tree. Betrayed, they finally disregard their mother's last order. That is their initiation into adulthood. I began to wonder, during my vigils at Florian's, whether Vitelli's desertion was not a more courtly version of this.

The friend I was looking for did not come to find me yet, inadvertently, I made other friends. I came to be such a regular at Florian's that, without realizing it, I slipped into Venetian *caffè* society. I stayed in Venice because I thought that Vitelli might relent and seek me there. I stayed because it was easy to be guided by Giovanni through his home waters. And I stayed because the architecture entranced me and I learnt from its palaces how better to design my own. It was in the six *sestieri* of Venice that I discovered traces of Donna Donatella in every woman I saw. I discovered femininity to be universally, though unevenly, distributed in all womankind. It did not diminish my love for Donna Donatella. While the green waters of the Rio della Guerra slapped at my water-gate, Donna Donatella answered my prayers at night. She fingered my spine like the keyboard of a spinet. She played melodies on my skin. Her hot fragrant breath filled my lungs. Her tongue licked me and her breasts rubbed my chest while I entered her and held her, rocking her endlessly towards the lagoon.

In Venice too, Maria of San Polo came to me, bearing traces of Donna Donatella woven like a tapestry on to her own. She was so readily available and responsive, lulling my more immediate needs with her voluptuous charms.

Every time she came to my lodgings, she assumed control of my house as though she were my acknowledged mistress, if not my wife. Entry into the Peacock Salon ensured the removal of her virtuous look and its replacement, as though by invisible mask, by a truly lascivious smile. I surrendered to her whims and my desires, and was pleased by her in every way except her sense of propriety, which insisted on being paid in coin every time she visited and in a ritual gift of a pair of ear-rings. At first I scoured the jewellers and antiquarian stalls. I spent many hours choosing opals, rubies, beryls and pearls, all of which she accepted with near indifference, tucking them away in her purse with scarcely more than a glance. When Giovanni informed me that her husband kept a jeweller's shop under the arcades opposite the fruit market of San Polo and that the jewels were destined to sit on his shelves, I dropped the romantic treasure-hunting and ordered him to buy me silver ear-rings by the dozen. Since Maria was not avaricious, she didn't seem to mind. No matter how close we got in our voyages of sexual discovery, she never forgot her final transaction. There was a routine to my life and also to my dissipation. I gambled and mostly won; my winnings were converted into priceless chattels, bought on the heirloom market by Giovanni. I whiled away a part of every day at Florian's listening to the strains of *Carnival of Venice* played by the Austrian orchestra in the square. Then I made love to Maria of San Polo who stocked her husband's shop with the fruits of her delicious sex.

Summer turned overnight to autumn and a tangle of crimson, russet and gold, then the leaves fell as though by order of a ballet master into the canals and floated and danced on the surface before subsiding into slime. The harsh raw winter returned, with its vaporous mists and its mystery, and I was still picking my way across the gossamer patterns of the spider's web. My life became as languorous as the seasons, following their patterns and their declines, sinking imperceptibly deeper into the muddy lagoon. I became almost a real Venetian, a lustreless pearl sitting in the cracked but once immaculate lining of the oyster shell, surrounded by treasures and globulous rotting slime.

⇒ XV ⇐

✦ In the hours after dinner, when the clouds of cigar smoke are at their densest and men have sated all their desires save the carnal ones, and there is a space of some several hours before bidding goodnight to wives and fiancées and setting off to gain satisfaction in the arms of a harlot or lover, man as a species is at his most selfless and benign. The dilemmas of distant continents become of sudden interest. The most intractable tyrants have been known to express a hypothetical interest in philanthropy. The world of politics spreads from the frayed edges of the home fields to a wider territory. Civic responsibilities that can otherwise lie dormant for twenty-two hours a day reawaken and stretch their limbs before sinking back into a stupor, banished to sleep on the threshold of brothels and boudoirs. It is always in the hours after dinner when guests of my own, or conscientious hosts, would lean across the wreckage of a dinner and ask, 'Now, del Campo, you lived in Venice in those historic years after the fall of Manin and before she joined the Kingdom, so tell us, what was the Serenissima like then? You have seen so much intrigue and excitement, won't you share some of it with us? There are not many men of action in our midst. Isn't that true?'

Truth is as elusive as a vapour. My beloved's face was more serene than any city, she stepped lightly. A breeze blew a wisp of hair into her mouth.

The Havanas and the port wine would circulate, together with brandy and goblets of black *amaro*. I knew that, in more sober moments, not one man around the table would have any genuine interest in what went on in a last corner of the Kingdom, renowned for its insipid aristocracy and its arrogance. This was not so when the wines had been passed freely, and layers of good food sat upon each other like layers of an exotic lasagna. The salamis, pickled mushrooms and aubergines lay under thinly rolled pasta tossed in a sauce of jugged hare and juniper berries, followed by ravioli stuffed with spinach leaves and ricotta cheese, then slivers of roast veal decorated with peas and ham, wild boar stewed for forty-eight hours with wine and herbs. There was chicken roasted on a spit because Monsignor Moreschi (whose maternal grandmother was rumoured to have been a peasant serving-girl) was present and he never much cared for any other meat. A form of pecorino and baskets of grapes cushioned on fig leaves was divided and demolished, succeeded by first one pudding and then another. These, I know, were provided in homage to myself, for I had a sweet tooth and a considerable fortune and many a worthy housewife tried to bribe me into her family by showing what agreeable attentions would be showered upon me should I choose to propose to one of her daughters.

I came of age in Donna Donatella's garden, kneeling in the damp grass. I was an unformed lump of clay wrapped in a coarse cloth. I was a stub of clumsiness. The skill of my fingers left me. Whatever I had been, I ceased to be. I have made myself into an image fit for her love. My only proposal is myself to her. I am the wedding ring to circle her.

'Yes, yes, del Campo,' Monsignor would chime in, as

was his wont, having heard nothing of the conversation, due to his deafness, but knowing the weight of his requests. Monsignor Moreschi lived a life as clear cut as the floor of the episcopal palace, where squares of white Carrara marble were interrupted with geometrical precision by considerably smaller squares of Lavagna slate. Such was his existence: a pure and uncomplicated expanse of goodness and ease, intercut by tiny regulated doses of contact with the outside world and its inherent evils. Evils which the Good Lord had chosen to dilute from demonic black to a more subtle charcoal grey, thus protecting his prelate's delicate nervous and digestive systems. During his sixteen-year reign as Bishop of Castello, an already unreasonable number of natural phenomena had seen fit to plague his office. Of these, the death of Giuseppe Mazzini, at a time when he had scarcely arranged his rooms and library to his taste in his new residence, then the death of Pius IX and all the rites expected of a conscientious bishop to accompany such a demise had drained him for many years. Pius was scarcely cold in his grave before Cardinal Monaco La Valletta had been sent by the new Pope to overwhelm him under the pretext of the inauguration of the sanctuary at Canoscio. The grey squares in the Bishop's life were all deaths and visits. The latter he classed together, regardless of whether, like Cardinal La Valetta, they came in human form, or, like the floods of '76 or the storm of '80 and the opening of the railway line to Arezzo, they were manifestations of the elements. In the Bishop's personal vocabulary, fires, lightning, earthquakes and the inroads of technology were all sent by the devil to test the faith of flocks of citizens and their weary pastors.

This left him with the white unruffled surface of his life lulled by ritual, meals and siestas. Although Monsignor was, undoubtedly, hard of hearing, he was also, just as surely, less deaf than he pretended. It suited him to ignore conversations that occurred around him. Using a pattern known only to himself, he regulated his answers to one of two. He either shouted, 'Yes, yes,' or he whispered disapprovingly, 'No, no. I don't think this is an appropriate moment.' Very occasionally, like an old sailor dipping into his boyhood sea-chest, he would say something that showed that under his narcoleptic mask a lively wit had been dozing. Usually, though, he either stirred up or stopped a conversation for no better reason than a ritual obeisance to his position. For the Bishop was even more fond of ritual than he was of chicken roasted on a spit.

I was fond of Monsignor Moreschi and I was intrigued by his occasional flashes of irony. I liked to think that, like me, he hid someone inside him who for reasons of his own he would not allow out. I have set out to show myself as I am. In the telling and the ordering of my tale I hope to clarify my actions to my own satisfaction and set my troubled mind a little more at ease. My main concern with this account is to disgorge the lives of other people I have inadvertently swallowed. When Vitelli invented me, he had not bargained for the monster he was creating. He thought that he was modelling a gentleman, but instead he made me into an instrument of destruction.

If asked to describe my entire life I could say that I thought I had tricked my destiny, but she tricked me. When asked to describe my work, I could say that I carved angels and their niches on various scales. Even my palace has a pattern of stone wings running through it. When asked to describe my love I could say Donna Donatella, the only woman whom I have truly loved. As to my friends I can tell you who they are and have been: Vitelli; my eldest brother Giacomo, who died of a fever; Giovanni; Guiseppe Nicasi – these are the closest and truest I have known. I could also, if called upon to do so, account for my life from the time I returned to Umbria to take possession of my estate to the present day. I do not say that I am proud of many of my actions, but I can recall them and I can explain the reasons that prompted me to behave as I did at any given time from my moving to Castello. With hindsight, I see that much of what I have done was foolish and wrong, and I would gladly surrender my life to correct it, though fate keeps no such pawnshops.

Notwithstanding all the above clarity, there is a foggy area of my life, a period shrouded in mist, I refer to my sojourn in Venice. During the three years I spent there, I glutted on its anecdotes and local history, I systematically stripped it of as much of its treasures as I could stuff into nine rooms and the salon of my apartment, and I absorbed a great deal of its apathy. Between my gambling and my half-hearted dissipation, I was aware of living in an occupied city. I was aware of signs of an Austrian garrison. I noticed a few of the most blatant signs of unrest but, for the rest, I must confess that I was blissfully unaware of witnessing anything historically interesting. I knew of marble lintels, brackets and overmantels, of pink-veined Portuguese cornices and plinths of red Verona and statues carved by the inspired hands of Giovanni Bon, Jacobello and Pier Paulo Dalle Masegne. I could describe the Gothic altar with statues of Bartolomeo Bon. I could tell of the four columns of alabaster brought from the Orient and sculpted with scenes from the New Testament in the Sanctuary of St Mark's. I had studied meticulously the winged lion on its monolithic column by the water's edge at the Riva degli Schiavoni and the statue of Theodore and his dragon beside it. Yet I could relate nothing of politics unless they were the politics of Doge Vitale Michele II who had brought the two huge columns from the East and erected them at the end of the twelfth century. Did my

Castellani hosts want to hear of the crusades? Did they want to talk of stone? If I unfolded my huge linen napkin and rolled out my old tools, would they be interested?

I had been self-consumed in Venice and self-absorbed. My master mated me to stone and Vitelli wed me to luxury; all I can say of my time in Venice was that I consummated my bigamy. Digesting stones with the gluttony of a condemned prisoner repenting of his crimes, I indulged myself in luxury in a way that I never would or would want to again.

I could no more answer questions on the subject of recent Venetian politics than I could describe the exact surface of the moon. It seemed that my only way into the probable attention and possible graces of Donna Donatella was via the dinner tables and ballrooms of her native Castello. So I suffered my ignorance to be jabbed and pricked and I suffered my conscience to do the same: I bluffed my way through such after-dinner surveys. The subjects that I could have spoken on, such as the exact condition of life on any one of my neighbour's estates as a share cropper or a daily labourer, I rarely ventured on, fearing to be relegated back to the darkness wherein even the mention of my sweetheart's name was taboo. I saw many men and women at those dinners, sitting around the walnut tables with their sturdily carved legs and their linen cloths.

Once, but only once, I came near to seeing the special loveliness of my love. Donna Donatella's best friend and travelling companion sat by my side, leaving me later to join my beloved. I grew to recognize all the faces by name; there were illustrious names and worthy names and names that were merely included out of kindness. I never noticed Dame Fate sitting at those dinners, sniggering as she must have been behind her fan, the brittle fan of a child's hand she has ravaged by famine, yet she was there, monitoring my discomfort. I wish and I wish that I could go back in years and see myself, Dame Fate or common sense and that of the three of us, one at least might have warned me that the very reason why Donna Donatella was so rarely seen was because she loathed the very pretensions I was so assiduously learning. It was true she never noticed me as a doting apprentice, but later I lost years by my falsehoods and my fopperies.

Perhaps, upon being asked about Venice then, in the troubled years between 1860 and 1863, if I had stood up and told the truth, word might have filtered back to her, that del Campo, though a fool, was an honest one. Perhaps she would have come to me sooner if I had spoken of my handful of real recollections instead of the borrowed rhetoric marinated in liqueurs. Would she have listened and felt any interest, I wonder, if I had spoken of the seahorses on that one night when I dined with her best friend? I felt her attention momentarily upon me. I felt her eyes touch my face in an acid burn and I strove to excel, to say something interesting enough to keep her interest. It was as though I felt the nearness of my love. Had I spoken differently, would she have carried the tale and kindled an interest in Donna Donatella's breast? I borrowed words and phrases from everyone around the table, empty, silly pronouncements that grew double hollow in my mouth. My mouth was full of pebbles but my nonsensical stammerings went on. She turned away from me and my husks of wisdom. My doubts will never end. They are like the palace which I see now that I shall never finish. From the west and the east there is no evidence of work still in progress or left undone. The north façade is nearly finished. If one were to settle for a certain plainness, one could say, it is done; but the south wing is open to the winds. It is a trepanned skull. It is my own head, leaking remorse and worry at certain points.

Giovanni has no patience with my present mood. He bore with me before, but now he claims that I am like a bored lover robbing an old affair of its past life. He says that I lick over my life like a fishwife picking the rotten shellfish out of her net, except that, he claims, my instincts are perverse. He says that I have a stock of rotten molluscs which I keep putting back into episodes that were fine until I interfered with them, tampering retrospectively.

'You are like an old roué who condemns sex once his organ goes limp on him, or a drunkard who condemns drink once the gout has crippled him. Instead of all your mournful scribbling, it would serve you right if I sat down and wrote my memoir of your life. That would not be weighted with regrets and doubts, I assure you. I would set down yours as you lived them, with as much enjoyment as anyone.'

If it is true that I am trying to erase my happiness, it is unwitting. My mind wonders. Giovanni cannot write a rival memoir to my own; despite all his advances, he still cannot write much more than his name. Perhaps he could equate my life, add up and subtract my pleasures and trials, multiply my assets and divide mistakes and give an answer to my doubts, a number, like the civic numbers the State allots to every house. When it is finished, even my palace will have a number, as though it stood in a street. It will never be finished though; it is part of the plan, a part that I didn't understand before, that it defies the final touch of a human hand.

If I had spoken of my palace, Donna Donatella might have heard of me sooner; or even if I had told her friend of the dead horse I found in the lagoon.

⇒ XVI ⇐

I was out one night with Giovanni. It was a summer evening lit by the pink light of his lantern into rippling pools disturbed only by his oars and the whirr of mosquitoes. My mind was all on churches and statuary as it had been since I had first discovered that Venice was not the sinister trap I had first taken it to be, but a stone-cutter's paradise: a continual unravelling marvel of carving. I mused upon the work of Girolamo Campagna whose style was very much that of my master's. I recognized the same method, though centuries divided them. I thought of my master with all his talents buried with him in a simple lead-lined coffin in the Campo Santo of Gubbio, in an unprominent place and with no statue to commemorate him, a man who had carved so many. I wondered if he would have died unknown and virtually unmourned if his work had been collected instead of broadcast across a hundred diverse cemeteries. His angels could be seen in many a chapel, and also in some fine churches, but who was to know that it had been the hand of my master that had cut them? I mused upon Campagna only because I had taken an interest in his work and pursued it through all the capillaries and veins of the city. My study was made easier by his signature, but no name or initial signed a work as well as the mark of the carving. I deduced that fame is only of importance during a man's lifetime; after his death his genius must speak for itself.

It was hot in the gondola – the nights were hot and close. Ever since the feast of the Redentore the waters of Giudecca had been full of boats. It looked as though dozens of small craft had mistaken the date and were searching hopefully for another party, another display of fireworks. Giovanni and I had two skins of Gioso wine and a flask of grappa, which one of his cousins swore was the finest of its kind. We also had a small basket of fruit and some bread and tobacco and we were making our way away from the crowds to the tranquillity of a deserted beach to 'amuse ourselves', as the deposed doge Foscari once wrote to a friend, 'in a boat, rowing to the monasteries'. All week the weather had been insufferably hot and Giovanni and I had taken to keeping our windows shuttered until dusk and then emerging to while away the night talking and fishing. Giovanni was still my servant, broadly speaking, but over a span of three years he had also come to be a friend. I could not sit with him in Florian's nor could I dine with him in most of the taverns of the day. He was never invited to the grand dances and dinners of my other friends, but I found great pleasure in his easy company, so I took to spending more and more time drifting across the lagoon that summer, either with him alone or with his infuriatingly businesslike cousin Maria of San Polo. Much to Giovanni's embarrassment, she charged a fee for joining us on these outings on the grounds that even if we did not use her carnally on these lazy evenings, we were depriving her of the fees of others who would.

'For the love of God, Maria,' he would say, 'don't you know what friendship is? Don't you see the difference between an assignment and an evening of brotherly talking?'

'Oh, Giovanni,' she would reply, very seriously, 'I do indeed know what friendship is, in that I have been rewarded, but I know that once a conversation takes place from below the waist, there is no question of brotherliness about any future discussions. As to real brothers and sisters, as you well know I have quite enough of them never to choose to be in their company. Why, even if the Signor Gabriele were my sister, what would be the point of rowing out in a gondola together with no one to witness our rivalry and no one to judge the winner?'

We were in the Peacock Salon at Campo della Guerra. Most of my waking hours were spent there in a little area in which Giovanni had contrived to make a circle of sofas and tables which became our only sitting room. As the months passed, the spare rooms of my apartment had been filling up with pieces of masonry, furniture and boxes of ornaments so beautiful and so plentiful that they would certainly have been confiscated had the ancient sumptuary laws still been in force. First the mosaic floors were covered with packets and crates, then the furniture, and lastly stacks began to rise up the stained silk lining the walls until, in some instances, the collection reached the crumbling ceiling cornice, which powdered and scattered across it all like a dusting of icing sugar on a splendid cake. One by one, the rooms were filled and closed. At first we left passages through the stacked goods like narrow channels through the treacherous lagoon, but these, too, silted up with clutter, and so each room in turn became an unnavigable morass, an island of busts and stones and statues. My landlord, happening to see a large wherry virtually blocking the Rio della Guerra, was perturbed to see an Istrian column, complete with massive plinth and pedestal, being heaved up the noble stairway to my rented *piano nobile*.

'What exactly is the illustrious signore doing with that pillar?' he asked the world in general. He stood on the stairs, thoroughly in the way and thoroughly pushed and shoved by the sweating carters. Then he stuck out his arm in front of him, as though wielding a sword and leading an imaginary army into a cavalry charge, and from his cramped angle of the side staircase he shouted, 'Halt!' in a voice so loud that it startled everyone, and caused several of the men to drop their load. The Istrian column suffered a hairline crack, the step it fell against lost a piece of *pietra serena* the size of my fist, and my landlord, who had never shown any other signs of character, found that he had startled himself more than anyone and developed a sudden and pressing need to take a nap. He shuffled up the stairs and scuttled across the vast landing without saying another word. Shortly afterwards, his manservant appeared and called down to us, 'Signor Paccagnella would like to place the courtyard at your disposal at no extra charge.'

So the courtyard took its turn and filled until it had the air of a disorderly museum, I thought; or like a great junkyard, Maria said. After the courtyard, I made use of my bedroom and Giovanni's chamber, and then I began to invade the Peacock Salon itself. I supposed I wanted to fill the house up completely to force myself away. Venice had a charm that held me in her spell. I was reaching the point where there was hardly room to squeeze past all my hoarded treasures, when I went with Giovanni to find some peace and found a seahorse instead.

Maria and Giovanni had had words and so we found ourselves alone, rocking through the night with a lantern at our prow and a level wake from Giovanni's skilled rowing, with a second trail of stirred water where my own hand was skimming the surface.

It was now at least a year since I had vowed to myself that no sooner did I hear of a suitable site than I would leave Venice and begin to build my palace on solid ground. Here was Vitelli's lesson serving me again; I was being two-faced, and this time to myself. I knew that the chances of hearing of a likely site were slim, so slim that I might just drift on with my life undisturbed. I needed a goad – I always have. When I believed that I knew where Donna Donatella lived, I thought one day I would go back to Castello and find her. Meanwhile I lay awake at night and worried about any marriage she might have made. She was older than me, a year or two at least. When I was fifteen she had looked like a grown woman.

Eventually, I sent a cousin by marriage of Giovanni to Umbria to find out how she was. As Giovanni so cruelly pointed out, she could have been dead. When my messenger returned, six weeks later, all his news was bad. He could not tell me whether she was dead or alive. Her family had gone; their villa had been sold. It was said that her brothers had been too deeply involved with the Vatican side and the Piedmontese had ousted them. It was said that they had emigrated. No one knew for sure. There were those who claimed that the family had resettled in Rome, others spoke with certainty of Paris.

I was twenty-five years old at the last day of San Silvano, then another spring and summer had hurried through my fingers as I sifted the salt water. I loved to lie thus, dreamily combing my fingers through the lagoon but the state of sewage was such inside the city that my nose killed the impulse even before my restless fingers began to twitch. Out towards the islands, though, the water was clear and cool and clean. Giovanni was humming a song quietly in the bows. The North Star was out and the constellations were all in their appointed places. My fingers had begun to ache. I thought, 'They are yearning for stone.' The water continued to slop across my hand and my mind continued to ponder Campagna's statue for St Anthony when my fingers touched home. At first, having wanted to feel something solid, I kept my hand on what I had caught.

Then it signalled to me that I was holding wax not stone. I dug my nails in deep, wanting to create a shape again, and felt an underwater squelch, a slimy giving way of putrid flesh accompanied by a foul smell, and Giovanni lurching and protesting as our gondola ran aground.

I pulled my hand out of the slough, sickened by it. There was a pause while Giovanni ran through his lists of beasts and saints: 'Wild boar's snout of a redeemer, St Ursula with the sagging tits of a lactating cat, pig Madonna, pig Christ.'

He unhitched his rosy lantern and carried it, teetering, towards me and what looked like a grey sandbank. Giovanni crossed and recrossed himself so many times that he burnt himself on his lantern. He touched the bits of his gondola that brought good luck, the *forcola*, the iron dolphin and the *cavai*, which was the only horse allowed on the lagoon, and he spat and kept the fingers of his left hand stuck in a gesture to ward off evil.

I knew before Giovanni did that we had collided with rotting flesh. I had touched it, gouged it, but when he shouted out, 'Oh, God, it is a horse!' my childhood phobia returned. The thundering of hoofs clattering sparks from cobbled alleyways, pressing children and men alike against the walls. Mad eyes, foaming mouths, monstrous jaws. Even the savage wolf of Gubbio had been tamed by St Francis, but a horse, the nearest thing to a dragon – a murderous wild beast came back to me. Not even St Francis had tackled a horse. The cloven hoofmark of the devil on a boy's shaved head multiplied and galloped through my veins. The remembered nightmare of a cavalry charge from which my comrades fled while I remained, stunned and petrified, to be taken prisoner, unarmed, for I had dropped my gun. When I first settled in Venice, its walls had haunted me with their relentless seeping of salts: the tidemarks reminded me of sweat glistening on a horse's flanks after it has bolted in frenzy and been collected. Hammer teeth in a cavern of froth, desperate eyes and its ribcage storming with fear.

Giovanni took the finding of the horse not in fear but in anger. It was an invasion of his territory, an insult. 'First the train and the railway, and now this, eh, horses in my lagoon. Never, no, signor, never, not in my lagoon.'

He shoved and pushed with his oar, cursing and protesting until we were disengaged. The horse moved in the water, jerked up and stuck two rigid legs in the air while swinging a stirrup into view with a booted leg jammed into it.

'It's not just the horse, Giovanni, there's a rider,' I whispered.

'You don't need to whisper, he can't hear you and nor can his seahorse.'

'Who do you think it is?' I asked him.

'Listen, how can I know any more than you? If he were alive, I would find out, if only to give him hell for riding in my waters. But the smell is making us both sick. Oh, God . . .'

Giovanni gagged over one side of the gondola while I leant over the other, careful to maintain our balance and stay above the festering sea.

Giovanni rowed home in silence. I washed my hand as much as I dared. When we came back within sight of the Redentore, the courting couples in their gondolas and the sightseers in theirs, I said, 'It's a bad omen, isn't it?'

'Terrible,' Giovanni said, giving way to tears. 'Terrible. We have to leave Venice. I have to leave my home.'

⇥ XVII ⇤

✠ After the incident of the rotting horse and its unknown rider, everything in Venice began to stagnate. Reason told me that July and August were putrid months and the dregs of the Republic of the Serenissima fermented every year with a fetid regularity. The stench and insalubrity of the city in the summer were notorious. The rich combated it by taking flight to the cooler, healthier meadows of the Veneto, while the poor learned to live with it. Once the swallows left, swarms of mosquitoes devoured whoever was too poor or too indolent to leave. I had been offered the lease of a pleasant enough villa on the left bank of the Brenta with a long low façade and the woebegone air of an army barracks dipped in ochre pigment to liven it up for the season. It had once been a convent and there was still something grim about it – a disapproving frown every time a carriage passed and kicked up clouds of dust. I could have borne the proximity to the road, but not the horses. I preferred a plague of mosquitoes and all the marooned sewage in the world to a residence built along a line of hoofbeats. My mind was so lazy, though, and my moods so lethargic, I do not know if I would have shifted from Venice that summer to any other more desirable villeggiatura.

The furthest my expeditions took me were to churches within the city, to statues within the churches to effigies on tombs, to monuments and shrines. Often, I found myself too apathetic to venture past the water-gate and the desiccated green powder of scorched water weeds on the top steps, followed by treacherously slippery mounds where slimy fronds concealed the lower ones. The water level was so low it was hard work to gain the junction with the Rio della Fava. When the tide was out, it was less like rowing than sliding over dead fish and debris. The oleanders were in flower in the courtyard, and there were lemon and orange trees each laden with fruit, leaves, and the occasional late flower. Giovanni had planted a jasmine in a great porphyry tub he had acquired from I know not where, and it flowered and filled that whole stone garden with its sweet scent. Each time a flower appeared on either of the orange trees, I sniffed the perfume as though it were a drug. For all its sweetness, I found the scent almost cloying in its natural state, something I never had or never would think of the distilled essence of orange flower that Donna Donatella wore on her skin.

During the hot, sultry days of summer, I confined myself voluntarily to my treasures. I had a collection of angels, carved in many types of stone. Each time a new delivery of curios arrived, the angels were shifted to the fore, like an advancing army. The oblique sun edged its way round the high walls of the surrounding palazzos, across the canal wall and then touched the great lion's head that grinned over the river door and crept into the courtyard.

By four o'clock, its rays would be warming the out-turned tips of wings and the crowns of heads; by five it would be teasing the orange and lemon trees, while still gently stroking the rampant jasmine, and by six, it would have warmed the stone of every angel, heated their bodies, as though they coursed with blood. It was a lazarine sun, not in the sense we used that word in Umbria, naming the fever words set up to cope with epidemics, but after the resuscitated man. There was no hint of sickness or disease, not even any fever, for just as the sun began to torment the more delicate flowers and bushes in the yard, dusk drew its horns in and sent it docile to hover in its daily senility over the sensuously reawakened bodies of Gabriel, Ariel Sariel, Raphael and all their lesser minions.

Giovanni and Maria never ceased to be disturbed by the way I stroked and touched the folds and curves of each carved stone. Maria used to say that if the Inquisition could see me so excited over my angels they would torture me for a heretic and a pagan. Maria had a jealous disposition; she objected to my lavishing such gentleness on anything other than her own delicate flesh. I had begun to drift away from her. I could still taste and touch traces of Donna Donatella in her silky flesh, but she was no longer the drug I craved. Like the city that bred her, she was diluted, watered down; an essence of an elixir that I craved in its pure form.

I was a gondola scooped out of wood, a man hollowed out of a tree trunk floating along a green and dirty channel disguised under a rippling carpet of rose petals. Maria stood upon the water with her virtuous smile making her seem as simple and devout as the Virgin of Santa Maria Zobeingo who when denied the use of the ferry walked across the Grand Canal to pray at her favourite shrine. Maria was standing quite easily upon the water, despite carrying a high scaffolding on her head comprised of baskets of silver and turquoise fish and another of figs and another of black silken aubergines and another of pumpkin flowers with parrots' beaks sprouting from their hearts and all topped with slabs of coloured marble – Carrara grey and white, Sienese yellow, Portuguese pink, Brescian red, travertine pink, Veronese red, greens and blues – balanced as easily as any girl might carry her load to the market.

'Gabriele,' she called to me, 'don't go. I have budgeted your time from here to eternity.'

The sun flickered images in my head. It heated my brain together with the stone and then left me tired. I counted myself athletic if I had the energy to stroll across St Mark's to Florian's to sip a cup of chocolate and watch the tourists clocking in and out of the miraculous spectacle of the square.

That summer I came to feel like a real Venetian. Each time the sun roasted my head I fancied that I might even have my assumed name down in the famous Golden Book. Almost all the true Venetian gentlemen had left the city. A mere handful was left, the derelict, decrepit and degraded. They rarely came to Florian's, though: it was shaming to be seen in the city in the summer: only Austrians and tourists were there. Even if a man or lady, a marquis or a marchioness, was stranded in the city, beached and abandoned, it was more shaming to be seen in public than anything that might have occurred to them hitherto and left them in their sorry state. For public opinion ruled far more effectively than the Austrian garrison. Society and its spies were the true rulers, and they had decided that it was not done to remain in the dowager Doge's lap during the summer months.

Thus I spent a solitary summer lording it over simple visitors as the one real specimen of Venetian society. I gave out no invitations, but I was pointed out to eager tourists of a certain class as one who might, if he chose to, invite them back to his Peacock Salon for dinner.

The stallkeepers, the antiquarian and bric-à-brac sellers, the Murano glass trinkets, the fans and the watercolours were all filling the square, crawling over the carcass of Venice like hundreds of curious maggots, leading parties of buyers into impossibly smelly alleyways there to tout their wares. Guides in profusion that belied any inadequacy in the education system appeared from behind every pillar and out of every doorway. German, Austrian, American, English, French and Italian tourists marched across Venice's graceful features, buying her souvenirs, breathing in her malodorous vapours, admiring her beauty, stroking her touchstones, peering at her pictures, learning her history, spending their money more freely than they had ever intended or imagined possible and then all returning through the same turnstiles to the outside world. For the most part I neither saw nor heard these summer visitors. It was as though the wintry fogs of the lagoon had stuck to my eyes, leaving them scarred with a permanent myopia, while the rasping winds of the Adriatic had struck my ears and stayed there, leaving them impervious to all but the chiming of local bells and the sing-song of local voices.

I was a drugged man as surely as if I had made my home in an opium den. I might never have noticed the tourist at all, had not my own inroads into the fortunes of the city been so deep as temporarily to embarrass Bastoni and his clients. Each year his club remained closed during July and August. Nobody knew where he went and I expect nobody cared, so long as he kept his perfectly balanced limp away from their own Palladian villas and quiet pastoral summers.

I sat sweating inside my elaborately wound cravat, musing on sculpture and stone while making typically Venetian decisions, such as should I have a second cup of chocolate, or should I switch to coffee? Should I smoke a cigar now, or should I wait another half-hour? I had grown so used to ignoring visitors that I do not know for how long the shadow had crossed my table before I looked up and came out of my reverie to see a friend leaning towards me. It was Damiano Rizzo sitting nervously on the edge of a toy chair in plush and gilt, built, it seemed, for a marmoset to perch on.

'Damiano, how come you are here?'

He shrugged and tipped his head from side to side in a way he had, which would have been droll had it not shaken up and loosed a further dose of his near lethal breath. Damiano was a good friend to me, but he had a certain shyness, due, perhaps to the circumstances of our first meeting. He always claimed that I saved his life at Bastoni's. He told me many times that he had never been so low, or so close to death. My first night had been nearly his last. The change in his luck made him believe that he owed me allegiance, which was both flattering and tiresome at times. When it became apparent that we were to be friends and that we would perforce spend time together, I tackled him about the dead fish he seemed to have inside him.

'You are not the first person to tell me this, and indeed I am at my wits' end to know what to do. My surgeon says the odour is emitted from my stomach and there is little I can do but live off gruel and herbal infusions. I have taken suicidal doses of teriaca, in fact I must be the best client of the pharmacy of the Golden Head, but what is the use, Gabriele, of poisoning myself with these vast quantities of gum arabic, fennel and amber if every time I open my mouth a sewer whispers on my breath?'

I felt very sorry for Damiano, yet it was self-interest that drove me to find a cure for his condition. When I say cure, this was not exactly the case but I found a quack who turned Damiano's breath from, say, the plague to a bad *grippe*. Such was the state of his breath when he accosted me so timidly at Florian's *caffè*. Without the cure, I would have choked immediately into cognizance of his presence; with it, I was able to ignore the sour-sickly waft that greeted me at so many Venetian street corners. When my turning of Damiano's luck at cards was compounded with my mitigating his evil odour, he declared himself eternally in my debt, and subsequently went out of his way to make my life easier and happier in many little ways.

Thus it was that Damiano came to inform me that Bastoni had taken the unprecedented action of opening up his club in the middle of summer. He had, it was said, some debts to pay and his coffers were low and a number of wealthy visitors from the Kingdom were in town and anxious to gamble. It was not known how much of the club would be opened, nor what would become of the losers, but without the cover of the fog and mist and darkness it was assumed that the channels of Sant' Ariolo would be left undisturbed. There was to be an extraordinary session. Twenty men only had been invited to play; Damiano was among them. Most of the others were outsiders. Since the games were masked, Damiano offered to surrender his place to me.

'I'll lend you my mask, and you can take a little essence of drains along with you, and lose occasionally, and no one will know you are not I.'

We played that night like partners in a grand quadrille, spinning slowly around the gaming tables, swapping partners in a fixed rotation. I had done as Damiano suggested and doused my cravat with some canal water and then doused my hair with a lime and bergamot pomade. Damiano always wore a gold mask with a ram's head and curling horns upon it. Those of us who knew each other's disguises teased him for this choice. To all accusations of cuckoldry he merely replied, 'I make no pretence at marriage and I have no wish to settle down. You may laugh because my mistress cuckolds me, but by doing so you tell me nothing new, whereas how do you know what your wives do behind your backs?'

I took the usual jests that evening for the ram's horns. I did not need to follow Damiano's advice about losing a game or two. I lost anyway, thrice and in a row. One more time and I would have forfeited my chance to win and have been forced to take the downward spiral into heavy loss.

The odds were high and the stakes higher due to my triple fault. Then a new partner came to me, and I began to win. I moved around every partner in the hall, winning and doubling, winning and doubling until the rhythm and the pace of that imagined dance quickened to a dizzy spin. My last partner was forced to play me at crippling stakes. I hardly noticed him at first – the wine and exultation had gone to my head. After the first game, he banged the table hard, causing all the assembled players to stop and look across. Bastoni came towards us, waving his hands as though grabbing at an explanation. Strange to say, he did not seem angry and the aura of cruelty that always hung around him seemed somewhat abated, as though something unusually pleasing had finally crept into his life and chiselled a way into his pumiceous heart.

My opponent spoke in a thick Venetian dialect. When he did so, I, too, looked across and studied him. I had not noticed him before; I had assumed he was a foreigner. At least one of my opponents had been a German, and another, I would be prepared to swear, was an American I had seen parading around Venice with a retinue of porters carrying trays like stretchers on which lay curios, decapitated statues, dismembered Madonnas, torsos of Christ.

'I have no more cash,' the Venetian said.

Those of us who were habitués of the club looked at Bastoni with interest. Here was the signal for blood and tears. Imagine our astonishment when our normally vicious host merely shrugged and asked, 'What can you bet then, my good man?'

'Land. I have land worth fifty thousand francs.'

'And what are we to do here? Play for it field by field and ditch by ditch?'

'I will wager the entire estate.'

'How do we know its true worth in these hard times?'

There was a long pause while Bastoni pondered this.

Eventually he said, 'I do not care for 10 per cent of anyone's estate. I have no love of ditches except for purely sepulchral purposes. Your opponent would have to agree to pay me two thousand, five hundred francs in coin tonight. Do you?' he demanded, turning sharply to me.

'I do,' I said, feeling an uncommon amount of emotion in my voice, which had answered quietly in the way I had before I began to wrap myself like an earthworm in the cocoon of a silk moth. My opponent looked up sharply and I thought I heard him sigh, perhaps with relief.

My opponent shuffled and I cut, then he dealt three cards each and the trump, tucked under the pack. Bastoni were trumps. When I saw the seven, half concealed under the pile, it seemed that I had already won. The woodman's clubs of the bastoni were my amulet, gnarled oak logs, ringed and cut like touchstones from my past. Then, for trick after trick, my own hand withered, bereft of trumps yet full of high cards that I was forced to sacrifice to my opponent. As the game progressed, I lost some of my intoxication from my previous games and the whiff of sour canal water irked me with its undertone of urine hanging in the air. As the game ended and the seven of bastoni was left on the table waiting for me to pick it up and use it as best I could in the endgame, which I already knew to be fruitless, it looked more like an arrangement of severed limbs than a pattern of loss. The stumps were the stumps of hacked-off legs. When it was over I didn't even count my cards, there would be no more than thirty points in my meagre pile of tricks.

We were playing to the best of three. If I continued with such poor luck for even half a game, I could be ruined. Bastoni hovered over me. My opponent sighed anew. My stomach turned. I shuffled; he cut; I dealt and turned up the king of denari. His face was proud but flat as the *schiacciato* panel I had restored in Urbino in the last winter of my apprenticeship. It had been a bitter winter plagued by frost. My master and I worked in a small room off the sacristy of the church. We were forced to stop often and swing our arms to get the blood back in our fingers. One section of a panel had been so damaged we had to carve it anew. The stone was cold and wet, clammy to touch and painful to my chilled fingers. Each morning the tools were like ice in my hands, although they warmed with use. The floor was cold and the room was cold and the stone was ungiving. Then it began to weep and the worked-out dust turned to mud. I prayed to Donna Donatella to warm the air, to lighten my lot. And my master said, 'We cannot work with the stone weeping thus. You must make a fire and heat the iron bars to dry its face!' The hot iron dried the stone and the small fire warmed the air and my hands that had despaired of comfort were warmed, too, and I was quickly ashamed of having lost my hope.

As Bastoni hovered behind me, gloating, I prayed again to Donna Donatella to bring sunlight to my hand. Just as the sun's face shone from the denari on the bas-relief face of the king of trumps, so the suns of denari shone in my hand. I picked up the ace, the three and a cluster of low suns to capture the points I needed. It was my game. We were quits. It was the best of three. My luck had returned and on the replay I won again.

And that was how I won my present estate in Castello and my opponent left that den a beggared man. I had no idea as the game progressed against whom I was playing; no more did I when his seconds arranged with me the signing over of the lands. I saw many names and titles in the deeds and finally my own false name was annexed to them. I became the owner of two thousand hectares of land and dozens of cottages. I became the owner of pasture, arable and woodland, with all the streams and springs, lakes and meadows, marshes and quarries of *pietra serena* upon that terrain.

That night I glided back from the gambling den to the Peacock Salon and Venice itself was like a peacock's tail fanned out and preened for all the world to see. As we paraded along the Canalazzo, Giovanni and I in a gondola laden not only with gold but the promise of land, I felt a great elation to be in that city of grandiose houses. To any eye other than a Venetian's it was a city of palaces, but in the Serenissima there was only one palace, the Palazzo Ducale; everything else, no matter how magnificent, was a *casa*, a mere house. We shimmered over the water burnished by the late evening light with sentinel 'palaces' on either side. The hosts of cornices, arches, crockets, carved bosses, finials, friezes, spandrels, balustrades ... To study the faces of Venetian buildings was to grow dizzy and drunk on stone. Here was a city of folly: a *folie de grandeur*, a madness of masonry, a meeting of dreams.

The air was full of wisteria and jasmine flowers, of wines and spices. The air was balmy. Giovanni lit his lamp, as did the other gondoliers. The *canalazzo* was full and overlapping with songs and fingered melodies. The lamps hovered and shook like giant fireflies. Lights glinted on the water's surface, reflected as hundreds of mirrors.

By the Rialto bridge the Angel Gabriel surveyed the scene and the white dove that was flying towards the Madonna embodied the pure delight of the unchaste Madonnas who had lived and loved in the intoxicating atmosphere of spilt wealth. It seemed that the treasures of the crusades had made the city pagan in its exuberance.

The evening light was like molten glass leaking out of the furnaces at Murano and the gondoliers' dipping oars were glass-blowers' pipes. The palaces were drawn up like a fleet of crusaders' galleons moored in the *canalazzo*.

From all over the city bells rang out like struck stone, making the air throb and vibrate in measured love-making. Balustrades of triple windows were bared like flaunted white-stockinged calves suspended from a garter-belt of masonry. And lattice-work was the criss-cross of a seagull's flight or the ribboned tracings of proffered corsets. I saw the blank daytime eyes of shuttered palace windows awake to the twilight, lit from within by thousands of candles rejuvenating centuries of wealth; displaying salons of silver, gilt, and blown glass, interiors of tropical wood, treasures from the East, the booty of pirates and crusaders kept by a harem of willing hands. The light was thrown out of the windows like the gold plates that in bygone days had been thrown into the canal as a gesture of wanton luxury.

From the taverns and the kitchens wafted the scent of frying olive oil, garlic and rosemary. In the patina on the canal's surface, before Giovanni's oar poked and stirred it, reflections of tables laid *alfresco* on terraces and balconies sparkled with their own candle flames.

At every junction, a bridge made a wedding ring with its reflection. The bridges were crowded, and the water's edge. Giovanni rowed us mid-channel with a procession of other craft in our wake. It seemed like a triumphant procession and I, the Doge, setting out to wed Venice to the sea with a golden ring. I was momentarily tempted to throw my own ring into the waters. But I was betrothed to another, to Donna Donatella. People say that blood is thicker than water, yet as the sunset turned the *canalazzo* red, deepening its surface to a glow of crimson, it struck me as a sign of kinship, bearing us along its artery, carrying us to its veins.

I would be leaving Venice soon, I knew, but it would stay like an aria from an opera, like a melody in my head, long after the performance was over, just as blood always returns to the heart.

✠ Despite all the evidence of my senses, I hoped to
encounter Donna Donatella in Città di Castello.
Reason told me she was gone; hope told me she would be
there. Reason told me to despair; hope told me to enter the
walled city in style the better to impress my phantom lover.
Giovanni's own despair at leaving the lagoon was tempered
by the extravagance of our departure. Nothing I could say
would persuade him that there might be any kind of real
life after leaving the Serenissima, but he felt that he might
survive if there was, at least, to be luxury. His gloom was
prodigious, his grief histrionic and his preparations almost
interminable.

Every piece of stone, every capital and every fragment of
every statue was numbered and labelled, listed and cata-
logued by Giovanni, myself and a scribe. Since this work
was numerically satisfying to Giovanni, he was forever
losing count. Or, perhaps, feigning to, so as to have the
pleasure of recounting, renumbering and relisting our
pyramid of miscellany. I began to feel that he orchestrated
these delays not just to indulge his mathematical fantasies
but to delay permanently our departure from his beloved
city. When I accused him of this, he pouted coyly and said,

'It is true. I cannot help myself. I am afraid. I have heard that this Città di Castello place is not on water and that it is locked away from the sea. There is no salt in the air and no salt in the bread. My cousin told me that there are brigands there who strip men naked in the night and slice their throats as easily as oranges. My cousin told me terrible things of your Umbria. You know how sad I would be to leave you, signor, but after my cousin returned with all his talk of forests and wolves and bears, I decided to keep you here by the lagoon.'

'Giovanni, what is this foolishness?' I remonstrated, as gently as I could.

'Foolishness? Is it not foolishness *not* to fear bandits and highwaymen when the roads are full of them? And then there are no raisins, no anchovies, no *fragolino* wine. The things that we take for granted here my cousin says are quite unheard of in your Città di Castello. He told me that in the weeks he spent there he never saw or smelt or ate a fish and he had to carry a pouch of salt around with him like smelling salts to revive his food.'

'Giovanni, it will not be like that.'

'Will there be fish? When you were a child, did you eat shellfish? And salt? Will the only salt I taste be in my tears?'

I thought for a moment and then I lied. 'Your cousin is not a gentleman; he doesn't know his way around. Of course there will be shellfish and salt. I vouch for it. After all, I did grow up there.'

I tried to imagine my mother's face, had she ever been confronted with a mollusc. She would not have known what to do with it. Thrift would probably have prompted her to keep it in a corner of our smoky kitchen where it would have rotted away. I remembered how I myself had suffered in my early days in Venice, struggling to swallow the slimy creatures of the sea. And I thought how Giovanni would suffer on the fare on which I had grown up.

Panzanella: a delicacy of stale, saltless bread steeped in water and raw onion rings. Instead of the light Austrian confections of Venetian bread shops, I thought of the heavy loaves of our native, saltless bread, which was in itself a treat to replace the daily ration of the leaden, gritty chestnut bread my mother baked on stones. I thought of the dull ache in the marrow of my legs, which came every winter until I was sent away to study stone. It was a nagging ache of hunger, transposed from my stomach to my shins. A pain produced not by the absence of fish but by the lack of any protein for my growing limbs.

Then I thought of the rare joys of quails' eggs in June and firm porcini mushrooms, gathered from the woods in October, grilled over hot ashes and peppered with the sharper tang of crimson-topped *bietole*. I thought of the feast we made one summer's night of a young hare, of the succulent bite of a songbird's breast, of the wild fruits of the forest and the wayside salads in spring.

Giovanni and I would not be scraping food out of a communal pot with our fingers in the stone hovel where I grew up. We would be ordering food from the city's market like a couple of grandees. We would eat like kings. We would feast on fresh pecorino every day. If the wine was poor, we would spice it with lemon and cloves until supplies of fine wines arrived to stock the cellars I would build.

'Giovanni,' I promised, 'whatever else you find in Umbria, I guarantee that we will eat well. I am taking you to a time of plenty. Every day will be like a feast day, you'll see.'

My servant was too Venetian to believe me. He believed what he saw, not what he was told of the world beyond the watery frontier of his own city. He was, however, somewhat appeased.

'I am doomed to follow you, signor, the omen of the seahorse leaves me no choice. I cannot take the step voluntarily. You must decide on the day of our departure, lead me away like a condemned man to the gallows. If I find a feast inside the noose, so much the better. We Venetians conquered the world once; we know what to make of strange things. It is the lack of water and the lack of salt that most distress me. We conquered the world with our ships. We walk on water.'

When my stone emporium was finally inventoried, packed and ready to be forwarded, we set off to conquer my world. I walked on air and Giovanni walked on waves, but for the duration of our journey we rode in a black-lacquered carriage panelled in gold and blue. Another cousin of Giovanni's had located it in Bolzano where it had been seized by the bailiffs from an impoverished English duke. The disgraced ducal crest was removed and skilfully replaced by my own fraudulent lily and crow in their respective quarters. A coachman and a footman were employed and dressed in a livery I designed for them.

In view of the brigands and their murderous designs, Giovanni insisted on having my stock of gold stitched into the upholstery of the carriage. This task was entrusted, in secret, to yet another of his cousins, who then padded my mattress of wealth with horsehair and flock with a final veneer of royal-blue satin.

We finally left in June, a week before the Redentore. Having delayed so long, I was in favour of staying on for that most delicious and spectacular of feasts, but Giovanni assured me that it would break his heart to do so.

'Since we must leave Venice, signor, I beg you to let it be now. It would bring me a sadness too great to bear to see the Redentore. I have taken my leave of the Ca' Contarini and I have taken my leave of all the places that

I love. I have taken my leave of all my cousins, signor, and if you do not want poor Giovanni to take leave of his senses, then take him away, now, while he has the courage to go.'

We set out at dawn in a cortège of gondolas; one for me, one for Giovanni wrapped in his black woollen cloak, one for the boxes of my most valuable effects and one for what Giovanni had deemed the most indispensable of my personal belongings. These trunks and chests and boxes were all shapes and sizes and more numerous than I had imagined, but Giovanni assured me it would be madness to travel without them. Since madness is a delicate subject to any Eugubino and one upon which we always feel inadequate to judge, given our civic badge of lunacy, I had concurred, against my better judgement. I allowed this convoy of cases to accompany us to Mestre where the once-ducal carriage was waiting.

As I had imagined, it was impossible to balance, let alone carry so many cases along pitted roads. Giovanni, who had not stirred in his gondola and whose only sign of life under his black shroud was the occasional tearful sigh, took no part in the loading of the carriage. The corner of his cape over his face was so wet from crying that it stuck to his features like a death mask. My own excitement at this new beginning in my life, combined with an anxiety produced by the proximity of the four black horses that were to draw us, made me impatient to get into the safety of the carriage and get my luggage off the quayside as fast as possible. To this end, I even shifted a couple of the chests myself and was astonished to feel how heavy they were. No matter how the coachman and the footman, and the three shouting porters they had hired to help them load up, grunted and panted, stacked and balanced, I had too much luggage. My coachman was determined to keep trying, and the morning threatened to be half over before we were on our way. The horses were nervous, a small crowd was gathering and the coachman's antics were becoming increasingly absurd.

'Send them back,' I told him. 'Let four of the smaller ones stay on the roof rack and send all the rest back to my apartment to be forwarded anon.'

I had no sooner spoken than Giovanni leapt to his feet with the speed of a whiplash.

'Not at all!' he shouted, seizing hold of a sea-chest. 'No, no, the matter is simple. Florido,' he said, shoving the coachman, 'go at once to that hostelry along the quay and hire a second carriage. And, Piero,' he ordered, turning the footman bodily towards the carriage steps, 'climb up and secure the first four boxes as my master orders, remove the others and prepare to load them behind us. And you,' he said, grabbing a bleary-eyed porter who had paused in his exertions to fill his clay pipe, 'you will go with the second carriage to guard my master's goods.'

'Me?' the porter asked, jabbing his pipe stem into his own wine-stained chest.

'Yes, you.'

'Me travel by land?' the porter insisted.

'Yes, you. Now don't waste my master's time and look to it,' Giovanni told the bewildered man and then, in almost the same breath, he turned to me and said in his most courtly manner, 'Now, if the signor will step into his carriage, everything will be ready in a matter of minutes.'

As though to illustrate his claim, a rattle of carriage wheels clattered over the cobbles accompanied by the beat of hoofs. To be sandwiched between two teams of horses was more than I could bear so I stepped into my ducal cage as gracefully as I could. Having sent away his gondola to be transported to him later, Giovanni joined me some twenty minutes later, having successfully loaded everything.

Once the wheels began to turn, Giovanni lost all interest

in our journey and again adopted his position of slumped grief. Despite the great heat that licked over our carriage as the day progressed, he kept his black cloak swathed around his face. And despite the grandeur and symmetry of Verona and Padua, he refused to give them more than a grudging and cursory glance. At Verona, I urged him to observe the Roman ampitheatre, a sight that he could never have seen before, but he would have none of it. Through the many days of our journey into Umbria, the most I could make him do was lower his black shroud a fraction and peer over its woollen edge. This he did, not for himself or through any curiosity or desire to look but as a way to please and mollify me. He did it in a way that implied that he of the serious mind, Giovanni Contarini of the broken heart in exile, was indulging his infantile and naïve master. And he, whose inane chatter and that of his many cousins had both cheered and plagued my life in Venice, set himself up inside a halo of silence. Within our carriage, it was a third passenger, who took up far more room than either Giovanni or me. It withered my own attempts at conversation, monologue or simple musing. It choked tunes in my throat, strangled whistling at birth and kept even humming or the tapping of my fingers along the brand new enamel of my windowframe to a minimum.

I might have despaired of my future life with this sullen creature by my side, were it not for the evening when I first discovered by chance, and then spied on, Giovanni enjoying himself as noisily as ever he was wont to do in Venice.

Giovanni and the coachman had struck up a friendship so sudden and so close it intrigued me. The two of them slept in my carriage: guards to the gold pieces sewn into its upholstery. I assumed that this camaraderie, enforced by the cramped space of two full-grown men sharing their sleep, had engineered their intimacy. Together with the footman, the three could be seen, roaring drunk and shouting jokes and lewd stories with such gusto that, twice on the course of our journey, the watch was called out to restore order. It was in Padua that I first observed their friendship. I was piqued, I suppose, to discover that Giovanni, who disdained to speak to me, and who tortured me with his silence, was as garrulous as Maria of San Polo with this coachman he hardly knew.

I compensated for the enforced silence of my days by spying on my employees by night. Sometimes, as I prowled around the courtyard of this or that wayside hostelry, I thanked God that I would shortly be engaged in building my palace. It was demeaning to be creeping around the outhouses and sheds of the places we stayed in. It was demeaning to be eavesdropping on my servants. It was demeaning to know that I felt any desire to do it.

It didn't take me long to discover that the bulk of my luggage, for my own personal immediate use, had been abandoned in Venice. It had never been boarded on to the gondolas or rowed across to Mestre. It had been left, from the beginning, with my stones and statues in the Peacock Salon. I had, I found out, the bare necessities required by a gentleman to travel and dine.

I had received many proofs to date of the inadequacy of my transmutation. I had often worried that my posturing was a mere veneer. Even when I ceased to fear that others would see through it, I was still aware of an uneasy lost boy, hidden inside the noble trappings of my disguise. Travelling, I learnt that the mask was grafting on to my face, was my face, and the ideas that I had learnt and gathered were taking root, bearing fruit, not as cuckoo scions, but as a unified, changed self.

My luggage had been left behind. In its place, Giovanni had brought enough Venetian fare to provision a warship and its entire crew. He had barrels of anchovies, packed solid with salt. He had barrels of raisins. He had small kegs of spices, barrels of Malvasio wine, crates of grappa, mixed boxes of dried meats, stuffed pigs' trotters and half-jars of oil and *fragolino*. Giovanni had laden my carriage and hired another to carry not my things but his food. As well as the dried fish and the dried figs, the hideous *stoccafisso* with its flat overused body and its gaping mouth, he had brought dozens of bags of salt. The second carriage lurched and struggled over the pot-holes in the road, not to carry my trappings but to transport Giovanni's stitched bags of saline crystals.

It was over the matter of these crystals that I knew, for sure, that I was metamorphosing definitively, both inside and out, into a gentleman. I had two great portmanteaux of clothes. I had trousers and boots, jackets for at least six different occasions. I had a dozen fine linen shirts and a dozen sets of undergarments. I had two dozen pairs of new kid gloves, a stack of cravats, a dressing-gown, a smoking jacket, even my smoking cap. I had, in short, everything including the pomades and potions that went towards dandifying my person. However, when I discovered that I had only these two great portmanteaux, only a dozen shirts, only two dozen pairs of gloves, then I, who had grown up with one tattered smock to my back and shoes like boats, who had never worn hose or underclothes and didn't even know what they were until Vitelli explained the niceties of a gentleman's attire, blanched with rage and flushed and felt a sense of outrage hitherto unknown to me. I felt an anger rising from my abdomen, suffusing my chest, choking my throat. For once, my reaction was entirely genuine. I was shocked to contemplate surviving on such a meagre wardrobe. It seemed, at the moment of my discovery, that life could scarcely go on with such deprivation.

Only later could I see that I still had more clothes, canes and hats with me than I had ever dreamt of in the past. Were I with my master in Urbino, the richness and variety of my clothes would have overwhelmed me. And yet, *en route* to Città di Castello, I could halt our journey for a whole day while I vented my anger on Giovanni for tricking me, and on circumstances that were obliging me to 'travel naked' through foreign lands.

Although from the time of my first planning this journey we fell out and disagreed over many things, on one both Giovanni and I agreed: that despite the so-called unification of Italy, the world beyond the Veneto, the alien places of Reggio Emilia, the Grand Duchy of Tuscany, Le Marche and any other state that we encountered, was a foreign country with foreign ways. Umbria itself was home to me, but Giovanni regarded it as neither better nor worse than other foreign places: somewhere barbarous, somewhere hideous and riven with danger.

He had wailed many times that 'poor Giovanni had taken leave of all his cousins'. However, I discovered that Giovanni's family was not so easily left behind. The coachman, my servant's sudden bosom friend, was his cousin; the footman, so mysteriously biddable, was another, as was the second coachman, the driver of luggage so conveniently found at Mestre. Even the rheumy porter, dragged reluctantly from the waterside who had feared to travel on land but had taken to it with a passion, was a cousin. The tentacles of Giovanni's family had a stranglehold upon me. It seemed that I had less to fear from bandits than I did from the more immediate band of the Contarini. Between them they had cheated me of the comfort of my clothes. Between them they had replaced my fine trappings with salt. They had salt to preserve the memory of Venice. They were smuggling salt past the barbarians just as St Mark had been smuggled past the Saracens in a barrel of salt pork. I was a vain man. I could have borne the loss of gold more easily than I bore the loss of my costumes.

Giovanni struggled to placate me. Nothing was lost, the

costumes would follow us. 'They are safe, signor. I swear on my mother's head, they could not be better stored. I arranged the layers of tissue myself, each sprinkled with lavender, each layered in your best and most secure trunks. They will follow on with your stone and my gondola. They really could not be better or safer, I swear.'

Giovanni's swearing was never reassuring at the best of times. His mother, unknown to me, had long appeared as a many-headed woman, one with a conveniently brushed scalp of silver hair waiting to be used as a perjury block by her wayward, lying son. He swore so often and so much on his poor mother's head that I felt she had to have many, or a minimum of two, budding from her frail, tired neck, or Giovanni would have worn away her skull. The steps of bridges and of certain churches and the steps that linked the alleyways and streets of Gubbio were worn away by constant treading. The pressure of a million feet had dipped the stone. The pressure of Giovanni's oaths would have done the same to any ordinary head.

We played a game, Giovanni and I: master and servant. We had been playing it for the three years of our time together. I played at being master, and Giovanni served me while making most of my decisions and wielding most of the power. Occasionally, to satisfy the gods of such relationships, I went through the motions of finding fault with some little thing. Giovanni displayed grief at my discomfort for whatever pretext I had trumped up, swearing all the while on his mother's head that he was not personally responsible. The inconvenience would then be satisfactorily dealt with by my most capable factotum and our life would proceed unaltered in its essence. *En route* to Umbria, I challenged Giovanni and his control of the reins.

He thought, at first, that my anger was in jest and played his part of the charade happily. He was used to me as I had been: del Campo, the helpless flesh of a mollusc; del

Campo, the stucco in his hands. I was the endless soft touch, the easy ride, the provider of all things. I amassed a fortune and Giovanni disposed of it – or as much of it as he could. Most of his expenditure was without my permission but was on my behalf. Much of the masonry and bric-à-brac had been found and bought by him. It is true that some of my money went to support his own family, keeping so many dozens of cousins afloat. They were like a network of plankton. Had the Contarini clan been bricks, there were enough of them dependent on my bounty to have constructed another wing of the Ca' Contarini.

I had watched them come and go, sidling empty-handed into my walled courtyard, clambering over my treasures like ants on a trail. They left, laden with bundles and bags, clutching their new treasures to them, concealing them in their rags, hiding them under their rough brown skirts, their raisin eyes narrowed in pleasure. This was the Venetian pleasure of pulling the wool over somebody else's eyes, of getting the lion's share. The food that they fancied was stolen from my kitchen would never have tasted as good had they known that Giovanni gave it away with my tacit consent.

That was in Venice. That was part of our pact. It was an arrangement that worked to our mutual benefit. I had no need of avarice: my money came to me easily and I was content to see it seep into the substrata of the city in the same way. I did not share the Venetian's delight in cheating, but I knew how short-measured my own stomach had felt for most of my life and I didn't begrudge them their trafficking.

On dry land, all I had in return for Giovanni's trickery was his insufferable sullenness. I left the lagoon a hostage of the Contarini tribe. I was the silly clucking hen that laid their golden eggs. By Arezzo, despite my shortage of fine plumage, I had become not only a cockerel but unafraid to use my spurs. My pouting, sulky servant entered Umbria with an abundance of salt and fish, but with his spirit as chastened and his complacency so shaken that the edge of his cockiness was gone for ever.

⇢ XIX ⇠

*And they said, Go to, let us build us a city and a tower whose top
may reach unto heaven; and let us make us a name, lest we be
scattered abroad upon the face of the whole earth.*

✠ The lands of Quarata stretched from the frontier of
the Grand Duchy at Volterrano almost to the plain
around the walls of Castello itself. They rose through the
oak-wooded hills to Muccignano and on beyond towards
Bólbina. Across the valley, they climbed past the watch-
tower of Ghironzo, along the ridge of Zeno Poggio and
down towards the valley of Petrelle and the estates of the
Marquises of Borbon. Wild cherries salted the green haze of
leaves; streams and cascades spluttered over rocks through
gullies lined with ferns and broom and wild thyme. A great
rumpled skein of fields was thrown haphazardly either side
of the twisting river, forced by the contours of the hills to
narrow and widen at their will. Hamlets and villages of hewn
rocks huddled under stone lips and over brows, clustered
around small Romanesque churches with squat *campanile*
that tolled the hours and their quarters, echoing their unsyn-
chronized time along the valley and into the thick woods of
the hills. These were the lands of Quarata, my lands. I held
the papers of my entitlement in my hands, but I knew, as
every peasant does, that land can never truly be owned. We
are the keepers of the soil, the curators of trees. We live and
die only to return to handfuls of soil.

In the heat of June, the hedges and wayside flowers were white with dust, as were the hems of every field where the dirt tracks were kicked over. My first task was to find a site for my future palace. The second was to find us lodgings nearer than the Tiferno Hotel in Città di Castello where we put up with much preening on arrival. It suited me to be seen for a while. I wanted people to start asking questions, and for Giovanni and his loquacious cousins to answer them. Only Giovanni, used as he was to my speech and that of his earlier employers, could understand or make himself understood. Since, though, of the four, he was the master of exaggeration, within hours of our arrival my fame had swept around the city and was spreading out towards San Sepolcro, San Secondo and Umbertide.

Three towers overlooked the Morra valley: Ghironzo, Quarata and Roccagnano. Each was five floors high, each visible from the others, each guarding a road. They had stood for six hundred years protecting the valley against marauders. They had passed through the hands of the Knights Templar, had been for and against the popes, supported the claims of *condottieri* and mothered the outlying villagers into their gathering skirts of impenetrable stone.

That summer, Giovanni and I travelled on foot, surveying the land, looking out for a sign to divine the site and transference of my palace.

I found the signs in the triangle between the towers, halfway up the hill on a wide plateau beside a spring of water. On the night that I found it, I did not return to Castello. I wanted to sleep out under the stars. I invited Giovanni to join me, but he still had not quite found his land legs or weaned himself from his tubs of salt anchovies. I could see that he wanted nothing more than to return to our waiting carriage and carouse with his cousins in the room that they shared at the back of the Tiferno Hotel, and which they had contrived to turn into a fisherman's shack.

I sent him away, to return on the morrow. My palace was to be a place where no one would ever stay against their will. It was to be a sanctuary. As I lay in the thick grass, my head nestling in a pillow of fresh spearmint, green mint and pimpernels, I watched the sun go down over the valley. There, looking out over the river, I would build a loggia of arches to catch the dying colours as they faded into the fields. There would be a four-arched opening, flanked by a further archway on either side. The lesser arches would lead on to balconies. The gateway to the sunset would lead into contemplation. This would be a loggia and a room that paid homage to Venice. The style must lap and border and layer across the sands of this room like an Adriatic tide. An echo of the Orient, of Byzantium, merged with the relative severity of our own Italian Renaissance style, and a trace of old Venice too; all this had to be there, but it had to be subtle. I did not want the fishwives of the *pescheria* flashing their silver and iridescent wares with shrieks and profanities. Nor did I want the sly, insistent chicaneries of the *merceria*, nor the flaunted wealth of the courtesans. There would, of course, be echoes of the Peacock Salon where I had been living for the last three years. But my room would have to be more than the shaking of a magnificent tail, more than the wonder of exquisite plumage unfolded and strutted out to impress the drab peahen. My room, which was growing by the minute and now had an L-shaped loggia running past stretches of closed stone to more arches cut away and stepping on to a series of balconies, had to contain both grandeur and simplicity. It had to merge with the landscape, almost become the landscape, blending the fine views all around, crossing over the lights, mixing the compass points, north, south and west. The ballroom, as it was to be, found its level. It would be on the first floor at the front, on the second floor at the back; it would be like a bridge across the palace, uniting all the disparate forces and elements of the landscape and terrain into a harmonious space. Light would be paramount. This would be the antidote to my prison cell. There would be windows on three sides: high, wide windows to drink in the daylight and to reflect and blend the three different views around each of the three ancient towers contained there.

To the south, where the land dipped away and rolled, I would plant a vineyard around the tower of Quarata. Beyond, the woods rose steeply, continuing in a great belt of forest up to the far crest, which was the Tuscan border. To the west, in the arc of the setting sun, the land fell sharply with crags where the broom and rock roses had insinuated roots through the fissures in the stone to grow precariously. Below this escarpment was the road to Cortona and Petrelle, which would keep me supplied. The valley was sharp here: the river ran swiftly through, lined with alders and acacias that seemed to lift the view back up the other side of the valley, with a few bedraggled cottages clinging to the rocks as though they had fallen in the water, pulled themselves out and were sitting now forlornly on the far side, trying to dry out in the sun. These dwellings straggled up the steep incline, cutting through the oak-woods to Roccagnano huddled round the second tower. Above the hamlet, an hour's walk away, lay Muccignano, a bigger, grander version of it, with proper streets and an illustrious history recorded in stone. It stood proudly on the hilltop opposite the palace.

As the fireflies danced in the twilight, I saw parts of the palace already in place and the views I saw were already seen as through the noble windows of its room. Where the hill ended and the sky began, all around the crest as it curved towards Castello, a row of oaks was silhouetted strangely, the branches seeming to flounder like the flailing arms of sailors falling off the edge of the known world. The summer breeze caught them and the dying day accentuated their isolation. I imagined them, highlighted, taking that top line and planting a great avenue of sentinel cypresses, garrisoning the valley for ever.

It was some twelve miles to Castello, which had become already a mere direction. I resolved to move to the direct vicinity of my building site. I would supervise it all in such a way that what might otherwise take several decades to build would be done in a handful of years.

I cast my eye again across the valley. The two churches of Morra rang their bells, picking up that of Roccagnano and Sant' Agnese and the heavy toll of Muccignano. I followed on beyond the cart-track, and back across the river, wading in the absence of a bridge, clambering up the far bank, running through strips of field divided into ribbons of corn, sweet peppers, tomatoes and sunflowers, separated by vines with a stranglehold over gnarled willow stumps. Where the fields dipped down to the riverbank, a trellis of melons and pumpkin leaves canopied the grass. Across the river the land rose again, traced by thin, shady finger-paths scraped through a tangled undergrowth of junipers, broom, heathers and ferns. Then the oaks climbed into a slope of chestnuts, broad spreading trees that had occupied the same place for centuries, shading the floor of the wood so effectively that only a mat of low grass and thyme could grow below them. Up and up the woodland rose, clearing twice to isolated ledges and small olive groves. This was the domain of the tower and castle of Ghironzo, which stood in their severe grey stone surveying the uneven lands they had tyrannized for so long. Time had been kinder to the fields and forest than to the buildings. The castle had begun to sink into the ground, its once noble halls reduced in places to heaps of *pietra serena*, each hewn by hand. I had spent more than an hour picking over these fine cornerstones, marking out potential quoins for the palace, selecting the finest and most regularly chiselled to form the cornerstones of my own edifice. It pleased me that the palace would rise on the plateau of the triangle of the towers with parts of the history of those much older buildings becoming an integral part of its new grandeur and elegance. There were three towers, three cards in each hand of briscola and there had been three tolls of the bell of San Francesco that signalled Donna Donatella's afternoon walk.

Where the spring erupted, it formed a pool, filled with a ghetto of amorous frogs. Their croaking reminded me of the croaking from beyond the wall on the day the war ended. A croak of freedom. The fireflies multiplied, hovered and sparked in the night. They were the gentlest of lights, magic lights with the bright excitement of distant fireworks brought closer for inspection and for admiration. They were gentle in their intent. They would come year after year, summer after summer, to this place with its screech owls and its faraway nightingale, its frogs and its aromatic grass. I was comforted, sandwiched between the stars and the glistening light of the fireflies, to have found a place where I could feel that I belonged. This was the home of which Vitelli had spoken, and home was somewhere I could always return. Regardless of what I or any future family were to do or learn, this site was where we would belong, now and always. I slept that night, dreaming of never leaving. My travels in the future would be from hall to hall, from room to room and from floor to floor. I dreamt, feeling that Donna Donatella would come one day and see the palace that would rise up before me and it would surprise and delight her as profoundly as the fireflies surprised and delighted me. It would draw her to it and touch her spirit so that she, too, would never want to go away. I dreamt of her fragrance, of the extraordinary shapeliness of the nape of her neck. If I touched that curve, it would be soft, I knew, but would it be warm to touch, or would it be cold as Palombino marble? The palm of my right hand ached, and my fingers quivered, longing to know, to feel, that mysterious skin.

She knelt beside me, staining her damask gown on a clump of mint. The fresh sting of mint masked the familiar scent of orange flowers and for a moment I confused Donatella's presence with that of other hands. I felt her warm breath on my cheek as she leant over me. She wore a garland of fireflies in her hair. She wore a necklace of live frogs who all obeyed her and hung decorously, scarcely moving their stretched limbs as they dangled from the gold chain round her throat. She wore a bodice which revealed so much of her breasts that questions that had riddled my nights were answered instantly. Her breasts were neither large nor small. They were shapely. They pointed upwards. They pressed against my chest. My heart stilled. The proximity of her breathing stopped mine. The stars above me beckoned me to join them. There was space in the galaxy for however many fragments into which I disintegrated. The stars were like handfuls of marble dust borne by the warm wind, clusters of *giallo antico* from Numidia and *cipollino* and the Statuario of the Northern Star from the marble mountains of Carrara. Then Donatella raised herself up on me, resting her weight on her index finger. The finger was long and white and delicate until it turned to iron. It was a file rubbing at my heart. It was a chisel tapping into my bones. It broke my first rib and chipped on, getting a rhythm that I recognized from my days of stone. But the chisel was unskilled and unsupervised: it broke another bone.

It found my heart and smothered it with mint, wrapped hastily in overlapping leaves, it stuffed torn grass into my lungs.

She sat beside me, tired by her work. From a cord at her waist she took an embroidered purse and snapped it open. It was empty except for two gold coins. These she tipped into the grass. Then she began to pick extraneous objects from my opened chest. She took, first, a piece of stone to blunt the chisel that cut through me. She took a salted anchovy, having first bitten off its head; she took a shrivelled orange, a toy gondola, a pair of boots, a deck of cards, a chisel, a glass jar of viridian pigment, a quill, a crust of chestnut bread, a quail's egg, four terracotta arches with plain pillars and the simplest design, each made of blocks. They were heavy and she had to strain with her two hands to lift them. When she had finished, she returned the dainty purse to its place at her slender waist.

The frogs around her neck grew restless and began to writhe. She shook her head and her thick hair tumbled around her face. She pulled out a tawny strand and licked it, threading it carefully through a blade of grass. Then she leant over me again and embroidered the wound in my chest. Every now and again, she leant back and looked at her work, holding her head sideways to see more clearly how the stitching was going. The frogs waited patiently, twitching their legs. When her work was done, she put the garland of fireflies where she had been. The screech owl in her purse gave a muffled call after she was gone. I tried to get up and follow her, but sleep would not release me from its embrace.

⤖ XX ⬸

✛ Twenty men were digging. They dug all day, every
day and the pit widened. It began as a trench a
hundred yards long, and then it widened. When it was
thirty yards wide and knee deep, the men began to tire.
They were used to drudgery. They had grown up on it;
they ate it and drank it and lived it every day. Their usual
work in the fields was no lighter than these twelve hours of
digging. It was the apparent pointlessness of their task that
disheartened them.

When a furrow was turned, seeds were planted, tares
grew and grain followed. Now they were scratching in the
dirt, beating the sun-baked mud with picks and spades. It
had taken weeks to get where they had, and what for?
That's what the men wanted to know. What for? They
knew they were scrabbling dust for the foreigner on the hill
and his gibbering minions, but they didn't know why.

'Are they Christians?' Primo Poesini asked his neighbour. 'Have you heard them? Singing and gabbling and
nodding and not a word of sense comes out of their
mouths.'

'It's the strangest thing I've seen,' his neighbour agreed,
'because they look like you and me.'

'Nah, they don't look like either of us.'

'They do too, more than the pedlar. And yet they say they're foreigners. I always thought foreigners were "them over there",' he said, pausing to rest on his shovel and jerking his head towards the frontier of the Grand Duchy. 'They say they're foreigners but they don't look foreign to my eye.'

'Your eye couldn't tell the difference between a golden oriel and a goldfinch if they were perched on the end of your bed.'

'What are you saying?'

'*Dio buono!* I'm saying they're strange and this digging is strange and that del Campo is stranger still: he starts off speaking Christian and the more he says the less you can follow it. You can stay with him until he gets to "palace" and then it's sheer guesswork. My wife has got it into her head that we're digging a pit into hell. She keeps me awake at night going on about it. I know we're not, but I couldn't tell her what we are digging to save my life.'

'How do you know it isn't to hell?' another digger asked.

'Well, it's obvious. If it was, we'd have started it in the valley and there'd be less far to dig.'

There were rumours that I was digging a lake, digging a crypt, digging for treasure, digging an underground vineyard. There were rumours that I came from the Grand Duchy, from Venice, from the Mountains of the Moon, from a pit of rivers that they call the sea. There were rumours that I was a soldier, a sailor, a priest, a duke, a bandit, a merchant, a prophet, a lunatic and an emissary of the devil. It was said that my carriage was made of beaten gold. It was said that I and my men ate insects. It was said that I was fabulously rich and had a hoard of diamonds stitched into bags which my man Giovanni guarded with his life. It was said that I had killed a hundred men in duels and kept bits of their bodies pressed in a barrel preserved in salt and the smell had filled their lodgings. It was said that I read spells out of a tin.

Half these things were said by Nunzia, in whose house we lodged, so the workers thought she should know. She watched us, even in our sleep; she watched us for the foreigners we were, sleeping under her roof, paying her money she could not refuse. But we paid so much money, so many coins, it made her deeply suspicious. And the house was full of food; indecent quantities of food that she cooked and we visitors wasted. She kept all our old food and sifted through it, looking for signs and portents in our leftovers. Beppe, her eldest grandson, came once a day and carried away our scraps, and Beppe saw strange things too, all of which he duly reported to be repeated from San Crescentino to Rocagnano.

The wages were higher than normal, so the work continued but it didn't seem to progress. Once the pit was three and a half metres deep, walls were erected inside it; thick stone walls with arched doorways and no windows. They asked what kind of man could spend such effort and money in order to live in a tomb? They didn't like it in the village or in the outlying hamlets. They didn't like it over the hill, but they kept digging for the wages they had come to regard as the wages of sin. They were so convinced of the futility of the project that once the first pit had been built and divided, they were hardly surprised when a second one was begun next door to it, as wide and long and deep again.

Tufts of wild chicory flowered on their spiky stems, mottling the fields with blue. The last of the blackberries were over, and the rosehips bulged scarlet on their briars. The workforce of twenty had doubled by August. By the end of September it would have doubled again. But by the end of September the rains would have turned the two pits into pools. Was I intending to live underwater? the workmen asked. The digging had already been stopped once to divert the spring water away. July had been a dry month, but August had brought the rain. There were several storms, sudden summer storms that crashed and shuddered through the valley, darkening the sky and pounding every tree, man and dandelion leaf with its great gusts of rain. The dry land drank in this rainwater gratefully, drenched only for the duration of the storm. Within minutes of the ensuing calm, the earth sipped the last of the rain on its face and left no trace of there having been any at all. The sun shouldered its way back through the clouds and shone as fiercely as before, denying the interlude of the storm, giving the impression of burning this late summer's day as relentlessly as any other.

The land was so dry that even the few inches of muddy water that had gathered on the pit floor drained away. It was the spring that had caused the flooding. The natural pool beside the pit had been dwindling week by week. The moss around its edge had turned a pale yellow. But each time it rained, although the water seemed to disappear much of it was gathering in the ground, feeding the spring pool, adding a tithe of water, however small, until it grew and searched out naturally any lower land to gravitate towards, to fill. The new pit was its perfect goal. It rained, it drained, and the pit floor, which had coped with the storm itself, became the object of this secondary rain.

The first time it happened I kept the men struggling in the mud. They slipped and cursed and wasted so much time that when another flood occurred I suspended the building work while a deeper pool was dug between the spring pool and the palace site. This would intercept the water and hold it, thanks to its great depth. The men had never had much faith in anything I was doing there – I suppose they had some hopes that my sanity would hold out, though, for some time at least. Without that, they would lose their wages. Leaving one hole to dig another, further away, leaving a pit that had been rigorously measured and overseen to dig another haphazard hole in the ground was worrying to my workforce. They did not see the logic of my drainage scheme. I gained a little ground with them, however, when the third storm came and the spring swelled, the new pool filled and our building site remained almost dry. It had worked, and I gained the first flicker of respect from some of the men who came up from the village each morning. They trudged up at half past five, and they trudged away, slowed by fatigue, after a day of what they saw as useless toil. They looked at me sometimes with suspicion blended with dislike. What right had I to waste their lives? What right had I, with my bags of crystals, to mock their labour and make them dig the whole day long to satisfy my idle caprice? They needed my money but they resented my leading them nowhere. After the drainage pit worked, a rumour began to spread among the many other rumours that maybe the foreigner not only knew what he was doing, but was going to do something beyond what a child would do playing by the river. Maybe this building thing was not the mockery it seemed, maybe . . .

As I sat through that first summer, waiting for the cellars to be dug, sitting, rising, walking, inspecting, I was more impatient than any of the diggers. Those first weeks and months seemed interminable. I watched the most minor transitions around the hummock of grass where I sat to view the proceedings. I studied the habits of the passing ants with such application that Vitelli would have been proud of me. The shackles of my prison days seemed a hundred times more bearable than the constraint of this waiting.

During those weeks I thought often and long of my old master. The palace would be the test of my apprenticeship. I knew my plans were a small part of what was needed.

Every great house has had its plans, but its greatness lies in the hands of its workforce, in the hands of the carvers and craftsmen. I had a vision of what I would do, but, one day soon, the challenge would be in the mastery of my hands. Often, in the past, I had banked with other masons, working as a team, side by side, masons from scattered towns gathered to restore some of the finest carving in Umbria. There were carvers sometimes who could no more draw an archivolt or pendentive than they could write their names, but in their fingertips they had the power to carve. They could cut at *pietra serena* like cheese. They used a hammer point with such ease I was ashamed to bank next to them. While I toiled at my first stages, some halfwit beside me would skim over his section with a square chisel and be ready for his skin of wine. Then I was grateful for my master's harshness. He kept me at my toil and he let me feel no pride so that I might one day excel. My fingers itched to be working, to regain their calluses, to caress dust and grain.

It was such a gradual process, watching my workforce sink underground. The first weeks were the worst. The loss of their feet the most disturbing. I had grown accustomed to see the world in terms of feet. I came from the earth and my own feet were firmly rooted in the ground, be it clay or sand or stone; it held me and ruled me. Sitting there, with gnats and butterflies circling round me as I surveyed the foundations of what would one day lift the earth into the sky, I was consumed by frustration. I had dreamt of seeing my palace rise. I had dreamt, too, of raising my palace. I realized at Quarata that part of my dreams had been me placing, with my own hands, one great stone upon another, carving, chipping, chiselling, blasting, splitting. My hands ached. My heart ached at the slowness of the progress.

At the end of September, when the rains came and

bucketed down, day after day, giving no pause for the sun to re-emerge and mop up the puddles, just raining, steadily and continually, I despaired. The drainage pit held, and the overflow trench I had built into it to take away excess water below the level of my cellars was effective. A trickle of water was diverted some eighty yards away to a grass slope that had grown noticeably greener since my crude engineering had made it the beneficiary of the spring. The natural spring and its tributaries were contained, but the unnatural deluge from the heavens had soaked and saturated the land around. The dirt floor of the cellars had turned to mud and the more the men trampled through it, the deeper the mud became. There were places where it sucked at a man's foot as though some gruesome animal were lurking in it. The mud pulled downwards and Giovanni and his cousins became afraid of it. It swallowed tools. There were two places where this phenomenon occurred, one more pronounced than the other. In the worst, a boy was caught up to his thigh and his thin cotton trousers were ripped off the leg that had been sucked in. He was dragged out by his mates and given a mouthful of grappa for the shock.

The dragon under the palace began its life that day. Giovanni, ever prey to fears of water gods, underwater monsters and the like, was all for calling it an omen, packing up and moving on. I explained to him in great detail the effect of fissures in the ground, under the top soil, in the rockbed and the workings of the underground water table. Giovanni's knowledge was eclectic, his concentration span erratic. Sometimes he could sit for hours and take in every word; at others he would block the simplest piece of information and seem incapable of understanding the most basic things. On the subject of the dragon, he was, as ever, unconvinced. He reminded me of his Venetian need to see before he believed. To which end, I endeavoured to lose and retrieve a dead hen to prove that the suction had a natural cause.

'Well, signor, we shall see. Let us hope this is so. What do I do, signor, if this dragon then bites off your hand, your arm, your—'

'It won't.'

'Well, signor, we shall see. Let us hope.'

'Hope!'

'Yes, signor, hope. Today I have discovered that there is hope even here in this tree place.'

Giovanni believed that trees existed exclusively to be stripped and sunk into his lagoon, his canals. Leaves, for him, were irrelevant, the great quantity of leaves in Umbria an affront.

'Really, signor, I tell you, today you have told me of this water table, of water under all this land, and I know now that this is the truth. I saw myself when the men dug the deep hole, it filled of its own accord with water. I was dying inside, signor. Now I know there is water under my feet, far under, but there, tonight Giovanni will get himself a girl, and bed her. Tonight Giovanni is a new man.'

Giovanni was happy, but the men weren't. They found my experiment distasteful, wasteful; and waste was unforgivable to them. They were not strangers to mud, sinking or otherwise: they worked in it through all the winters of their lives. There was nothing new or interesting in mud. The little respect that I had gained on my drainage pool was lost when I dropped a perfectly good hen on a perfectly clean piece of rope, made a fool of myself straining to retrieve it and then pulled it back up covered in grey clay. When Giovanni applauded, I saw him sink in the eyes of the diggers from courtly buffoon to barrel-organist's monkey. I saw them shake their heads as they walked away. It was a hen that I dropped down and a hen that I pulled up. What was so clever about that? Had I pulled up a plate of steaming hot polenta with a sauce of wild boar and tomatoes or even a chicken casserole, now that, as I overheard Primo Poesini say, would have been something. As it was, I spoilt the makings of a good broth.

⇥ XXI ⇤

✦ When October brought some respite from the rains
and the autumn sun warmed the ground, a trench
was dug around the outline of the south wing. It was filled
with stones and mortar, and by November the first layer of
stones took their place. The first cornerstones from Ghironzo were positioned and set, and the frustration of the
summer vanished, channelled into an excitement that knew
no bounds. After the men had left, I walked around the
south wall, and I walked along it, climbing up and down
where the gap for the doorway was. I had prepared the first
quoin myself, squaring it as my master had taught me,
reinitiating my hand to the seduction of stone. It was *pietra
serena* from Ghironzo hewn, perhaps, six hundred years
before my time. It had been cut well, but with the weath-
ering it needed resquaring. To take the cornerstone out of
the twist I found the two lowest corners and then made a
draft between them with an inch chisel and a mallet. Then
I chiselled down three corners bit by bit. Skimming until
one face was level then taking all my measurements from
that, squaring the edges. There were masons at the quarry
who could have done it, but I wanted to do it myself and
I did.

Every day, between seventy and eighty men came up to work, fortified by the sour local wine and a sense of purpose. I hired oxen from everywhere I could. The field crops were over, only the chestnuts needed gathering and the olives had to be picked and pressed. The year's wine was fermenting, the corn had long been sold and stored, the fields were fallow until the spring. This was a time of eking out; for the day labourers there was never much work in winter. It had been so for my father and all our neighbours. It was so everywhere that poor men worked another's land. The palace, which had been so unpopular in the summer, became better than chestnut bread as the winter progressed. Men who had never hoped to work in regular employment took home a weekly wage. Journeyman builders who were forced to scour jobs from town to town could climb the hill to Quarata and return home knowing that what had begun would take not weeks or months but years to complete, and in those years their time and skills would feed their families, lifting them from the uncertainty of other times into prosperity.

Half the workforce was sent to the quarry on the track to Poggio to hack out the stone. It was also their task to load up the ox carts with pilfered stones from the fallen properties that littered the estate. Together, we moved a mountain. I had not been in my element with digging and measuring. It reminded me too much of the descent into the Etruscan tombs with the guttering candle. Once we began to raise walls, I was master of my trade. The masons knew about stone, but I knew more. We began to work together as a proper team; I led, and they followed. Their wages and the wine were always there, but they followed me as well, I hope, because they sensed that I knew where I was going. A brotherhood began. The palace bound us. It became a focal point for the entire village.

As the winter dug its claws into Quarata, we adapted as

an army would in a state of siege. The building site became a camp. The second coachman, so hastily hired at Mestre, had returned, after an unnecessarily long stay in Castello, together with his carriage and Giovanni's drunken cousin. He was almost as reluctant to leave as he had been to come. I mentioned to Giovanni (something I would never have done before the incident of the salt and raisins) that it was to return empty but for one crate, whose dimensions I specified, which he could send back to his bereft family in Venice.

This left me with a staff of three: Giovanni, Florido his cousin, the coachman, and Piero his cousin, the footman. I had feared that Giovanni might be like a fish out of water, but he had the qualities of a crab. Once he had adapted to his new surroundings he moved on land with an extra sense and made himself as useful in Umbria as ever he had been in Venice. He was never popular with the local men. They eyed his dark curls, his indolent sea-water eyes, his sensuous lips and soft hands with instant suspicion. As time progressed, and their sisters, daughters and even their wives began to eye Giovanni, too, drawing their own, more favourable conclusions, he became the scapegoat of their discontents.

Florido had become as essential to me as Giovanni. I would never mount a horse, never ride one. Florido kept the four horses of my carriage, and he kept them away from me. I needed him to cover the distances. He kept the four mules and the three carts that were used for general carrying. I felt a gratitude to him, a fondness for him for handling those horses, for setting off daily with Giovanni to get me all the things I needed and bringing in the artisans from Lugnano.

The frosts came early in that winter of 1864, they froze the ground solid and sprinkled it daily with a powder of St John's white, frescoing the stiff, trampled grass and driving us into winter quarters. In it I saw marble dust and the chemical salts of Venice pushing into the Umbrian landscapes. The artisans and the labourers, who had come from far away, had been sleeping out in the fields, under trees, in ditches and in makeshift shelters of planks and boards. As the New Year approached, I had a row of huts built for them and we kept a log fire burning round the clock. The sour wine, though as welcome as ever, was not enough. Florido set up a camp kitchen in the frozen maze of the cellars. Soups, stews and roast game filled the night air and kept the team harnessed to the job more effectively than any of my dreams.

I remembered my own days spent in the field, days spent in chilled churches, chiselling stone with hands bitten raw by the winter. I cleaned so many angels then, and I often prayed that one would warm my fingers and feet, bring me a cup of warm broth, a place to lie at night other than the cold straw of some miserable, draughty shed. My old master drew the work from me with his harshness. Only in the latter years of my apprenticeship did I toil out of love for the stone itself and what I could make of it with my own hands and my tools. Yet the memory of those days did not allow me to be a good master: I was too soft and would have spoilt the workmen – the palace would have never grown under my management. But there was Giovanni, my other half, who kept the men working, chiding them away from the bonfire when they lingered there too long and showed the makings of a pasha in his dealings. Between us we cracked an even pace.

I do not know what Giovanni did, togther with fat Florido and Piero, but the workmen were always relieved to see me returning from my trips. The land had already claimed me, it had whispered to me that it was my home. Gradually, after days spent at the terracotta works in Siena, the workforce began to claim me too. It was the first time in my life that I had ever truly felt that I belonged. I had wanted to belong once in my mother's skirts, but she had always pushed me away, and long before the tallying. I remember being moved on to make way for a baby sister, of being shoved forcibly aside and looking on.

I had my one stone hut, a sentry box built on a lip of hill overlooking the site. It had a slab of Sardinian granite for a seat not unlike the shelf I had once shared with Vitelli, only shorter. It had two pillars either side of its entrance; with these I whiled away the long hours of my watching, carving them in the way of the crypt pillars of the Church of St Veronica, where I had worked once for many months.

Piero kept a supply of sticks and logs beside this hut and I had a small fire burning in the open air, which warmed the stone as pleasantly as in any drawing room. I sat upon a blue satin cushion from my coach with my tin of drawings beside me, poring over future glories, adding and subtracting curves and lines. The longer the actual palace took to grow, the more ornate its interior became on paper. I was impatient to get on. So impatient that sometimes my journeys to Siena soothed my nerves. The terracotta works were full of decorations, finished artefacts that I could touch and see. I took in my own designs and began the process of forming the plaster moulds into which the terracotta for Quarata would be packed and baked.

I drew one hundred diverse designs, from the simple pillared arches of my dream of Donatella to elaborate frieze blocks of angels' wings, with all the flowers of the fields that I had sifted so restlessly through my hands that summer. The terracotta works were quick. From one month to the next they could produce hundreds of pieces, which they crated, numbered and named and sent by ox-drawn convoy to the palace site. We stacked it in ever-growing mounds. By February the first window spaces could be clearly defined as gaps in the wrapping stone. There would be three hundred and sixty-five windows: one for every day of the year. Each window would have a terracotta surround. Each surround was made up of seventeen pieces, each piece took a strong man to lift it. Later it would take two men to lift them into place.

Each new idea was drawn on a clean sheet of paper, and new ideas sprang from existing plans, breeding like rabbits in a pen. My master had told me that I should see every job complete in my mind's eye before I began it! I saw the palace and I saw its parts but only the parts were complete. Perhaps that is why the old plans were the dearest to me; the piss-stained Bible pages were sacrosanct. I believed that every idea that had grown out of my prison cell had to be honoured in the house. Some were less than realistic, but I studied those the hardest, inhaling the old nostalgia for Vitelli and the cell and the undying vision of Donna Donatella. Sometimes I asked myself what the chain of my doing would lead to.

I had seen and fallen in love with Donna Donatella. I longed to be noticed and admired by her. I had seen and fallen in love with life and I longed to be a part of it. I had studied hard to become a gentleman. I had played hard to accrue the wealth to build the palace and take my place in society. I had done it all for love of Donna Donatella, but where was she? Had I lost her in the shadow cast by the rising stone?

Life was passing me by as I transformed a hillside with the stone. I had made an elaborate water-clock with my ditches, but the monstrous stone shell was only shoulder high and only then in places. It would take years to complete. It would be years before it dazzled anyone. It was as insubstantial as the palaces of the fireflies. And when it was finished who would see it? I had set tongues wagging in Castello and set rumours racing around Lugnano and every village within a radius of fifty miles. Yet no clues as to the whereabouts of Donna Donatella and her family had come my way. I had sent out spies to discover her whereabouts and met with nothing but blanks and disappointment. Her brothers were disgraced, her father, frail. Rumours and counter-rumours had left a trail of false information. She had emigrated, died, married, become a nun, given birth to triplets, moved to Emilia, gone to Genoa, set sail for the Indies, succumbed to the ague. I followed up every rumour and every lead to no avail.

I knew for certain that I had seen her in the garden of her father's house in Castello. The house was now boarded and had been empty for years. I knew that her father owned another property north of Petrelle. It, too, was empty but for a custodian and his three daughters. In the end it was Giovanni who gave me news of Donna Donatella. An uncle of hers had sent word that the two of them would be returning in the summer to put the castle in order. The custodian was to make it ready from the end of May.

'Are you not proud of me, signor, for getting this information of your beloved?'

It was midwinter and skylarks were rioting in my ribcage. Words were beyond me.

'You should be proud of me, signor, I had to bed all three of the daughters to get this information for you.'

Words became the flowers and spices of a summer garden; their scents and colours rose and swooped.

Thou hast ravished my heart, my sister, my spouse; thou hast ravished my heart with one of thine eyes, with one chain of thy neck.

'You are smiling, signor, you are unkind to Giovanni, you should not smile so. Those girls have hair on their faces and they live almost exclusively on raw onions. I drank of their sour breath for love of you, signor, to tell you she comes.'

Make haste my beloved, and be thou like to a roe or to a young hart upon the mountain of spices.

⇝ XXII ⇜

✤ I made a chart of all the days until May and set myself the task of dredging the sand from the banks of the Tiber at Santa Lucia, before Castello, through an hourglass and into the mortar of my dream. Eighty men were not enough. I sent Giovanni out with Florido and the coach to recruit stonemasons and bricklayers, stone-cutters, carpenters, joiners and smiths. They travelled from village to village offering bribes, from hamlet to hamlet with a purse of gold coins to lure men and boys away from their kitchens to Quarata. By the time Donna Donatella arrived, we had to have reached the second floor at least, not just on the south wing, but everywhere. The entire structure had to rise. It had to rise with supernatural speed. It had to show its coming grace. I had to do it.

The men were working flat out, toiling through hail and snow. Their wages had increased and I had instructed Florido to feed them well with plenty of fat and meat.

'Give them all they can eat. Make them strong. My life depends on it, Florido.'

The camp kitchen now employed four boys to help my coachman–cook. Potatoes and onions, cornmeal and flour, chestnuts and beans, sheep, pigs and whole cows were delivered up for Florido's stews and roasts.

I had a hundred pairs of working gloves made to enable the men to keep up their speed despite the cold. I had their winter clogs replaced and changed the straw they stuffed inside them for goose down. I kept the seamstresses of Morra, Lugnano and Ronti busy stitching thick jackets for them. The carvers, in particular, suffered from the cold, standing still for hours at a stretch. I had fires built around the palace at night to prolong the hours of light and enable the work to progress into the dark winter evenings. I thought of every way I could to accelerate the pace. There was an air of frenzy at the site and the walls were rising faster than they had ever done. It still wasn't enough, if we were to have the semblance of a palace ready by May.

I chose to make the three towers of my edifice rise independently of the rest. I would construct and finish them, so that their height could hint at things to come. The towers were to be six floors high. Each tower differed in its conception, but all three were to end with cupolas. Each one would be open to the four winds, two with windows, one without, and each would be a place to look at the stars. I thought of Gubbio and its towers. The square tower of San Giovanni with its open-arched *campanile*, the tower of Sant' Ubaldo, the octagonal tower of the Madonna del Prato and the defiant pointing finger of the Palazzo dei Consoli crenellated and crowned. I thought of Gubbio and its race, pitting rival factions against each other, goading the others on to strain themselves past any natural strength. If the *ceri* were carried in a single procession, their carrying would be short-lived. It was the element of the race that gave the *ceraioli* their prodigious strength. In Gubbio, men died lifting. They died running, too.

I kept a basic team of builders to raise up the walls with all the carriers and mixers of mortar, shovellers and levellers they needed. I kept fifty men at the old quarry at Poggio and started a new quarry nearer to the house, hacking out *pietra serena*, and I put forty-five men to work on the towers. I split the latter into teams, each of fifteen men and boys. Some were to work on scaffolding, some to carry, some to winch, some to lay. I offered a prize every day of a goose and a hen for whichever team finished first and second. Most of the men didn't return home that winter, except on Sundays, and the geese and chickens were more welcome than wages at home. I gave each team a name, after the three look-out towers that had once protected the valley, Ghironzo, Roccagnano and Quarata, and I gave them each a patron saint to spur them to victory and hold their loyalty. Following the rites of Gubbio, I gave them each a coloured neckerchief to wear as they worked: gold, red and blue. And as in Gubbio, at the *festa* of the Ceri, I gave them the chance to prove their manhood, their love, their strength, bravery, dedication and conquest of fear, performing superhuman feats. I told myself it was a homage to the Ceri. But was it profanity? I don't know.

There were days when I saw my building site in a state of near hysteria and the spirit of competition so ingrained that no one spoke except to call for the next stone, and no one rested in the day, though at night the workmen lay sleeping around the campfire consumed by exhaustion. I sat one evening on a board by the fire and watched. I watched the sleeping men and noted their haggard faces, their limbs twitching in their sleep, their hands cut and bruised. There had been many minor accidents and two more serious ones in the last three days. There were always some, it was inevitable, but the trouble with the present injuries was the knowledge that they could have been avoided. I looked into the flames leaping into the darkness and I fancied that I saw a great tower, high as the Tower of Babel, and men were falling from all its floors like shaken ashes, tumbling and screaming through the air. When I looked more closely, they were my men; I recognized their faces one by one. They fell in profusion, but their faces stopped in slow motion, upside-down and sideways as they fell. There were Giuseppe and Primo, Marino, Luciano, Terzo, Urbino, Tonino, Mario, Gianni; they were all there, falling into the heap of crushed bodies on the ground, which was the fire, glowing, throwing out the looks of betrayal that each man gave me as he burned.

'Move back from the smoke, signor, it's in your eyes. I thought for a moment you were crying,' Giovanni told me, touching my shoulder as he spoke, motioning me back from the flames.

'I'm killing them, Giovanni,' I whispered.

'Killing what?' Giovanni asked, looking around anxiously and stamping his feet as though whatever it was I was killing might still have a few survivors who might be making ready to climb up his legs. He moved away a little.

'Killing what?'

'The men.'

'It's true,' Giovanni stated in his most matter-of-fact way. 'Some of them won't last much longer like this. Put them on short shifts, that's the answer.'

Florido was waving to him from the roasting spit. Giovanni took his long black cape in one hand and flung it over his shoulder, giving him an elegant but mysterious appearance. He stepped over the recumbent figures of the workmen, lying wrapped in their coats, a human lagoon with Giovanni walking over it. Then he called back, hardly bothering to turn, giving the next man in his path a slight shove with the toe of his boot as though to ascertain whether there was enough life left in the victim to benefit from the new regime.

'Shorter shifts.'

I had not been crying, as Giovanni had supposed. The

fire was hot and the smoke had caught me. I had been feeling remorse for the state of my men, but in a sentimental guilt-ridden way that indulged myself and in no way benefited them. I was a sentimental man; Giovanni was practical. He came across sometimes as callous or even cruel, but in his practicality he was more human than I, for all my operatic heart-searching. Shorter shifts were the answer. In Gubbio, no *ceraiolo* was asked to carry a candle for more than a few minutes at a time; one went in and another went out, working in teams, but working in staggered relays. It was obvious: the men must work and rest at frequent intervals. The teams would have to be bigger. After Giovanni left me, I felt ashamed to see what a fool I had been, and to see how easily a fool can become a tyrant, and a tyrant cruel. I didn't want Quarata to be like the Duomo of Florence where hundreds of workmen lost their lives in constructing the giant cupola. The Duomo had three colours too: green, pink and white. Quarata's colours, though stolen from Gubbio, would not be tainted by death. The Mariangeli boy was already splinted up and gessoed, and Terzo had a pirate's cut across his cheek from a rogue sliver of stone that narrowly missed his eye.

Next day, the shorter shifts began. Piero, who had any number of undefined jobs, now had a job of his own. He was the time-keeper. He rejoiced in his new role, calling out the changes in the echoing, rolling voice of the Venetian watch. He had been the least expansive of the Venetian team, following Giovanni and Florido round like a hunting dog, anxious for errands to fulfil. Now he took as much pride in his new role as if I had made him Mayor of Castello. By the afternoon of his first day, he had purloined a drum from one of the huts and taken to beating out the changeovers as though at a great civic pageant.

My repentance at the sacrilege of borrowing elements from the Ceri and transposing them to Quarata was short-lived. By the evening of Piero's first day with his drum, while the bonfires around the palace shell threw light on to the racing workmen and torches stood out in their iron holders, lighting up the four corners of each tower, I taught him the drumbeats of my youth. I taught him the rhythm of the Ceri, the rhythm of passion. I taught him to beat out the secret of life, the way to victory through running feet, TUM-tata: TUM-tata TUM TUM / TUM TUM. I taught my Venetian minion what only the Eugubini are supposed to know and he beat the rhythm of lovemaking into the air, into the stone.

The three towers grew, layer upon layer, to the cupolas of the sixth floors, to the place of vaulting where the palace had first begun. I opened my tin and took out the drawings, the first designs, the first flights of my imprisoned fantasy. The vaulted ceilings of the sixth floor cupolas were so ornate that no one could fail to be impressed by the workmanship that would go into them. Even Donna Donatella would stand in awe when she saw the Gothic carvings that were to adorn them.

During that winter, while my men slaved, I had not been idle. I had taken out my tools, my square chisel, my mallet, my hammer and my files, and worked together with four stonemasons to fashion the pillars and the capitals, the pediments and the arcs and bosses – so finely worked I longed for my master to see them too, as a lover of stone and its craft. Donna Donatella would admire it, but my master would have known that I had seduced the blocks I worked from. The foliated pillars were the pale grey of the mists of Burano, the colour of woodsmoke filtered through trees, the gentle grey of the bedrock of Quarata, of *pietra serena* quarried centuries ago, plundered from the ruined halls of Ghironzo. It was the stone I knew best and it sang for me. In early April, when the teams of builders finished the structure of the three towers of Babylon, we were ready to dovetail our stone to their vault.

The first room of my dreams would also be the first room of the reality. While the building proceeded, we finished the interior of the east tower, the tower of the wind. Its floor was inlaid with marble; pink Portuguese, white strips from Carrara, yellow Sienese, mottled agate green from India. It was inlaid with great intricacy at its centre and in two bands around the edge of the room, but most of it was the gentle pink of the local travertine, polished to a smoothness that brought out the subtlety of its Umbrian hues. It is the pink of Assisi, the pink of the first light over the hills, the pinkness of flesh, gentle and comforting to the eye.

The tower of the wind had four windows, each taller than a man, each framed in terracotta, whose ornamentation was focused at the brackets of their lintels. The bulk of the frame was plain, with a touch here and there of decoration. The effect was to be of music, building up by an accumulation of notes. The beauty would emerge through numbers. The ceiling was to be the focal point of the tower, a homage to the heavens leading up to a perfect dome, which would be painted with pure lapis lazuli, powdered and imported from Afghanistan. I had bought it myself from Venice, from a merchant on the Riva degli Schiavoni. It had cost as much as gold dust. When the east tower was finished and the cypress windowframes were in place, the glass puttied in and the gesso dried on the walls, I applied the luminous lapis lazuli myself, layer upon layer, painting it on with a badger brush as though I were caressing the skin of Donna Donatella herself. When the linseed base in the paint had finally dried, I applied the constellations of gold leaf, burnished with amber. When Orion and Jupiter, Venus and Mars, the Milky Way and the Great Bear were all there on the cupola, I painted in the Northern Light, bigger and brighter than any other star. I painted the Pole Star, my master's star, my star, on 15 May, the day of days, the day of the Ceri. Then I waited for the arrival of my beloved, in the room that was ready for her.

⇒ XXIII ⇐

O my dove, that art in the clefts of the rock, in the secret places
of the stairs, let me see thy countenance, let me hear thy voice;
for sweet is thy voice, and thy countenance is comely.

✠ The tower of the wind was ready, but Donatella
didn't come. The first two weeks seemed like a
reprieve; more work could be done, the spiral stone staircase fitted in its entirety so it curved up, as sensual as
vertebrae, beneath the pink stone through the skeleton of
the east tower. There was time to begin the details on the
south tower and to raise up the wrought-iron carapace of
the west. For the west tower followed the concept of older
villas with a male and female tower, the one cloaked in
masonry, the other open to the air. The female tower was
like a pergola on a parapet, a place where jasmine would
grow from pots and twine their supple stems around the
ornate iron with fine white blossoms to scent the summer
nights.

I had not expected to be given this extra time. Two
weeks at the pace we had reached meant a great stride
forward with the other towers. But when May passed and
June came and there was still no word of Donna Donatella
or her uncle coming to Petrelle, I began to sicken and the
work to slow. Giovanni tried to comfort me: 'There was
bound to be some waiting. The girls at Petrelle say Donna
Donatella's uncle is an erratic man. He has been known to

arrange and cancel visits in the past. He has not been to the castle for five years, though, so they are sure he will come. It's just a matter of when.'

I was not comforted. I abandoned my sentry box on the hill for a new perch in the tower of the wind. Each window was indented in the thick walls, and each had a pink travertine marble seat. I chose to sit in the south bay, with the warmth of the sun on the back of my neck. Sometimes, I surveyed the building works below me, but mostly my mind was turned inwards and I chose to read the books that I had studied with Vitelli. I also pored over the texts of our *papier mâché* playing cards and, more and more, I numbed my mind by playing patience with the briscola deck.

Nor was there comfort in my cards. The days of turning up my good fortune from the pack had gone. Far away from any realistic hope of seeing my beloved, there had been two cards that fell time and again for me. They were the seven of denari and the three of cups, Genesis 21: 6, 'And Sarah said, God hath made me laugh, so that all that hear will laugh with me ...' to verse 20. In prison the second had seemed glued to my hand. Vitelli said it was unnatural because, no matter who dealt, the three of cups always fell to me with its text from Genesis 24. It was *my* text, I was Isaac and Rebekah was my beloved.

And Isaac went out to meditate in the field at the eventide: and he lifted up his eyes, and saw, and behold, the camels were coming. And Rebekah lifted up her eyes, and when she saw Isaac, she lighted off the camel. For she said unto the servant, What man is that walketh into the field to meet us?

All through that summer, I lifted up my eyes but I saw no camels coming. The road was white with dust from the comings and goings of my own ox carts. Many of the drovers who came had passed by Petrelle; they were all asked for news and were full of gossip, but none was about my beloved. Her uncle had vanished and taken her with him. I started to resent and then to hate her uncle. I felt he was cheating me. I sat in my tower and brooded, concocting bitter thoughts. I grew careless of the building. Giovanni climbed up and down the stairs, chiding, asking, coaxing as though I were a sick falcon in my nest and needed luring down with a morsel of fresh meat.

'The new batch of terracotta, signor, it excels all others. It is the capitals of the loggia columns. You must come and see, you will be amazed, I swear, on my mother's head, you have not seen such fine pieces yet.'

I was off my food. He tried another bait.

'The west team have left the tower and they are working on the back wall of your library. They seem to be blocking in the fireplace. Perhaps you should come and see, signor, before it is too late.'

I didn't care. What good was a fireplace if she would not come to warm herself beside it? What good was anything without her? He shook the jesses in his hand, hinting at flight.

'There is talk of an Etruscan tomb unearthed in Trestina. The drover who told me says a suit of golden armour has been unearthed. And there is a chalice, so he says, of the purest gold engraved in marvellous designs. He says the finder wants to sell, today—'

The east tower was my cup of gold, a chalice within a chalice, a shield within a suit of armour, a treasure laid for her. She didn't come. She wouldn't come. What use had I for other finds?

Giovanni knew how to break down resistance, though. He had practised the skill in the markets of Venice, haggling over prices with the merchants there. He was very Arabian in his doggedness. Perhaps he had heard me speak of my old master's obsession with Etruscan finds and my own frightened quests for gold. Or perhaps he knew too well my avarice for things. And he knew my pride; he knew that, eventually, I would be bound to follow his golden bait. How could I let some other collector buy any of the treasure that I was amassing for Donna Donatella? How could I let slip something that one day she might come to hear about?

The heat and the sense of anticlimax took its toll on the workforce. Many of the men had taken to returning home in the evenings, and many failed to come back. It was never an exodus, just a slow seepage. Without the precise instructions I had been giving every day, many were unsure of what they should be doing. Giovanni braved the grey spiral stairs time and again, but when it finally dawned on him that I would not be rallying for a while to my cause, he made his own decisions rather than lose the workforce. He kept me informed.

'We are stuck now to get the floor joists in without the whole middle falling down – you would have to show us how. I know you did something clever on the first floor, but Giovanni wasn't concentrating then and I don't trust any of the masons to do such a big job without you. So, we will wait,' Giovanni told me. 'And meanwhile, I have the men building a walled garden. Florido says that he could do with a more sheltered place to keep his herbs and vegetables. He says the wild animals keep coming and digging them up where they are. With a walled garden, he would be happy and you could set your fruit trees to grow. Gain some time, signor, like you're always telling me. And . . . well, Piero really wants something new to drum about, he's got quite used to that drumming now, he's a bit lost without it. And—' Giovanni was never discouraged by my lack of response. He looked at my listless person, sniffed disdainfully at the pissy cards he had tried many times to hide, and continued. 'I heard today that Donna Donatella's family have quite a collection of Etruscan things. You know the man in Trestina never did sell his golden cup. He was probably asking too much for it. I thought it was ridiculously cheap, but it was probably too much. What would Giovanni know about such things?'

He paused, making me aware of him by his silence, neither leaving nor speaking as he slouched by the door, his tongue between his teeth, his eyes half closed.

'It's probably lucky, signor, that you have so many ways to introduce yourself to Donna Donatella and her uncle, when they come. Giovanni Contarini would have bought that cup and kept it to give to the uncle. He's a greedy bastard from what the custodian's daughters say. He digs, but he doesn't spend. He'd covet a chalice like the one in Trestina. He'd be impressed. Well, as I say, it's probably lucky you've got so many other *entrées* there. You can't row a boat without an oar.' He waited again, pretending not to see me or to be thinking about me at all. The relative quiet imposed by the midday heat was pierced by the cries of the masons calling out to one another, yodelling their names over the background effervescence of crickets in the yellowing grass.

'Of course, if they did arrive tomorrow, you've probably already worked out how to get them here. You'd need a plan, what with him being a recluse and so stingy. It doesn't sound like they keep much company over there, either – just close friends, so I'm told.'

Luring me down from my eyrie was relatively easy. Luring Donatella's uncle to my unfinished house would be another matter. My life had progressed via such a bizarre route that I had assumed that if links were missing in my chain, Providence would join them. There had been nineteen links in my prison chain: I had imagined each link to be a hurdle, a challenge to surmount *en route* to my beloved. My master's voice came back to me: 'A chain is as strong as its weakest link.' They were words so often repeated that I had blocked them out. It was galling to be so endlessly dependent on Giovanni for my ideas, but he often saw things I did not. Once he had mentioned this weak link, I could think of no other. As he had known I would, I bought the Etruscan chalice.

Where would I keep it, Giovanni wondered. I bought a cabinet from an antiquarian in Castello and three chairs. I bought a writing table and a small case for my books. A floodgate opened. A dozen and then a tide of antiquarians tracked me down, pursued me, sold me their wares. I began to accumulate furniture and panelling, doors and tapestries, screens and settles, tables, desks and chairs. Giovanni encouraged me mercilessly.

The summer passed, and still Donna Donatella did not arrive. Giovanni became, temporarily, the overseer at Quarata. He bequeathed me Piero to serve as my factotum in his stead. It was Piero and I who found the first heaps of furniture and had them carted to the storerooms we had made on the site at the back of the south wing. It was Piero who had picked up the Castellano dialect from the workmen and found himself at his ease in town, who asked his way around, driving the coach, presenting me and generally keeping me company. And I liked Piero, not least because I felt that, more than anyone else, he had been moved by the drum. The rhythm had entered his blood. His drumsticks were idle now and the tattoo was over, but Piero, like me, still carried it in his veins: TUM TUM / TUM TUM.

For an entire year I had shunned society. I had established myself as an eccentric and a recluse. I knew that rumours had spread and taken root; my wealth was becoming legendary. I knew that mothers all over northern Umbria were anxious to catch me and marry me to their daughters. I knew that many husbands and fathers had been nagged half to death to engineer meetings with me, make appointments and get me home and wed. I had avoided them like the pox. I was aware of them because rumours course both ways, but I hadn't wanted any of their schemes or stratagems until it dawned on me that advantages could flow two ways. When Donatella came, I could be already established as part of the circle that she would naturally rejoin. I could be so fêted that I would be at every gathering and if so, I would be bound to meet her, sooner or later, when she returned.

After my brief depression at her failure to materialize at Petrelle, I recovered sufficiently to see that my life was meaningless without her and I lived on hope. 'If' was an impossibility. I had to believe in 'when'. When she came, when she saw the palace, when she finally noticed me, I would awaken once and for all from my dream. The palace was my token of love, as were the rows of pomegranate trees I had planted in the autumn for her slippered feet to wander among in years to come. I had waited all my life. I would wait again. Nothing could damp the flame of my faith and desire.

Many waters cannot quench love, neither can the floods drown it: if a man would give all the substance of his house for love, it would utterly be contemned.

I had the drawings for a suite of rooms in the south wing sketched over The Song of Songs. They were her rooms. They were on the second floor. I ordered the materials needed to finish them, from the floor tiles and marble inlays to the mosaics of her dressing room, to the gesso mouldings of her boudoir, the Venetian drapes, even the orange trees for her balconies. The winter to come would not be wasted, and when she came in the following year, I would have not only the east tower but a throw of rooms in which to woo her.

Meanwhile, I gathered every crumb of information I could find about her from her old friends and neighbours in Castello. I carried the image of her like a fresco ingrained so deeply on my memory that it touched the bone. She was slender and her neck was long and arched. Her face was poised and shapely in its curves. Her cheekbones were high, her nose straight and long and her eyes slightly aslant, almond-shaped, speckled hazel and grey. Though her eyes were clear, they did not reflect the light, they drew it in. Her skin was fair with a faint glow of sunlight, as though bathed in amber. Her hair was neither blonde nor brown: it was the colour of the husks of ripe Indian corn, streaked by the summer strand by strand. It conveyed a sense of plenty: it filled me with awe. The nape of her neck was covered in ivory down. Her lips were full and sensual. They were crimson, when I saw them, stained, perhaps, by the pomegranate she was eating. She was picking each grain out with a pin, savouring them with intense concentration. In repose, she seemed unnaturally still. When she smiled, her whole face was illuminated from within.

She looked across the garden once and saw me kneeling by the broken stone. She flashed a smile at me as sudden as lightning and as quickly gone. Her fingers were long and delicate, and her slippered feet were tiny to my eyes. When she walked past me, she left in her wake a scent of orange flowers. When she walked past me, I was struck dumb.

My eye was trained to memorize beauty. I memorized hers, reproducing her face and hands and neck in every detail, transposing her flesh to stone. And every stone I carved I longed to imbue with the elixir of life, to seduce and caress her flesh in place of the unforgiving grain.

In Castello I learned that Donna Donatella was fond of dancing. She had danced with every eligible bachelor in the town and eluded marrying any of them. It was generally agreed that a girl shouldn't dance so well unless it was to catch herself a husband. It was generally agreed that she had a quiet voice and a graceful figure. A judge some ten years older than myself, whose face was as mottled and veined as a piece of Veronese marble, whispered to me that when Donna Donatella laughed, she arched her neck and rippled out a sound so unsettlingly sensual that he remembered it still and pulled it out of his mental archive sometimes to guide him through the long hours he spent in court.

In Castello, I learned that Donna Donatella had an orchard of her own. That she had a love of bees and fruit. I heard of her nectarines and figs, apricots and oranges. She had lemon and mandarin trees, which bore fruit in such abundance that she took baskets of it to the orphanage of the nuns of Santa Clara. I learned that her mother had died of a fever when Donatella was still a child. Her two brothers were older and few spoke well of them. They had fallen from favour during the war and had carried some treachery into the city that was hinted at but never named. I heard that despite their misdemeanours Donatella loved them.

Their father, I was told, had nurtured his daughter like a prize fruit. He distilled into her strange and exotic qualities unnatural in a lady of Castello: she spoke Latin, Greek and French. She played the spinet. She had a singing teacher from Naples who trained her voice. Her father, poor man, worshipped her and turned a blind eye to her faults: when she was not grafting potted trees, and perverting nature by making pears grow on an apple branch, she wasted entire days in reading books. Had her mother lived, I was assured, this would not have been allowed.

Donna Donatella went her own way, followed by a whiff of orange-flower water and the chill breath of disapproval from the city beyond her garden walls.

I learned from a matronly lady with three daughters of her own that Donatella had an aversion to wearing boots and shoes. 'My seamstress used to live with them, so she should know. She said it started when Donatella was still a child. She refused to wear shoes. She insisted on slippers. Satin slippers embroidered all over the toes. A motherless girl with the airs of a Chinese empress. Inside and out, traipsing round that orchard, tramping over the ashes of the bonfires she had lit to keep the frost off her trees. Well, sometimes she'd smoke out half the city, depending which way the wind was blowing. If it was easterly, we couldn't open our drawing-room windows to air the room. Imagine! That was Donatella for you. More silk gowns than she'd ever need in a month of Sundays and never without some horrible trapped bird in her lap, splinting its wing, if you please! The stains, apparently, were unwashable.'

One of the carters who delivered supplies from Castello, came once with his uncle to give the old man a ride. It was Giovanni who discovered he had once been Donna Donatella's gardener.

'She had a way with trees. She could mix them. She'd take a shield bud off one tree, make a cross in the bark of another and slip the shaved bud into it. Then she'd tie it round with gut and in the spring a new one would grow. She got it from a book, she said. It used to worry me. You know, a girl in the garden doing unnatural things.'

'Did you know her long?'

'Oh, yes, she was a little thing when I started. She used to follow me around: wet slippers in the dew and her nurse behind her, always complaining. Sometimes she gave her nurse the slip and went around with her brothers. I caught them once, boiling snails in a coal bucket. The Frenchies were in town then and, as you know, they'd eat the dirt from under their shoes if it was served in a fancy sauce. The snails kept crawling out of the colander they were in, away from the heat, and she and the boys kept putting them back in. Making some French thing, they were, and the snails all for getting out and them all for forcing them back in ... Mostly, though, she was for mending up little things, not tormenting them. She had a soft heart for songbirds and a way with flowers.'

'Did she talk to you much?'

'Oh, yes, she had her days of talking. Sometimes you'd think she didn't know how and some days she didn't know how to stop. And she gave me things. She gave me all the fruit I could carry home, and clothes for my kids. She gave me a mountain of her old slippers for my girls ... not that they could ever wear them – not for the size. But they were made of woven gossamer.'

'What did you do with them?'

'The missus sold them. Sometimes they'd be worn to shreds, but mostly they were like new: shiny and worked in coloured threads. They fetched a bit on the market. They helped, you know.'

'Has she ever come back?'

'I wouldn't know. And I wouldn't know where to. The house was sold. They've gone. And you should see the orchard now, all run to ruin.'

One by one I added the new tesserae to my mosaic.

I took to visiting with a vengeance, dandified once more, rolling up to other villas and apartments in the ruined duke's carriage, sending Piero ahead of me with a lantern to light my footsteps to the great chestnut doors of the grandees of Castello. Piero and I had an understanding. He knew it was a game I was playing, which linked back into something more visceral than I would ever find in the salons or round the tables of this local gentry. At every door, Piero ignored the great clanging bells and beat out our own code, knocking it with his hard knuckles on the wood: TUM-tata / TUM-tata / TUM TUM / TUM TUM.

☞ XXIV ☜

✠ Fears and anxieties are like aches and pains: they cancel each other out. My earlier worries of being unmasked, of being caught out and declared an impostor had almost faded next to my concern at discovering the whereabouts of Donatella. Clucking enquiries into my past struck me more as an unwarranted intrusion into my privacy than a potential risk. I was Gabriele del Campo, Garibaldini, ex-prisoner-of-war, one-time captain of the Red Shirts, born in Piedmont, with distant family in Ravenna, long-time citizen of Venice. I was all these things; I believed in them myself: why shouldn't others believe in them too? I was no longer worried about what or who I had come to be. If anything, I was more concerned about what or who I had ceased to be.

My master's death had been a great shock to me. I had known for many months that he was dying: his lungs were full of marble dust, the muscles in his face had collapsed and a hand more skilful than either his or mine was sculpting him out from the inside. Then the flesh was filed off his bones, square chiselling everything from his face but his bare skull stretched over with parchment. His breath was smothered by the particles of dust, his words as choked in powder as his hair, brows, lips and nostrils had always been after a day spent carving. In making statues, he made himself look like one – as I suppose I did as well – but he was the one I saw: a macabre courtier, the chalked face, the whitened bone.

As he died, he tried to tell me many things. His eyes searched for me, as though by longing they could speak. His throat grated strangely and he wheezed, filtering his last weeks through the stone dust. He didn't die in peace. He had wanted to talk, to say something. He clutched at my sleeve with a grip that surpassed any strength I'd thought could be left in his emaciated body. He clawed the cloth around my wrist and drew me closer to him. He was trying to whisper, but he could only wheeze. So he fought, inwardly, and struggled and wheezed again. I had, of course, seen people die, but never as slowly or as laboriously. I wanted him to live. I didn't want to be alone. I was twenty-one and I had nowhere to go. I stayed with him. I waited until they buried him. I helped to carry his coffin, yet I never made him his own headstone. He died, and I left as though the eleven years we had spent together were a bag that could be left behind. And yet he left his mark on me; he filled my bag with stones, and travels with me no matter where I go.

I am Gabriele del Campo, but the boy I had been had disappeared without a trace. Even the angels I had carved were signed with my master's mark. Only my mother and my two younger sisters could have saved me from a state of never having been. Soon after I arrived from Venice, I took the carriage, with Florido driving, and guided him towards Gubbio. I avoided the city itself, its magic was too strong for me to meet, so we skirted Monte Ignano and the high grey walls and the entrance of Sant' Ubaldo, driving up beyond the city to the crossroads, a mere beaten track, which led up to the hamlet of my birth. I left Florido to fend for himself and took off on foot to find my mother. It was nearly an hour's walk to our cottage. I knew it well and noticed the few changes on the way. A willow tree that used to bend over the stream had fallen and left a jagged stump. The rotting chestnut board that served as a bridge had broken and not been replaced. A strip of land that had once been used for corn lay abandoned and full of thistles. Most things had remained the same, though, down to a tangle of everlasting sweet pea that sprang up yearly by the shrine, and the drifts of acacia fluff that gathered in a dip of alder roots. Bulrushes still grew where they always had; a broken gate lay propped against a stone where it always had. Taddeo's cottage had been reclaimed by the land but, beyond it, wild strawberries struggled through the rocks in exactly the same places I remembered them.

When I arrived my mother was in the garden tying up bundles of thorns. She didn't hear me approach. I didn't want to walk up behind her and startle her so I edged my way round her small plot of ground. She was struggling so hard with her twigs, she was muttering under her breath. '*Dio buono*, be good!' she hissed, at the recalcitrant bundle. She used to say the same to me when I was little and she held me by my ear and scrubbed me at the cold-water tub. A scent of fresh bread was in the air, blended with chicken dung and boiled spinach.

'*Salve*,' I called out.

My accent was foreign. My mother looked up and stared at me; she said nothing for some time. I moved closer and she stepped back.

'*Salve*,' she said, grudgingly, and returned to her tussle with the kindling.

I stood where I was, waiting for her to say more, to ask, to recognize me, to suspect that I was her son. She said nothing, not even looking up. I remembered my last disastrous visit so many years ago.

'I'm looking for your son, I—'

'He's dead.'

'No, your younger—'

'He's dead.'

'I'm looking for the boy who went away to cut stone.'

'They're all dead, all my sons.'

'But, the youngest, when did he—'

'What difference does it make if they're dead?'

'I knew him.'

She didn't look up. She wasn't interested. She wrestled with the thorns, forcing them to bow to her will. She tied them grimly. She had nothing more to say and wanted nothing more to be said. She finished a bundle, tied round with a reed, and then started another. She was stubborn.

'Do you know me?' I asked her, not daring to call her Mother. She didn't look up at once, she worked on, and then lifted her head slowly and turned it away again.

'No, signore. Why should I? You are a foreigner.'

'May I come in?' I asked, taking a step nearer.

'The girls have gone,' she said flatly. 'One dead and one gone so you won't find them in there.' She jerked her head towards the cottage. 'Someone has wasted your time, signore. There is nothing here for you. Good day.'

She bent back over her work, scrabbling the prickly wild plum twigs into order, tying them up. I waited. She was not going to break the silence again. I waited to make sure and then I said, 'Your son made some money; he asked me to bring it to you.' As I spoke, I drew out a pouch of coins I had been carrying and moved my arm towards her.

My mother stepped back again, her voice came as a hiss, her eyes narrowed in anger. 'Go away, signore, and never come back. Take your money with you. Do you think I have worked all the days of my life on the edge of existence and kept my balance for you to come now when my life is almost over and push me over the edge so easily? Go away.'

'But your son. I promised . . . The gold is yours.'

'Go away.'

'Look at me, signora, look at my face. Don't you know me?'

My mother looked once more into my face, keeping her eyes on mine for longer, lingering to show the full disdain of her expression. She didn't recognize me, not even with a flicker of doubt.

I did not know how to please her, or how to get close to her but, like a piece of stone I had studied, I knew where her flaws were. I knew her weak points and I knew how to tap expertly in just the right place to split her open. If I had asked about myself alone, she would have been indifferent, but I included my elder brother in my question. My mother had never been able to resist talk of him. He had been her light and her hope. One day the Blessed Virgin would reunite her with him; meanwhile she would honour the Madonna and wait.

'I will go, signora, and leave you in peace, but first I must ask you one question and you must answer it truthfully, swear by the Blessed Virgin. Did you love your sons?'

My mother looked around her, as though there might be spies hidden in the trees, then she moved a step towards me and said, 'My eldest boy, Giacomo, I loved more than all the world. He was strong and quick and funny and born with a braided cord that bound him to my heart. I cut his cord when he was born, but something kept my Giacomo near me, when I worked, when I washed, slept, carried and nursed my others, it was Giacomo, always him. He died of the fever. I buried him down the hill in the Campo Santo, they made me, I would have kept my boy here with me, but they made me, they came and took him away. My love is buried with him, it is inside his crate. I wrapped it around him to keep him company in the other world. After he was gone, my love was gone.'

She wrung the words out of her like water from her linen sheet; her lips were frayed. As she spoke, they twitched out of their usual tight line of disapproval and relaxed into a disturbingly loose, vulnerable set. I longed to lean over and kiss, to bend down and touch her brown, furrowed face. Her grey linen dowry seemed to have wrung out the tenderness I had always believed she kept hidden in her dour chest.

'And your other son, the one who went away? Did you miss him?'

'I couldn't forgive him for living when Giacomo died. He was the cuckoo in our nest. He had to go. I didn't miss him. He could have gone with the fever and left me Giacomo. He had to go anyhow.'

'How do you know that? Why did he have to go?'

'It was written in the stars.'

She had spoken, she was done, she turned to make her way back to the ramshackle stone hovel with the smoky kitchen where she had supper to prepare before nightfall.

'How do you know he is dead, the younger son?'

She didn't turn back, she walked on towards the parched stone steps that led up to the kitchen. From under the house, a stale stench of confined livestock wafted out. The giant sage bush at the base of the steps was in flower.

'It was written on the wall.'

She walked on, climbing slowly up the stairs, grown old, limping slightly. I was afraid. The wall to me was the prison wall and any writing on it was the calligraphy of bullets. What did my mother know of all that? How could she know it? There was something uncanny about her: she had always known things about me as a boy, catching me out for things I had done but she could not possibly have seen.

'What wall?'

She turned round again now, sharply. She was tired of me, she wanted me gone; we had made a pact, she had spoken and I should be gone. Her dark eyes flashed this to me.

'A list of names was written on the wall, the boy's name was on it. I can't read, signore, and nor would I want to, but someone told us the boy was dead.'

She pushed her kitchen door open and shoved it shut behind her.

I left my pouch of coins on the stone ledge of the rough steps my mother had just climbed. She could keep it or leave it or bury it. I needed to leave it. Then I made my way back down the hill through the woodland. She had not said 'my boy' was on the list, she had said 'the boy': the cuckoo she had reluctantly reared and had been glad to see the back of. I stopped by the shrine of the Blessed Virgin at the bend before the streams and touched the little statuette. It was gesso and a flake of blue dress crumbled in my hands. I felt myself momentarily back against that wall, remembering.

It seemed that there was a sudden chill mist, and frogs were croaking. It seemed that the coarse grass under my feet had turned to trampled mud and cobbles sprinkled with vetch. It seemed that the blue hills on the horizon had compacted and merged to form a high stone wall. I was standing before it, clutching at stray memories of my mother. Then the bullets came and I fell. I fell through the cobbles, through the hands of soldiers. I fell through my boyhood. I fell through open fields and through tunnels of Etruscan tombs. I fell through tufa, through crumbled lime. I fell through the *campanile* of Sant' Ubaldo, through the drums of time. I fell through water, through a dead horse. Then my body became a chisel, forged and hammered out of steel, folded and folded until every part of me cut through stone. I made a mountain of dust as high as Monte Ignano. Then I ran round it three times. Then I put the dust in my handkerchief and beat the panel of my memories, carved in stone, and the dark dust was driven into the hollows of the carving to help it read well. Grasshoppers sang. A cock crowed. My feet felt their way downhill over the ridges of dried mud, finding their way home. Finding their way back to the place where Donna Donatella could find me.

Then I picked a few of the long sweet-pea stems with their puce, papery flowers and headed back to Florido. I saw the carriage nestling by the edge of the oakwood. Florido was sleeping in the grass. Somewhere behind me a cuckoo called. I paused and then strode on. It was June in Umbria. There would be cuckoos calling on the edge of every wood.

⇒ XXV ⇐

✦ 'And Jacob served seven years for Rachel; and they seemed unto him but a few days, for the love he had to her.' Genesis 29:20. This kept flicking up and arresting my attention as I leafed through my drawings. It irked me: I removed it from the tin. It was a page with a drawing of a cabinet, an octagonal room to keep treasures in. In prison, it had been dear to my heart, and I had chosen the text specially. Seven years had not seemed like an eternity then. It was a rogue page of Genesis that had somehow escaped the *papier mâché* process of the playing cards. However, by keeping it separate, I seemed to imbue it with a deeper significance. I had set myself the task of executing all the plans of all the drawings in my tin, but I made an exception of the octagonal cabinet and burned it. I could wait a summer at a time, but the thought of waiting seven years, even though I was sure my love surpassed that of Jacob's, was unbearable. And it was all right for him – he had Rachel there in the same household while he laboured, while I had only my dreams and the empty castle of Petrelle with the three onion-breathed daughters of the custodian to sustain me.

Giovanni's loyalty to my cause also bore the strain of

THE PALACE   235

time. The middle daughter from Petrelle bore him a son, an enchanting black-haired boy with Giovanni's curls and smiles and his same lazy way of observing the world through half-closed sensual eyes. I was godfather to the boy, who was named after me, and after some hard-nosed bargaining with the girl's father, who looked half-witted but was as sharp as an animal trap under his bleary leer, his daughter, Maria, was married to Piero with much pomp and circumstance. Giovanni had already weaned the girl off raw onions, and Piero was delighted with his bride, moustache and all. He even got her eating anchovies and taught her to add raisins to her pasta sauces. They were the first family to take up residence in the palace, with married quarters in two rooms on the ground floor of the east wing. Giovanni and Florido, who were next door, knocked through the communicating wall, re-establishing the Venetian ghetto there, a small maritime court with chubby Gabriellino as its infant king.

The palace was progressing well. The building had assumed a steady pace, slowed only by excessive cold or, more seriously, by drought. It had seemed, when our trenches were flooded and the spring overflowed, that there would never be a lack of water at Quarata. It was, potentially, a Venetian palace. Its very name spelt water, AQUAR-ATA, a place of abundant water, and yet, the summers killed my plans. The more we built, the more water we needed. We needed it to wash the stone, to cut the marble, to mix the mortar, to sluice out the dust. By July, the sweltering heat cut back the spring to a mere trickle so we had to buy water; to import it. The teams of oxen dragged up great oak barrels of it. During the first year, this sufficed, but by the second and third, the incentive to bring up our supplies had waned, which slowed down the builders. Money no longer had the instant allure of the first year. There was a new prosperity in Morra – the palace was seeing to that, sending wages down month after month, buying lengths of cloth and willow clogs, cradles and chairs, picks and spades and bowls; things that had been lacking before and that only money could buy. Once they had been bought and the polenta and chestnuts and fresh bread were always on the table, there was no need for more. I had my workers, but I didn't have enough water from June to September and sometimes October.

In the third year, I offered a barrel of water for a barrel of wine. That worked. We never had a shortage again, although Giovanni was worried we would run out of wine. I pointed out all the hectares of vineyards in my domain. He reminded me that they were all under the *mezzadria*; half the wine would go to the men who worked them, the other half to me. It was enough. The building fever became contagious. All over the neighbourhood, people began to expand their cellars to accommodate the coming wine.

When Gabriellino was three, Giovanni and Piero began to fret. They shared their fatherhood of the boy, taking their responsibilities seriously. Giovanni came to me.

'Signor, I must speak to you of Gabriellino's birthright.' Giovanni, I knew, had a habit of going through my things. He had always hated my tin of texts because of its smell, but since he was drunk, I feared that he had been reading them and was coming now to claim some biblical right. Giovanni had changed greatly since our move to Umbria. It would not have surprised me if he had suddenly got religion.

'We need water, signor. You must make a lagoon. Gabriellino must learn to row. We are gondoliers. He must learn to walk on water.'

Sometimes, when the nights were still and the grass-hoppers sang in the poppy fields that our fieldworkers had unearthed, I would lie down and contemplate the stars. I looked for myself, not searching for a name, but a role, a reason to be. I could only ever come up with the builder of the palace, the architect, the would-be lover of Donna Donatella, the would-be friend of Imolo Vitelli. And sometimes I wondered what others thought I was, not by name but again by role and reason to be. Giovanni had ceased to take advantage of me or I of him, I hope, and we had grown closer.

'You must make a lagoon,' he said, as though it were a simple matter for a mortal. 'Gabriellino needs it.'

After he left me, I wondered how many men it would take to dig out a lake, and what machinery could be brought in or devised to assist it. I wondered how much money it would take and how many years. Like stepping stones, my thoughts crossed to how much money I had left and how much I had already spent. I had amassed a fortune in Venice, but in the four years of our Umbrian building, I must have run through a lot of it. How much?

On two wings the palace had reached the fourth floor, the final floor. It was ready to be roofed. There were to be thirty-six separate roof structures, one for each card of a briscola pack. The year before the far slope of Zeno Poggio had been felled and the wood seasoned so that the tall oaks could become the beams and joists. For the main beams, I had thinned an ancient chestnut grove from the lands below Muccignano. Some of the trees were three hundred years old; it seemed like desecration to cut them down. But a building must be sunk with stone and float with wood, and my obsession with the palace had already run to crime. I beat my chest a little, shed a crocodile tear, and the great chestnuts were cut down.

There followed weeks of stock-taking during which I realized just how loyal and capable Giovanni Contarini had been. I even began to believe that his claims to being part of the great Contarini family were true: he had the makings of a captain of industry. I would have buried my gold under a tree and dug out what I needed week by week but he had invested it in the Monte dei Paschi bank and kept it turning over in stocks and bonds. He had also kept some back from me and financed ventures in Venice that had brought in more than triple the initial outlay. It was as though he had turned his sacks of salt into diamonds. The visions that for days had been plaguing me of having to return to Venice and trying my hand at Bastoni's vanished. I wouldn't have to gamble again. Giovanni had managed my lands and my finances so well that I could roof the palace and deck its halls, lay out its gardens and make a lake and never need to move from Quarata again. Gabriellino would get his gondola and a settlement besides.

'Giovanni,' I said, when we were alone and the full impact of his brilliance had sunk in, 'what can I do for you? What can I give you to repay all you have done?'

'Follow your dream, signor,' he said, and smiled, flipping the curls from his forehead. 'All my life I grew up gliding past the great palace of the Contarini. My father told me of what could have been. I longed for it. I yearned for it, more than for any other thing. I could not even imagine another palace; there is no place in Venice for anything new. I was trapped in the failure of possession. I learned to make things slip through my hands as quick as sardines, backwards and forwards, that was easy, but to make something, signor, that would stay for ever, that would haunt boys like me and make them feel the grandeur of God and the immortality of man.' He smiled, pleased by his words, by the length of them and the rich music they acquired in his mouth.

'You have shared your dream with me, signor. There is no greater gift. You have made it mine. I need you to follow it. When Donna Donatella steps into this palace, she will shudder at the best cards you have ever been dealt and you will hold her heart in your hand. That, signor, will make Giovanni a wealthy man: a Venetian wealth, which is the massing of beauty.'

In that moment I wanted to tell Giovanni many things. I wanted to tell him the truth. When I started to speak, he put his finger to his lips.

'If you make a lake and a field of lilies, she will come soon.'

⁓⧉ XXVI ⧉⁓

✛ Three hundred men and twenty oxen dug out the
lake in a clearing in the woods to the south of the
palace. I chose a place where a natural stream could feed it.
We dammed and diverted the stream and then the works
began, repeating on a greater scale the first digging of
foundations. This time there was less despair. The palace
had become the pride of Morra. People came from all over
Umbria to admire it in its unfinished state. I entertained
them from a palanquin equipped with chairs and settees,
tables and cut-glass decanters of cordial and sparkling wine.
When the new digging commenced, rumours began to
circulate that it was the beginning of another edifice. Its
depth and breadth were alarming. But a spirit of hope had
entered our enterprise and the men hoped that this new
dig was not the onset of madness.

While the digging progressed, I sent an agent to the
Lowlands to enquire about lilies and to bring back a stock
of bulbs. He sent word that there were many varieties and
supplied a list. I chose them by their names alone: marta-
gon, star-gazer, arum, tiger lily, enchantment and many
others. Ten thousand bulbs were crated in peat and sent by
ship to Livorno. We ploughed the land on the far side of

the lake, still dry and still being dug, and planted the fat, garlic-shaped bulbs in shallow pits.

As I supervised their immersion into the trampled clay, clods of it stuck to my boots, weighting my feet until each step felt as though I were dragging shackles and chains. My mind turned back to the nineteen links that had once joined me to Vitelli and an image of my cell mate came to mind; a sense of him.

A visitor arrived and called out my name. I turned, expecting one of the many curious Castellani who had taken to visiting the site, but was stunned to see, across the gaping earthworks of the lake, the man who made me. It was Vitelli, grey-haired and frailer than he had ever been, but unmistakably Vitelli. We moved towards each other.

He wanted to hold me at arm's length, to look at me. I wanted to hold him in my arms. We embraced, clumsily, then he led me away from the men to hide the tears that were shaking me. Vitelli walked me in a one-sided frog-march, supporting me as he strode along, talking all the while, holding me up until the shock allowed me to stand on my own feet alone. Doing, in fact, what he had always done.

'You have done wonders, Gabriele. I knew you would. I hoped. It all seemed so improbable that it somehow had to be true. And you have transposed something Venetian here, it is remarkable. And this?' he asked, sweeping his arm behind him towards the receding pit.

'It's a lagoon.'

Vitelli laughed, then stopped and laughed again. He let go of my arm and held my head against his shoulder.

'Yes, a lagoon,' he said, letting me go so suddenly I stumbled backwards and brushed against a prickle of junipers. 'I should have guessed: the geographical catalyst moves a lagoon into the landlocked forest. Quite inspired and worthy of the place. You know, Morra is a place of thinkers. It got its name from the Romans: *dimorra*, a stopover. It was where Hannibal stopped over to review his strategy before marching on to Lake Trasimeno and thrashing the Romans. Now you are building your own Trasimeno – scaled down, of course. It must be the only scaling down you have done. I'd no idea the palace was going to be so vast.'

We had reached the plateau around it. Vitelli strode across. I had never really seen him in the open air. I didn't know he strode. Our cell had always forced him to shuffle.

'Vitelli,' I said, as soon as I had recovered my senses, 'where have you been?'

'I have been watching you, Gabriele. I've been around.'

'But why? Why, when I have missed and needed you so much?'

'Missed, but not needed. You needed to stand alone. You found your gondolier by yourself and I take off my hat to you for him,' he said, taking off his hat. 'I am tired,' he announced. 'I need some wine. Let us sit down and when I have recovered from my walk, you must show me around the manifestation of your brain. Lead me into its chambers. I have waited most impatiently for this day.'

I guided him to the palanquin and poured him some Rubesco which he drank down, holding his glass at a tilt for more.

'Chance is a master craftsman, Gabriele. It chooses its tools and uses them to finish its design, regardless of what we do or want. You cannot carve stone with a paintbrush, or paint a canvas with a chisel. Chance twinned us, long ago, in that cell. It chained me, a man once full of life who had grown tired of it, to a boy who had never lived it. It chained your thirst to my sated bursting point. It shackled you, the stonemason's apprentice so in love with the unknown lady Donna Donatella, to me, her favourite cousin.'

'What are you saying? What—'

'Why didn't I tell you? Why didn't I say, through all those nights when you described your love for her?' He sighed. 'If you had known, back then, in the prison, that she was in love with another, that she was betrothed to another, would you have built the palace?' I bowed my head. I ached. The wine inside me curdled.

'She is free again, Gabriele,' he said gently, touching my arm to regain my attention. 'She is a widow. She loved her husband with a strength almost as great as your own. He married her for her money, he didn't really care for her. After he died, she went abroad and travelled for a year. She has returned now. Before the New Year she will come back to Petrelle. To live there. She has changed. Fate has twisted her into the thread she is, ready to weave her into this tapestry. You must lead her into the palace as you will lead me now. The rest is in the hands of chance.'

I showed him the entrance hall with its high ceilings and long, high windows, each with a place below it for an orange tree. I showed him the patterning of the pink travertine of the floor cut out of a single block from Assisi and sliced. I showed him the staircase rising up through all four floors in cantilevered magnificence. White unpolished marble from Assisi, each step as thick as my body and rounded by an even hand. I showed him the railings of the stairs copied from a bridge in Venice. I showed him the landings, which were great slabs of white travertine four yards along and two foot thick, of which it had taken an engineer from Arezzo to mastermind the hauling into place. I showed him how the rooms flowed around the stairwell and beyond, from wing to wing and into the unfinished wing, returning and spreading like myriad veins running back into an artery. I showed him my library, with its walnut panelling and fitted shelves and the bestiary of carvings that adorned the columns between the books. I showed him my books, proudly, almost shyly, needing him to approve of them as much as of anything he saw. I showed him unfinished rooms, with bare stone walls and gaping holes where chimney-breasts would stand. I showed him finished rooms with velvet drapes patterned with the acid stains of Venetian dragons. I showed him the riches I had stored in the Peacock Salon of San Lio and the courtyard by the canal of the Rio della Guerra. I showed him pilasters from Istanbul embedded in the plasterwork, panels by Renaissance masters sunk into the walls. I showed him mosaic floors with pictures from the Greek myths that he had first told to me, and stones with inscriptions incised in them by my own tools.

I showed him the banqueting hall, unfinished still, but offering all the views it had been built to show. I led him on to the loggia, through the four arched windows that rose five yards high in the west wall. We stood by the four terracotta arches of the loggia, identical to those inside the room, but open to the air, and I told how their simple shape had come to me in a dream. I took him up into the tower of the wind and told him how we had raced to finish it. I filled his head with so many visions and such a wealth of shape and form that I could see he was reeling.

When he had lingered long enough in the tower of the wind to touch the fine carving at the base of its vaulted ceiling, I said, 'Now I will take you to Donatella's rooms.'

The doorway was more finely carved than any other in the house. I had worked for many months upon its cornice. There was an angel on either side, each with the face of Donatella as I had seen her as a boy. They knelt and held between them an orange tree. Around the frame were pomegranates and lilies. Between the angels I had incised a text from The Song of Songs. Vitelli read it out as we stood in front of it. He had been almost speechless during the tour.

'Awake, O north wind; and come thou south; and blow upon my garden, that the spices thereof may flow out. Let thy beloved come into his garden, and eat his pleasant fruits.'

⇥ XXVII ⇤

✠ Vitelli was staying at the Tiferno Hotel in Castello.
I did not let him return there. I had overtired him
with my tour. That night he retired early, almost too
fatigued to eat. By morning, he seemed much recovered
and we talked again. He told me what I had already seen
for myself: he was a sick man. I pressed him to stay with
me and he told me he had hoped I would make the offer.
Then I gave him a choice of rooms. He said he had already
chosen the east tower because it was less dusty than the rest
of the palace.

'I am used to dust,' I told him. 'I grew up with it; my
master died of it. While the works continue, it will always
be here. It sits in a patina over everything. The women
wipe it away continually, but to no avail. It's in the air, in
my hair, in my eyes, it gets in the food. We eat and sleep
and drink it: the gritty taste of Quarata.'

'Hmm, well, I don't want to die of dust, and your tower
of the wind was miraculously almost free of it, so I shall
make my sitting room on the first floor, my study on the
second, my bedroom on the third, and because you have
built such a quantity of rooms, I shall float around in the
other three with no use for them but a sense of space, and

sometimes, Gabriele, we shall sit and look at the stars from the top room and set all the ills of the world aright over a bottle of brandy.'

The arrival of Vitelli transformed the palace. It turned almost overnight from a building and camping site to a residence. The catacombs of unfinished rooms were boarded off from their more finished brothers. In deference to my guest's dislike of dust, the structural building of the south wing was halted. It seemed but a slight decision at the time, not one that would doom it to incompletion. My menagerie became a household. The cats, dogs, rabbits, hens, geese, ducks, pigs and the pet wolf that Florido had reared from a cub were suddenly penned in instead of roaming around the cellars and the grounds. And the artisans who had set up their camp in the basement of the south wing, spilling out with what looked like a gypsy encampment into the young vineyard, tidied their sacks and tools and their multicoloured bundles of belongings. They took their laundry off the rosemary hedge that Florido had planted, tucked their camp followers into their quarters or sent them back down to the village. They contained their music and merriment each night to a reasonable level instead of the debauched revelry that had long been their wont.

The Venetian ghetto, access to which was via a flight of steps from the wide downstairs alleyway dividing the north and south wings, was also restored, outwardly, to order. The discarded barrels of anchovies, which gave the far end of the alleyway – at the point where it opened out on to the downstairs loggia – the air and smell of a quayside, were stacked neatly by Piero either side of the steps, leaning against the wall in two undulating pillars. The Venetians had absorbed Maria from Petrelle into their midst so effectively that she excelled them in littering the area around their nest, re-creating an alleyway of the Serenissima with mounds of rubbish putrefying in colourful strata. Offerings were always ready at the altar of a sea breeze, loose bits of paper and cloth to travel away and colonize surrounding neighbourhoods, infiltrating faraway places with the detritus of sifted treasures and an essence of fish. At Christmas and Easter and New Year, at the Feast of the Redentore and the high days and holidays of the Lagoon, Giovanni, Piero and Florido decorated the alleyway and its surrounding stone with paper bunting and strips of ribbon, with tinsel and holly, broom and juniper. When the festival finished, the decorations remained. They tore and flapped and greyed in the dust, turning this corner of my still unfinished magnificent palace into an ageing slum.

With the advent of Vitelli, everything changed. I awoke in the morning to the swishing of brooms. Every room and hallway was being swept out. Every scrap of rubbish was gathered by the boys with long sharp sticks. Things that were decomposing were shovelled up and burned. The feathers and heads of innumerable chickens were incinerated. The great pots and cauldrons for the workmen's stews were scoured with ashes. The materials that were strewn around the forecourt were neatly stacked. The sacks of lime, gesso and *scagliola* were confined to specific rooms.

Breakfast, which had come to be coffee and fresh *ciacia* bread served in the ghetto while I discussed the day's plans with Giovanni, appeared for the first time in the virgin breakfast room, to which Giovanni led first me and then Vitelli as though this were an everyday occurrence. A feast of fresh rolls and croissants, coffee, milk, chocolate, honey, butter, cherry jam, slivers of pecorino and a bowl of fruit sat on the pristine Burano lace cloth with Limoges plates I had not seen since the day I bought them from their Lyonnais owner, as he struggled to keep the bailiffs from his water-gate along the Grand Canal.

Florido, who for four years had been camp quartermaster, supervising the four boys and three women who fed the troops, turned over his command to his chief assistant and became my chef. His coarse leggings, big boots and hessian apron were handed down and replaced by a long startling-white apron that reached down to his ankles and gave him the clinical appearance of a surgeon in search of an operation to perform. The great kitchen, which had been one in name only, was brought to life. Several large oak trees were sliced and carried into an anteroom, the fire was started, the spit oiled, the grills set up and tables moved. A marble slab, less thick but no less long than one of the landings, was positioned on legs in the centre of the flagstoned floor and Florido came into his own.

Within the week, some twenty rooms that had been empty were fully furnished. Persian rugs had been unrolled, furniture unpacked, curtain poles in gold and ebony were nailed up. Statues, plinths, paintings, engravings, tapestries, scrolls and miniatures all found their way upstairs. I had forgotten them although I had hunted each of them down, once – they had been stored for so long that they had sunk into a general store. As each piece emerged it seemed to belong as though it had been made for Quarata. Rooms that had no life beyond their shape acquired a character so marked they looked as though they had always been as rich and that I had inherited them intact instead of building them. And because they had such character, they suddenly demanded names. Vitelli was their godfather. We baptized them together: the Blue Room, the Red Drawing Room, the Venetian Room, the Arab Room, the Chinese Room.

Before Vitelli came, there had been my rooms, the library, the ballroom-to-be, the kitchen-to-be, the ghetto, the workmen's sheds, Donna Donatella's rooms and the three towers. The tower of the wind I rechristened Vitelli's Tower. The workmen's sheds, which were the basement and part of the first floor of the south wing, were vaulted with lilies carved on crests under each pediment. They were fine, light, beautiful rooms into which the workmen had moved one winter when their crude sheds had proved too cold for them. The term 'sheds' stuck, and always would, just as Piero's corner would always be called the ghetto.

Vitelli loved the palace; he roamed around it touching its walls with infinite tenderness. Where my hand had carved, his hand caressed.

When we were in prison, I had thought Vitelli pitied me. I knew he liked me and I hoped he was proud of me then. We had an affinity. Because he had given me the word, it replaced the one I would have used, replaced somehow the idea of it too. I loved Donna Donatella with such a force that it swallowed up the word love. I had not thought about my relationship to Vitelli in terms of how I felt about him or he to me since my Venetian days. He was the mountain from which I cut my stone. He triggered my ideas. I had missed him. I had missed him from the moment when he took his leave and sent me out from the prison gates to make my way to Venice. And it had hurt so much more to think that he hadn't missed me. While we were shackled to each other he had given me his time and his knowledge. Yet as soon as we were free to go our own ways, he'd disappeared. I had honoured his memory, loved his memory and missed him. I was relieved, but confused to discover that Vitelli had secretly watched over me and missed me too.

In prison, he had always been reticent about himself, about his family. I had learnt not to ask questions about them. I could ask anything about his ideas, but nothing about his feelings. At Quarata, he seemed to need to speak. When he wandered around the house, it was mostly on his own. When he walked through the nascent gardens and grounds, he liked to have me with him.

One day, we had been strolling through the walled garden admiring the last of the autumn fruit which the new trees had gallantly put forth. He had many plans for the gardens which he discussed with me at length. He had a passion for fountains and, at his insistence, I had the men lay pipes all over the grounds. Taking a leaf from my master's book, I used the baptismal fonts I had amassed in Venice, drilled by the marble cutters to grace the pools and bowls that took their place around the palace. The first of these was already playing water, much to Vitelli's delight.

We sat down on the *pietra serena* lip of one such pool and paused to survey the view while a thin autumn mist crept across the hillside, curling into the terraces, masking the pomegranate avenue with its scarlet pom-poms; smothering the Indian bean tree Vitelli had bought on a trip to Arezzo, veiling the grey wall of the garden and funnelling out towards the forecourt. There was a chill in the air, creeping up with the mist and sponging up the heat from the dying October sun.

'Before I met you, Gabriele, I lost my son.'

I didn't know he had had a son.

'I married young and happily, but then I took a mistress who stole all my time. My mistress was politics. I was so enamoured of them, they came between my wife and me.

'Remember I told you of the rising of '48, of its failure and how Garibaldi and the others had to flee? I didn't tell you then that I was there, nor that it was a campaign of two years' duration. From Nice to Milan, to Bologna, to Romagnola and into Rome. They were exciting times for Italy and for me. I was drunk on our victories and on the chance of freeing Italy once and for all from Austria. People everywhere were giving up so much for the cause. I knew it hurt my family to be away. My son was ten. My wife wrote to me, she begged me to return, she needed me. But the force of France was sent against us. We had been beaten back from the south. We held the city and the people were for us, ready to die for the cause. I believed in the cause, Gabriele, as something that would alter all our lives, mine, my son's, my wife's, the entire country's. Garibaldi says men are reformed 'by example more than doctrine'. His doctrine was one word: "*Avanti*". Forwards. We had to go forwards. There was no turning back. I wrote to say I could not return, not yet, I couldn't let my comrades down.

'All through the month of June '49 we held out in Rome, besieged by the French. On the *festa* of St Peter and St Paul, the French mounted their final assault.

'We lost. We lost, Gabriele. The odds were stacked against us. Some of us left by night on the first of July, following our leader and his promises. He promised us "neither pay, nor quarters, nor provisions; I offer hunger, thirst, forced marches, battles and death". He spoke the truth. We fought our way back through Italy to the Alps, harried and persecuted by the French, the Austrians and the Spanish.

'It was not until September that Garibaldi set sail for Elba, loved but defeated for the time. He lost his wife in that campaign; and I lost mine.'

Vitelli paused and scratched the stone with his fingernails.

'When I returned to Piedmont, to my home, my wife had died of fever. My son had had to bear her death alone. I let him down and I let her down and there was no turning back the clock to tell her how much I loved her ... I let her down. It was my son who'd last written to me. His letter came through the siege. "Come home, Mamma needs you." I thought that she could wait, that he could wait. I thought she would understand.

'When she sang, her throat quivered like a quail's. When she played the mandolin, the air around her stopped as though the whole world were caught in her thrall. When she walked, she swung her hands like a toy soldier. When she laughed, tears filled her eyes. When she cried, it was always silently. She was frail, but she hid her frailty. She was afraid of sickness, of darkened rooms. She spent her hours in the gardens. She loved flowers so much, she'd say, "They are my life." She asked our son to send for me. I wrote back, "soon". But soon wasn't soon enough and she had died.'

✦ Donna Donatella was coming to Umbria, to Quarata. I felt as though her feet were running already over the hill from Petrelle, tripping over the stones, beating up the white powdery dust on her way through the woods to visit her cousin Vitelli, to visit me.

The hawthorn berries were crimson on their stems and the scarlet hips were balancing on their briars; the oak leaves were russet, their twigs swollen with galls. The acorns were heavy on the trees, the walnuts were dangling in their green cases ready to drop. The last shrivelled blackberries, sprinkled with lime, were lining the tract. Mare's tail and bracken, heather and cyclamen and dozens of coloured fungi covered the underwood. Snipe and woodcock, partridge and pheasant scuttled through the undergrowth, falling prey to Piero and his battalion of huntsmen and hounds, stocking the larder, filling the spit.

Vitelli and I spent many weeks in the woods, watching the final dredging of the lake and then watching it fill, inch by inch, after the stream was diverted back into its pit. It looked as though it would never fill and standing over it became less of a pleasure than a frustration. It was a puddle, a muddy puddle that kept seeping into the summer-parched ground. Finally the earth began to offer up its juice. I would have gladly turned my back on it, but Vitelli kept returning; worrying around the site, wanting to leave his signature in trees. He ordered an avenue of cypress trees to lead down from the forecourt of the palace to the lake. Where the land was marshy, he chose a glade of mixed conifers to climb up the slope to a clump of wild cherries. From the lower end of the lake, beyond a belt of lilacs, he left an escarpment of oaks and then a mile of walkways lined by box trees. Around the palace itself, beyond the place where lawns would be, there were more cypresses, six deep.

'A hundred years from now, people will see your palace and my trees. It is comforting to know they will be here after I am gone.'

For a month he had tree fever. Vitelli knew the names of trees I had never seen: wellingtonia, cedar of Lebanon, *Magnolia grandiflora*, ginkgos, and date palms. He laid out an olive grove, on the north slope that stretched down to the river, and a nut walk of hazels beside a meandering stream. He designed the remaining gardens into geometrical patterns, lining the pathways with hibiscus and oleanders and trellises of jasmines. He made a knot garden of white roses, another of aromatic herbs. Then he set me to design pergolas in stone or in iron, as intricate as the designs of the towers. These he had planted out with wisteria and vines, clematis, honeysuckle and climbing roses. For the pools of the fountains, he found nympaeas, goldfish and speckled carp.

He worked so hard, designing, ordering, checking measurements and spacing out the grounds that I feared for his health. I didn't know what ailed him, nor did he say, but it was clear that he was weakening. His breath was short and his eyes were overbright. At dinner his colour was always high, while at breakfast and through the day his skin had an ashen look. Sometimes when he was standing about the grounds, or climbing stairs, he would pause and hold his side. If ever he felt observed in this, he would shrug and smile; when not, he held himself, cradling his ribs and whispering. During conversations, he would drift into snatched minutes of sleep, waking with a sad, hollow look in his eyes.

When I urged him to rest, to tell me his plans and let me see to them, he shook his head. 'This garden is my last will and testament. I have nothing else to leave. Next summer, it will flower and I would like to see it then. I shall walk in this garden with my cousin Donatella. Would you deny an old man his pleasure?'

When the lagoon was finished, he took many of the workmen to plant stones in the garden. On the terraces, he devised balustrades and steps that were so elaborate they had arches and alcoves, niches for statues, columns and platforms and built-in seats. He raided the storerooms for busts and statues, urns and plinths. Carpets of turf were laid, and carriageways of slate.

By mid-December, the frosts were severe. Every morning they draped Vitelli's garden in thick crystals. The cold made the stonework weep and then ice over, polishing it to a glaze. He often looked at the gardens from the palace, moving around from room to room and floor to floor to see how each part looked from above, leaving his footprints in the icy dust. He usually lingered a little over breakfast, talking quickly through his plans for the day, enlisting Giovanni to organize the men and run his errands. He had been working non-stop for two months, not resting even on Sundays. One day, the breakfast-room fire had burned itself down to a steady glow despite the early hour, and when Vitelli had finished staring out of the window on to the parterre, instead of wrapping his woollen cloak around him and striding out, he draped it over his shoulders and sat down by the glowing embers.

Vitelli's and Giovanni's relationship had been circumspect for many months. Each was a little wary of the other and each, perhaps, a little jealous. Like passing gondolas, they came so close to crashing, their varnish would graze, but they knew how to steer their own courses so skilfully that neither craft was damaged. By winter they had progressed from sparring partners to friends.

Giovanni said of him, 'Your Colonel Vitelli is the devil himself for explaining things. I think he'd explain the stars down out of the sky. He never asks a thing but he must tell you why and all its internal workings. He's a man of reason, if ever I saw one, and the reason is chewing him out. It's sucking his bones, signor. Have you seen how thin he is?'

'Giovanni, bring me some brandy, will you, and cigars. I'll be staying in today,' Vitelli said.

Giovanni was as surprised as I, but we said nothing. Vitelli said nothing, staring into the fire. A long time passed, during which Giovanni stayed, waiting, curious for an explanation. When the brandy was not forthcoming, Vitelli looked up. 'I'll be staying here now until my cousin comes. It is too cold to garden any more.'

When Giovanni left the room, I ventured, 'You are ill, Vitelli. Can't I call you a doctor?'

'Hmm!'

The fire seemed to absorb him completely, to exclude me, and then, if I stared hard into its hot ashes, to draw me in.

'She will be here soon. And soon I shall be gone. There was a time when I loved this land, when I knew it well. I wanted you to have Quarata. Sit still now, and I'll tell you something.'

I stopped fidgeting.

'I lost my son before I met you. He was your age and not unlike you in his looks. He never quite forgave me for being away when his mother died, and I never forgave myself. It made it very hard to talk. I have told you I was a gambler. I used to be almost as lucky as you. I lost my touch at the wrong time, though, and I lost my son. He was with me in the skirmish that landed me in gaol. I took a risk and lost. Almost half my men were killed that day. And my son with them. The enemy held the high ground but their men were tireder than mine. They had been hard pressed since dawn. Our numbers were even, or so I thought. There was a rumour, in our lines, of reinforcements having been smuggled up. I gambled that was a bluff. I gambled and they won.

'After the Papists took me, I didn't want to live any more. I knew they had orders from their masters, the French, to shoot their prisoners. I hoped they would shoot me.

'That morning, Gabriele, when you left for the firing squad, I ached to take your place. I remember so clearly as you walked to the door how much you looked like my son. I thought for a moment you were he, being led away so slowly. I thought if only I had a chance to begin again, to be a father again, how different I would be. And then they brought you back and gave me that chance. I lived again through you.

'I knew, by then, that sooner or later the Cause was bound to win. The French would be ousted, Italy would be united and free. My love affair with politics was over. There were two people left in the world whom I cared about. You and my cousin Donatella. I was chained to you and you to her.'

Giovanni came clattering in with the decanter of brandy on a tray. Florido's wolf had got loose and was pushing to come through the door with him. Giovanni was at pains to control it. Vitelli stared back into the fire. His cheeks, normally so pale, were red from the heat. After Giovanni left, cursing the wolf in the corridor as he made his way back to the dining room, Vitelli stirred and poured two drinks. 'Here's to the New Year,' he said, and sipped some brandy, 'and here's to so many things.' He drained his glass and shuddered. 'When she comes, she will tell you this land was mine. I have told her I gave it to you as my son.'

'Yours?'

'Yes.'

'Then why?'

'You won.'

'But why, Imolo?'

'You always won. I wanted you to have it. I knew you'd win. I hadn't bargained on your staying in Venice for so long. Nor had I realized how empty my life would be after the prison. I—'

'But I was waiting for you. Why didn't you find me?'

'I found you, Gabriele.'

'Yes, but why didn't you show yourself?'

'What was there to show? *Avanti*, forwards, it's the only way to go. You were going forwards, but I was going nowhere. I hadn't been to Quarata since I was a boy. It was to have been for my boy, not for me.'

'But I beggared you.'

'Near as dammit!'

'Why couldn't we have come here together, built this together?'

'I wanted you to build your palace. I needed you to. You wouldn't have done it unless you were alone. Now that you have so nearly finished, I am here. I have written to Donatella to tell her I am ill. She will come soon and she will come often. She knows that I love you more than all the world. She is close to me. She will come every day. You will have till the summer to win her. You have only to guide her footsteps to her rooms. I have told her about the palace and the lagoon and the gondola. And about the garden.

'I want you to remember me in things you can touch. I told her you had built the palace as a homage to love. She writes that she hopes you will show her round every room.

'She will be here in three days now. I must rest before she comes. And remember, you have loved her all your life as a shadow. Do not love her as a dream, love her as a woman and you will fulfil what you have begun. But when she gets here, you must see her as a woman with her feet on the ground.' He wrapped his cloak around him and rose. 'I am tired.'

For most of the next three days, Vitelli slept. I took out my tools from the chest under my bed and chose the set of chisels I liked best to handle. Then I took the pair of silken slippers that Maria of Petrelle had taken, at my request, from the chest of Donatella's things stored at the castle. In the imprint of her slippers I traced her footsteps in stone, chipping out her tread with my tools. Making her footsteps walk towards her rooms, across the marble and terracotta floors to the chimney-breast. I had Giovanni light the fires in her apartments and through all the freezing house in readiness for her call. There were many footprints to make, dipped into the stone. I had to work day and night, chipping in the cold by candlelight, bringing the angel I had dreamed back to earth. Each imprint would exactly fit her foot. The dips must not be deep enough to make her trip, they had merely to convey the sensation of the stone.

How beautiful are thy feet with shoes, O prince's daughter; the joints of thy thighs are like jewels, the work of the hands of a cunning workman.

As I punched the first shavings out of the porous travertine, Vitelli's voice lingered in my head, swaddling my thoughts like a sea mist. It lulled me, as it had once lulled me in our cell, and it spurred me on.

'Donna Donatella will arrive on the day of San Felice. You will be thirty-one years old to her thirty-three.'

The marble was weeping condensation from the cold. Giovanni's fires had not yet reached the corridors.

'You have proposed to her in stone. You can woo her with your work, but you must find words as well. Donatella has been shackled to a man who was mean in spirit, avaricious of tenderness, a miser of words and gestures. Words are the bricks and mortar of love. Daily, life can wash away the sands of love and leave a man or woman bereft of anything but an empty stave. Words are the nuggets that stay and give comfort, tiding lovers over, from one ford to the next. Take nothing for granted. Once she is yours, woo her still and be generous of spirit, it is a far greater gift than all the gold and stone in Umbria. I hope to live to see you wed and the lilies bloom before I die.'

I rubbed the wet dust from the stone.

Make haste, my beloved, and be thou like to a roe or to a young hart upon the mountains of spices.

'You must bury me in the cemetery at Morra and carve an angel for my tomb.'

An angel whose legs were as 'pillars of marble, set upon sockets of fine gold: his countenance is as Lebanon, excellent as the cedars. His mouth is most sweet: yes, he is altogether lovely'.

The eight sides of the worn beechwood handle of my chisel are moulded to my hand. The travertine will press against the arch of her feet. Her feet will follow where my hand has been. Then my hand will follow where the stone has caressed her.

'Gabriellino is the only child in your house. He has not

learned yet to walk on water. He will walk in the rose gardens with Donatella. He will help to win her. She would dearly love a child of her own.'

I have grazed the terracotta, chipping away slivers so that their undulations do not bruise her slippered feet.

Once, I could not raise the silk of her skirts even in my dreams. Then I raised them nightly. When she comes, I shall raise them again and again in the rooms I have crafted for her. I shall draw out the rhythm of the stone and fill her with it. I shall love her as a woman: the only woman I have ever loved. If the seed cannot take in her womb, it will not be through want of trying. 'I am my beloved's and my beloved is mine.'

I am three footsteps away from the threshold of her rooms. When the least roughness of these dips is filed away, all work on the palace will cease. At sundown, Piero will beat his drum to that effect.

Donna Donatella is coming and I know now that the south wing will never be finished. It was always a dream house, and like a dream, it has no end.

All Pan Books are available at your local bookshop or newsagent, or can be ordered direct from the publisher. Indicate the number of copies required and fill in the form below.

Send to: Macmillan General Books C.S.
          Book Service By Post
          PO Box 29, Douglas I-O-M
          IM99 1BQ

or phone: 01624 675137, quoting title, author and credit card number.

or fax: 01624 670923, quoting title, author, and credit card number.

or Internet: http://www.bookpost.co.uk

Please enclose a remittance* to the value of the cover price plus 75 pence per book for post and packing. Overseas customers please allow £1.00 per copy for post and packing.

*Payment may be made in sterling by UK personal cheque, Eurocheque, postal order, sterling draft or international money order, made payable to Book Service By Post.

Alternatively by Access/Visa/MasterCard

Card No.

Expiry Date

Signature

Applicable only in the UK and BFPO addresses.

While every effort is made to keep prices low, it is sometimes necessary to increase prices at short notice. Pan Books reserve the right to show on covers and charge new retail prices which may differ from those advertised in the text or elsewhere.

NAME AND ADDRESS IN BLOCK CAPITAL LETTERS PLEASE

Name

Address

8/95

Please allow 28 days for delivery.
Please tick box if you do not wish to receive any additional information.